Mayne Reid, Edmond Morin, Harrison Weir, Julian Portch

The Forest Exiles

The perils of a Peruvian family amid the wilds of the Amazon

Mayne Reid, Edmond Morin, Harrison Weir, Julian Portch

The Forest Exiles
The perils of a Peruvian family amid the wilds of the Amazon

ISBN/EAN: 9783337382407

Printed in Europe, USA, Canada, Australia, Japan

Cover: Foto ©Andreas Hilbeck / pixelio.de

More available books at **www.hansebooks.com**

THE FOREST EXILES;

OR, THE

PERILS OF A PERUVIAN FAMILY AMID THE WILDS OF THE AMAZON.

BY

CAPTAIN MAYNE REID,

AUTHOR OF "THE BOY HUNTERS," "THE YOUNG VOYAGEURS"
"THE DESERT HOME," ETC.

WITH TWELVE ILLUSTRATIONS.

BOSTON:

TICKNOR AND FIELDS.

M DCCC LXII.

CONTENTS.

(5)

6 CONTENTS.

THE FOREST EXILES.

CHAPTER I.

THE BIGGEST WOOD IN THE WORLD.

Boy reader, I am told that you are not tired of my company. Is this true?

" Quite true, dear captain — quite true."

That is your reply. You speak sincerely? I believe you do.

In return, believe *me* when I tell you I am not tired of yours ; and the best proof I can give is, that I have come once more to seek you. I have come to solicit the pleasure of your company, not to an evening party, nor to a ball, nor to the Grand Opera, nor to the Crystal Palace, nor yet to the Zoölogical Gardens of Regent's Park — no, but to the great zoölogical garden of Nature. I have come to ask you to accompany me on another "campaign" — another " grand journey " through the fields of science and adventure. Will you go?

" Most willingly, with you, dear captain, any where."

Come with me, then.

(7)

Again we turn our faces westward ; again we cross the blue and billowy Atlantic ; again we seek the shores of the noble continent of America.

" What ! to America again ? "

Ha ! that is a large continent, and you need not fear that I am going to take you over old ground. No, fear not that. New scenes await us — a new *fauna*, a new *flora* — I might almost say a new earth and a new sky.

You shall have variety, I promise you — a perfect contrast to the scenes of our last journey.

Then, you remember, we turned our faces to the cold and icy north ; now our path lies through the hot and sunny south. Then we lived in a log hut, and closed every cranny to keep out the cold ; now, in our cottage of palms and cane, we shall be but too glad to let the breeze play through the open walls. Then we wrapped our bodies in thick furs ; now we shall be content with the lightest garments. Then we were bitten by the frost ; now we shall be bitten by sand flies, and mosquitoes, and bats, and snakes, and scorpions, and spiders, and stung by wasps, and centipedes, and great red ants. Trust me, you shall have a change.

Perhaps you do not contemplate *such* a change with any very lively feelings of pleasure. Come, do not be alarmed at the snakes, and scorpions, and centipedes. We shall find a cure for every bite — an antidote for every bane.

Our new journey shall have its pleasures and advantages. Remember how of old we shivered as we slept, coiled up in the corner of our dark log hut and smothered in skins ; now we shall swing lightly in our netted hammocks under the gossamer leaves of the palm tree or the feathery frondage of the ferns. Then we gazed upon leaden skies, and at night looked upon the cold constellation of the Northern Bear; now we shall have over us an azure canopy, and shall nightly behold the sparkling glories of the Southern Cross, still shining as bright as when Paul and his little Virginie with loving eyes gazed upon it from their island home. In our last journey we toiled over bleak and barren wastes, across frozen lakes, and marshes, and rivers ; now we shall pass under the shadows of virgin forests, and float lightly upon the bosom of broad, majestic streams, whose shores echo with the voices of living Nature.

Hitherto our travels have been upon the wide, open prairie, the trackless plain of sand, the frozen lake, the thin, scattering woods of the north, or the treeless, snow-clad " Barrens." Now we are about to enter a great forest — a forest where the leaves never fade, where the flowers are always in bloom — a forest where the woodman's axe has not yet echoed, where the colonist has hardly hewed out a single clearing — a vast primeval forest, the largest in the world.

How large, do you ask ? I can hardly tell you. Are you thinking of Epping, or the New Forest ? True, these are large woods, and have been larger at one time ; but if you draw your ideas of a great forest from either of these you must prepare yourself for a startling announcement ; and that is, that the

forest through which I am going to take you is *as
big as all Europe !* There is one place where a
straight line might be drawn across this forest that
would measure the enormous length of two thousand
six hundred miles ; and there is a point in it from
which a circle might be described with a diameter of
more than a thousand miles, and the whole area in-
cluded within this vast circumference would be found
covered with an unbroken forest.

I need scarce tell you what forest I allude to; for
there is none other in the world of such dimensions
— none to compare with that vast, trackless forest
that covers the valley of the mighty Amazon.

And what shall we see in travelling through this
tree-covered expanse? Many a strange form of life,
both vegetable and animal. We shall see the giant
"ceiba " tree, and the " zamang," and the " caoba,"
twined by huge parasites almost as thick as their own
trunks, and looking as though they embraced but to
crush them ; the " juvia," with its globe-shaped fruits
as large as the human head; the " cow tree," with
its abundant fountains of rich milk ; the " seringa,"
with its valuable gum ; the caoutchouc of commerce ;
the " cinchona," with its fever-killing bark ; the
curious " volador," with its winged seeds; the wild
indigo ; and the arnatto. We shall see palms of
many species; some with trunks smooth and cylindrical — others covered with thorns, sharp and thickly set ; some with broad, entire leaves — others with
fronds pinnate and feathery, and still others whose
leaves are of the shape of a fan ; some rising like

naked columns to the height of a hundred and fifty feet, while others scarcely attain to the standard of an ordinary man.

On the water we shall see beautiful lilies — the snow-white *nymphs* and the yellow *nuphars.* We shall see the *Victoria regia* covering the pool with its massive waxlike flowers and huge circular leaves of bronze green. We shall see tall flags like Sara-cen spears, and the dark-green culms of gigantic rushes, and the golden *arundinaria,* the bamboo, and "caña brava," that rival the forest trees in neight.

Many a form of animal life we may behold. Bask-ing in the sun we may behold the yellow and spotted body of the jaguar — a beautiful but dreaded sight. Breaking through the thick underwood, or emerging slowly from the water, we may catch a glimpse of the sombre tapir or the red-brown capivara. We may see the ocelot skulking through the deep shade or the margay springing upon its winged prey. We may see the shaggy ant bear tearing at the cones of sand clay and licking up the white termites ; or we may behold the scaly armadillo crawling over the sun-parched earth and rolling itself up at the ap-proach of danger. We may see human-like forms — the *quadrumana* — clinging among the high branch-es and leaping from tree to tree like birds upon the wing ; we may see them of many shapes, sizes, and colors, from the great howling monkeys, with their long, prehensile tails, down to the little saïmiris and ouistitis not larger than squirrels.

What beautiful birds too ! for this forest is their

favorite home : upon the ground, the large curas·
sows, and guans, and the " gallo," with his plumage
of bright red ; upon the trees, the macaws, and par·
rots, and toucans, and trogons ; in the waters, the
scarlet flamingoes, the ibises, and the tall herons ;
and in the air, the hawks, the zamuros, the king vultures, and the eagles.

We shall see much of the reptile world, both by
land and water.   Basking upon the bank, or floating
along the stream, we may behold the great water
lizards, the crocodile, and caïman, or the unwieldy
forms of the *chelonia* — the turtles.   Nimbly running along the tree trunk or up the slanting lliana, we
may see the crested iguana, hideous to behold.   On
the branches that overhang the silent pool we may
see the " water boa," of huge dimensions, watching
for his prey — the peccary, the capivara, the paca,
or the agouti ; and in the dry forest we may meet
with his congener, the " stag swallower," twined
around a tree, and waiting for the roebuck or the
little red deer of the woods.

We may see the mygale, or bird-catching spider,
at the end of his strong net trap among the thick
foliage, and the tarantula at the bottom of his dark
pitfall constructed in the ground.   We may see the
tentlike hills of the white ants raised high above the
surface, and the nests of many other kinds hanging
from high branches, and looking as though they
had been constructed out of raw silk and paste-
board.   We may see trees covered with these nests,
and some with the nests of wasps, and still others
with those of troupials and orioles, — birds of the

genus *Icterus* and *Cassicus*,— hanging down like long cylindrical purses.

All these, and many more strange sights, may bc seen in the great forest of the Amazon valley ; and some of them we *shall* see — *violà !*

CHAPTER II.

THE REFUGEES.

UPON a bright and lovely evening, many years ago, a party of travellers might have been seen climbing up that Cordillera of the Andes that lies to the eastward of the ancient city of Cuzco. It was a small and somewhat singular party of travellers ; in fact, a travelling family — father, mother, children, and one attendant. We shall say a word of each of them separately.

The chief of the party was a tall and handsome man, of nearly forty years of age. His countenance bespoke him of Spanish race ; and so he was. He was not a Spaniard, however, but a Spanish American, or " Creole ; " for so Spaniards born in America are called, to distinguish them from the natives of Old Spain.

Remember, Creoles are *not* people with negro or African blood in their veins. There is a misconception on this head in England and elsewhere. The African races of America are either negroes, mulattoes, quadroons, quinteroons, or mestizoes ; but the " Creoles " are of European blood, though born in America. Remember this. Don Pablo Romero — for that was the name of our traveller — was a Creole

a native of Cuzco, which, as you know, was the ancient capital of the incas of Peru.

Don Pablo, as already stated, was nearly forty
years of age. Perhaps he looked older. His life
had not been spent in idleness. Much study, combined with a good deal of suffering and care, had
made many of those lines that rob the face of its
youthful appearance. Still, although his look was
serious, and just then sad, his eye was occasionally
seen to brighten, and his light, elastic step showed
that he was full of vigor and manhood. He had a
mustache, very full and black ; but his whiskers
were clean shaven and his hair cut short, after the
fashion of most people in Spanish America. He
wore velvet pantaloons, trimmed at the bottoms with
black stamped leather, and upon his feet were strong
boots of a reddish-yellow color — that is, the natural
color of the tanned hide before it has been stained.
A dark jacket, closely buttoned, covered the upper
part of his body, and a scarlet silk sash encircled his
waist, the long fringed ends hanging down over the
left hip. In this sash were stuck a Spanish knife and
a pair of pistols, richly ornamented with silver mount-
ings. But all these things were concealed from the
view by a capacious poncho, which is a garment that
in South America serves as a cloak by day and a
blanket by night. It is nearly of the size and shape
of an ordinary blanket, with a slit in the centre,
through which the head is passed, leaving the ends
to hang down. Instead of being of uniform color,
several bright colors are usually woven into the
poncho, forming a variety of patterns. In Mexico a

very similar garment — the serapé — is almost uni
versally worn. The poncho of Don Pablo was a
costly one, woven by hand, and out of the finest wool
of the vicuña; for that is the native country of this
useful and curious animal. Such a poncho would cost
twenty pounds, and would not only keep out cold, but
would turn rain like a " mackintosh." Don Pablo's
hat was also curious and costly. It was one of those
known as " Panama," or " Guayaquil " — hats so
called because they are manufactured by Indian
tribes who dwell upon the Pacific coast, and are made
out of a rare sea grass which is found near the above-
mentioned places. A good Guayaquil hat will cost
twenty pounds; and although, with its broad, curling
brim and low crown, it looks not much better than
Leghorn or even fine straw, yet it is far superior to
either, both as a protection against rain, or, what is
of more importance in southern countries, against a
hot tropical sun. The best of them will wear half a
lifetime. Don Pablo's " sombrero " was one of the
very best and costliest; and this, combined with the
style of his other habiliments, betokened that the
wearer was one of the " ricos," or higher class of
his country.

The costume of his wife, who was a dark and very
beautiful Spanish woman, would have strengthened
this idea. She wore a dress of black silk, with velvet bodice and sleeves, tastefully embroidered. A
mantilla of dark cloth covered her shoulders, and on
her head was a low, broad-brimmed hat, similar to
those usually worn by men; for a bonnet is a thing
unknown to the ladies of Spanish America. A

single glance at the Doña Isidora would have satisfied any one that she was a lady of rank and refine-
ment.

There were two children, upon which, from time
to time, she gazed tenderly. They were her only
ones. They were a boy and girl, nearly of equal
size and age. The boy was the elder, perhaps thir-
teen or more — a handsome lad, with swarth face,
coal-black eyes, and curly, full-flowing, dark hair.
The girl, too, who would be about twelve, was dark
— that is to say brunette — in complexion. Her eyes
were large, round, and dreamy, with long lashes, that
kept the sun from shining into them, and thus deep-
ened their expression.

Perhaps there are no children in the world so
beautiful as those of the Spanish race. There is a
smoothness of skin, a richness in color, and a noble
"hidalgo" expression in their round black eyes that
is rare in other countries. Spanish women retain
this expression to a good age. The men lose it
earlier, because, as I believe, they are oftener of cor-
rupted morals and habits; and these, long exercised,
certainly stamp their lines upon the face. Those
which are mean, and low, and vicious produce a
similar character of countenance; while those which
are high, and holy, and virtuous give it an aspect of
beauty and nobility.

Of all beautiful Spanish children, none could have
been more beautiful than our two little Creole Spaniards, Leon and Leona ; for such were the names of
the brother and sister.

There yet remains one to be described ere we
2

complete the account of our travelling party. This one was a grown and tall man, quite as tall as Don Pablo himself, but thinner and more angular in his outlines. His coppery color, his long, straight black hair, his dark and wild piercing eye, with his some-what odd attire, told you at once he was of a different race from any of the others. He was an Indian — a South American Indian ; and, although a descendant from the noble race of the Peruvian incas, he was acting in the capacity of a servant or attendant to Don Pablo and his family. There was a familiarity, however, between the old Indian — for he was an old man — and Don Pablo that bespoke the existence of some tie of a stronger nature than that which exists between master and servant ; and such there was in reality. This Indian had been one of the patriots who had rallied around Tupac Amaru in his revolu-tion against the Spaniards. He had been proscribed, captured, and sentenced to death. He would have been executed but for the interference of Don Pablo, who had saved his life. Since then Guapo — such was the Indian's name — had remained, not only the retainer, but the firm and faithful friend, of his bene-factor.

Guapo's feet were sandalled. His legs were naked up to the knees, showing many an old scar received from the cactus plants and the thorny bushes of acacia so common in the mountain valleys of Peru. A tunic-like shirt of woollen cloth — that homemade sort called "bayeta" — was fastened around his waist, and reached down to the knees ; but the upper part of his body was quite bare, and you could see

the naked breast and arms, corded with strong muscles, and covered with a skin of a dark copper color.
The upper part of his body was naked only when
the sun was hot. At other times Guapo wore a
species of poncho like his master; but that of the
Indian was of common stuff, woven out of the coarse
wool of the lama. His head was bare.

Guapo's features were thin, sharp, and intelligent.
His eye was keen and piercing; and the gait of the
old man as he strode along the rocky path told that it
would be many years before he would show any
signs of feebleness or tottering.

There were four animals that carried our travellers
and their effects. One was a horse ridden by the
boy Leon. The second was a saddle mule, on which
rode Doña Isidora and Leona. The other two animals were not mounted. They were beasts of burden, with " yerguas," or pack saddles, upon which
were carried the few articles that belonged to the
travellers. They were the camels of Peru — the far-
famed lamas. Don Pablo, with his faithful retainer,
travelled afoot.

You will wonder that one apparently so rich and
on so distant a journey was not provided with animals
enough to carry his whole party. Another horse at
least, or a mule, might have been expected in the
cavalcade. It would not have been strange had
Guapo only walked, as he was the arriero, or driver
of the lamas; but to see Don Pablo afoot and evidently tired, with neither horse nor mule to ride upon,
was something that required explanation. There
was another fact that required explanation. The

countenance of Don Pablo wore an anxious expression, as if some danger impended ; so did that of the
lady ; and the children were silent, with their little
hearts full of fear. They knew not *what* danger, but
they knew that their father and mother were in
trouble. The Indian, too, had a serious look; and
at each angle of the mountain road he and Don Pablo would turn around and with anxious eyes gaze
back in the direction that led towards Cuzco. As
yet they could distinguish the spires of the distant
city and the Catholic crosses, as they glistened under
the evening sunbeam. Why did they look back with
fear and distrust? Why? *Because Don Pablo was
in flight, and feared pursuers.* What ! had he
committed some great crime? No. On the contrary, he was the *victim of a noble virtue* — the
virtue of patriotism. For that had he been con-
demned and was now in flight — flying to save not
only his liberty, but his life — yes, *his life ;* for, had
the sentinels on those distant towers but recognized
him, he would soon have been followed and dragged
back to an ignominious death.

Young reader, I am writing of things that occurred
near the beginning of the present century, and before
the Spanish American colonies became free from
the rule of Old Spain. You will remember that these
countries were then governed by viceroys, who rep-
resented the King of Spain, but who in reality were
quite as absolute as that monarch himself. The
great viceroys of Mexico and Peru held court in
grand state, and lived in the midst of barbaric pomp
and luxury. The power of life and death was in

their hands, and in many instances they used it in the most unjust and arbitrary manner. They were themselves, of course, natives of Old Spain — often the pampered favorites of that corrupt court. All the officials by which they were surrounded and served were, like themselves, natives of Spain, or " Gachupinos," (as the Creoles used to call them;) while the Creoles — no matter how rich, or learned, or accomplished in any way — were excluded from every office of honor and profit. They were treated by the Gachupinos with contempt and insult. Hence, for long, long years before the great revolutions of Spanish America, a strong feeling of dislike existed be- tween Creole Spaniards and Spaniards of Old Spain ; and this feeling was quite independent of that which either had towards the Indians — the aborigines of America. This feeling brought about the revolution which broke out in all the countries of Spanish America (including Mexico) about the year 1810, and which, after fifteen years of cruel and sanguinary fighting, led to the independence of these countries.

Some people will tell you that they gained nothing by this independence, as since that time so much war and anarchy have marked their history. There is scarcely any subject upon which mankind thinks more superficially and judges more wrongly than upon this very one. It is a mistake to suppose that a people enjoys either peace or prosperity simply because it is quiet. There is quiet in Russia, but to its millions of serfs war continuous and eternal ; and the same may be said of many other countries as well as Russia. To the poor slave, or even to the overtaxed subject ·

peace is no peace, but a constant and systematized struggle, often more pernicious in its effects than even the anarchy of open war. A war of this kind numbers its slain by millions; for the victims of famine are victims of *political crime* on the part of a nation's rulers. I have no time now to talk of these things. Perhaps, boy reader, you and I may meet on this ground again, and at no very distant period.

Well, it was not in the general rising of 1810 that Don Pablo had been compromised, but previous to that. The influence of the European revolution of 1798 was felt even in distant Spanish America, and several ebullitions occurred in different parts of that country at the same time. They were premature; they were crushed. Those who had taken part in them were hunted to the death. Death! death! was the war cry of the Spanish hirelings; and bitterly did they execute their vengeance on all who were compromised. Don Pablo would have been a victim among others had he not had timely warning and escaped; but, as it was, all his property was taken by confiscation, and became the plunder of the rapacious tyrant.

We are introduced to him just at the period of his escape. By the aid of the faithful Guapo he had hastily collected a few things, and, with his wife and family, fled in the night. Hence the incompleteness of his travelling equipage. He had taken one of the most unfrequented paths — a mere bridle road — that led from Cuzco eastward over the Cordillera. His intent was to gain the eastern slope of the Andes .

Mountains, where he might conceal himself for a time in the uninhabited woods of the Great *Montaña*, and towards this point was he journeying. By a *ruse* he had succeeded in putting the soldiers of the despot on a false track; but it was not certain that they might not yet fall into the true one. No wonder, then, when he gazed back towards Cuzco, that his look was one of apprehension and anxiety.

CHAPTER III.

THE POISON TREES.

Following the rugged and winding path, the travellers had climbed to a height of many thousand feet
above the ocean level. There was very little vegetation around them. Nothing that deserved the name
of tree, if we except a few stunted specimens of
queñoa trees, (*Polylepis racemosa*,) and here and
there patches of the Ratanhia shrub, (*Krameria*,)
which covered the hillsides. Both these are used
by the mountain Indians as fuel, but the Ratanhia is
also a favorite remedy against dysentery and blood
spitting. Its extract is even exported to European
countries, and is to be found in the shop of the apoth-
ecary.

Now and then a beautiful species of locust was
seen with its bright-red flowers. It was the " Sangre
de Christo " of the Peruvian *flora*.

Don Pablo Romero was a naturalist, and I may
here tell you a pleasant and interesting fact — which
is, that many of the earliest patriots and revolution-
ists of Spanish America were men who had distinguished themselves in natural science — in fact,
were the " savans " of these countries. I call this a
pleasant fact, and you may deem it a curious one too,
because men of science are usually lovers of peace

and not accustomed to meddle either in war or poli-
tics. But the truth of the matter is this — under the
government of the viceroys all books, except those
of a monkish religion, were jealously excluded from
these countries. No political work whatever was
permitted to be introduced ; and the people were kept
in the grossest ignorance of their natural rights. It
was only into learned institutions that a glimmering
of the light of freedom found its way, and it was
amongst the professors of these institutions that the
" rights of men " first began to be discussed. Many
of these noble patriots were the first victims offered
up on the altar of Spanish American independence.

Don Pablo, I have said, was a naturalist; and it
was, perhaps, the first journey he had ever made
without observing attentively the natural objects that
presented themselves along his route. But his mind
was busy with other cares ; and he heeded neither
the *fauna* nor *flora*. He thought only of his loved
wife and dear children, of the dangers to which he
and they were exposed. He thought only of increasing the distance between them and his vengeful enemies. During that day they had made a toilsome
journey of fifteen miles, up the mountain, — a long
journey for the lamas, who rarely travel more than
ten or twelve, — but the dumb brutes seemed to exert
themselves as if they knew that danger threatened
those who guided them. They belonged to Guapo,
who had not been a mere servant, but a cultivator,
and had held a small " chacra," or farm, under Don
Pablo. Guapo's voice was well known to the creatures, and his " hist ! " of encouragement urged them

on. But fifteen miles was an unusual journey, and the animals began to show symptoms of fatigue. Their humming noise, which bears some resemblance to the tones of an Æolian harp, boomed loud at intervals as the creatures came to a stop ; and then the voice of Guapo could be heard urging them forward.

The road led up a defile, which was nothing more than the bed of a mountain torrent, now dry. For a long distance there was no spot of level ground where our travellers could have encamped, even had they desired to stop. At length, however, the path led out of the torrent bed, and they found themselves on a small ledge, or table, covered with low trees. These trees were of a peculiar kind, very common in all parts of the Andes, and known as *mollé* trees. They are more properly bushes than trees, being only about ten or twelve feet in height. They have long, delicate pinnate leaves, very like those of the acacia, and, when in fruit, they are thickly covered with clusters of small, bright-red berries. These berries are used among some tribes of Indians for making a highly valuable and medicinal beer; but the wood of the tree is of more importance to the people of those parts as an article of fuel, because the tree grows where other wood is scarce. It is even considered by the sugar refiners as the best for their purpose, since its ashes, possessing highly alkaline properties, are more efficient than any other in purifying the boiling juice of the sugar cane. The leaves of this beautiful tree, when pressed, emit a strong aromatic smell ; and a very curious property ascribed to it by the more ignorant people of the mountains will be illustrated by the dialogue which follows : —

"Let us pass the night here," said Den Pablo halting, and addressing himself to Guapo. 'This level spot will serve us to encamp. We can sleep under the shade of the bushes."

" What! *mi amo !* (my master!) Here ? " replied the Indian, with a gesture of surprise.

" And why not here ? Can any place be better ? If we again enter the defile we may find no other level spot. See ! the lamas will go no farther. We must remain therefore."

" But, master," continued Guapo, " see ! "

" See what ? "

" The trees, master ! "

" Well, what of the trees ? Their shade will serve to screen us from the night dew. We can sleep under them."

" Impossible, master — *they are poison trees !* "

" You are talking foolishly, .Guapo. These are *mollé* trees."

" I know it, señor ; but they are poison. If we sleep under them we shall not awake in the morning — we shall awake no more."

And Guapo, as he uttered these words, looked horrified.

" This is nonsense ; you are superstitious, old man. We must abide here. See ! the lamas have lain down. They will not move hence, I warrant."

Guapo turned to the lamas, and, thinking that their

movements might influence the decision of his master, began to urge them in his accustomed way. But
it is a peculiarity of these creatures not to stir one
step beyond what they consider a proper journey.
Even when the load is above that which they are accustomed to carry, — that is to say, one hundred and
twenty pounds, — neither voice nor whip will move
them. They may be goaded to death, but will not
yield, and coaxing has a like effect. Both knew that
they had done their day's work; and the voice, the
gesticulations, and blows of Guapo were all in vain.
Neither would obey him any longer. The Indian
saw this, and reluctantly consented to remain; at the
same time he continued to repeat his belief that they
would all most certainly perish in the night. For
himself, he expressed his intention to climb a ledge,
and sleep upon the naked rocks; and he earnestly
entreated the others to follow his example.

Don Pablo listened to the admonitions of his retainer with incredulity, though not with any degree of
disdain. He knew the devotedness of the old Indian,
and therefore treated what he considered a mere
superstition with a show of respect. But he felt an
inclination to cure Guapo of the folly of such a belief; and was, on this account, the more inclined to
put his original design into execution. To pass the
night under the shade of the mollé trees was, therefore, determined upon.

All dismounted. The lamas were unloaded; their
. packs, or *yerguas*, taken off; the horse and mule
were unsaddled; and all were permitted to browse

over the little space which the ledge afforded. They were all trained animals. There was no fear of any of them straying.

The next thing was to prepare supper. All were hungry, as none of the party had eaten since morning. In the hurry of flight, they had made no provision for an extended journey. A few pieces of *charqui* (jerked or dried beef) had been brought along; and, in passing near a field of " oca," Guapo had gathered a bunch of the roots, and placed them on the back of his lama. This oca is a tuberous root, (*Oxalis tuberosa*,) of an oval shape and pale-red color, but white inside. It resembles very much the Jerusalem artichoke, but it is longer and slimmer. Its taste is very agreeable and sweetish — somewhat like that of pumpkins, and it is equally good when roasted or boiled. There is another sort of tuberous root, (*Tropæolum tuberosum*,) called " ulluca " by the Peruvians, which is more glutinous and less pleasant to' the taste. This kind is various in form, being either round, oblong, straight, or curved, and of a reddish-yellow color outside, though green within. It is insipid when boiled with water, but excellent when dressed with Spanish peppers, (*Capsicum.*) Out of the *oca*, then, and *charqui*, the supper must be made; and for the purpose of cooking it, a fire must be kindled with the wood of the mollé.

For a long time there was a doubt about whether it would be safe to kindle this fire. The sun had not yet gone down, and the smoke might attract observation from the valley below. If the pursuers were on their track, it might be noticed; as upon this lonely route a fire would indicate nothing else than the camp of some one on a journey. But the stomachs of our travellers cried for food, and it was at length resolved to light the fire, but not until after sunset, when the smoke could be no longer seen, and the blaze would be hidden behind the thick bushes of mollé.

Don Pablo walked off from the camp, and wan- dered among the trees, to see if he could find some- thing that might contribute a little variety to their simple supper. A small, broomlike plant, that grew among the mollé trees, soon attracted his attention. This was the *quinoa* plant, (*Chenopodium quinoa*,) which produces a seed not unlike rice, though small- er in the grain, whence it has received in commerce the name " petty rice." The quinoa seeds, when boiled, are both pleasant and nutritious, but especial- ly so when boiled in milk. Previous to the discovery of America, " quinoa " was an article of food, sup- plying the place of wheat. It was much used by the natives, and is still collected for food in many parts. Indeed, it has been introduced into some European countries, and cultivated with success. The leaves, when young, can be used as spinach, but the seeds are the most sought after for food.

Don Pablo having called Leon to assist him, a quantity of the seeds were soon collected into a ves- sel, and carried to the place which they had chosen for their camp ; and, as it was now dark enough, the fire was kindled and the cooking pot got ready. The Doña Isidora, although a fine lady, was one of those who had all her life been accustomed to look after her household affairs : and this, it may be remarked, is a somewhat rare virtue among the Peruvian ladies, who are generally too much given to dress and idleness. It was not so, however, with the wife of Don Pablo. She knew how to look after the affairs of the *cuisine*, and could dress any of the peculiar dishes of the country with the best of cooks. In a short while, therefore, an excellent supper was ready, of which all ate heartily, and then, wrapping themselves up in their ponchos, lay down to sleep.

CHAPTER IV.

THE SUPPER OF GUAPO.

I HAVE said all ate of the supper. This is not strictly true. One of the party did not touch it; and that was old Guapo. Why? Was he not hungry like the rest? Yes, as hungry as any of them. Why, then, did he not eat of the charqui and ocas? Simply because Guapo had a supper of a very different kind, which he carried in his pouch, and which he liked much better than the charqui stew. What was it? It was " coca."

" Chocolate," you will say, or, as some call it, " cocoa," which should be called, to name it properly, " cacao." No, I answer; it was not chocolate, nor cocoa, nor cacao neither.

" It must have been cocoa nuts, then." No, nor yet cocoa nuts. The " coca " upon which Guapo made his supper, and which contented his stomach perfectly for the night, was an article very different from either the cacao which makes chocolate or the nut of the cocoa palm. You are now impatient to hear what sort of thing it was, and I shall tell you at once.

The coca is a small tree, or shrub, about six feet in height, which grows in the warmer valleys among the Andes Mountains. Its botanical name is *Ery-*

throxylon coca. Its leaves are small and of a bright-
green color, and its blossoms white. Its fruits are
very small scarlet berries. It is a native plant, and
therefore found in a wild state ; but it is cultivated
by the planters of these countries in fields regularly
laid out, and hence called " cocales." This plant is
raised from the seed ; and when the young shoots
have attained the height of about eighteen inches
they are transplanted and put down again at the distance of about a foot apart from each other. Now,
as these little bushes require a humid atmosphere,
maize plants are sown between the rows to protect
them from the sun. In other places arbors of palm
leaves are constructed over the coca plants. When
no rain falls, they are watered every five or six days.
After about two and a half years of this nursing the
coca bush is ready for use ; and it is the leaves alone
that are valuable. These are gathered with great care,
just as the Chinese gather the leaves of the tea plant ;
and, as in China, women are principally employed in
this labor. The leaves are said to be ripe, not when
they have withered and turned brown, but at a period
when they are fullgrown and become brittle. When
this period arrives they are picked from the tree and
laid out on coarse woollen cloths to dry in the sun.
When dried, they remain of a pale-green color ; but,
should they get damp during the process, they become darker, and are then of inferior quality, and sell
for a less price. When fully dried, they are carefully packed in bags and covered up with dry sand,
and are thus ready for the market. Their price, on
the spot where the crop is produced, is about one

3

shilling English per pound. They are therefore full as costly to produce as tea itself, although the coca bush will yield three crops of leaves in one year — that is, a crop every four months ; and one hundred plants will produce about an arroba (twenty-five pounds) at a crop. The coca plant will continue to give fresh leaves for a long period of years unless attacked and destroyed by ants, which is not unfrequently the case.

Now, why have I so minutely described the coca bush ? Because that, in the economy of the life of those Indians who inhabit the countries of the Andes Mountains, this curious plant plays a most important part. Scarcely one of these people is to be met with who is not an eater of coca — a " coquero." With them it is what the tea tree is to the Chinese. Indeed, it is a curious fact, that in all parts of the world some stimulating vegetable is used by the hu-man race — tea in China, the betel leaf and the nut of the areca palm among the southern Asiatics, the poppy in the East, with tobacco and many like things in other countries.

But the coca not only supplies the Indian with a solace to his cares ; it forms the chief article of his food. With a supply of coca an Indian will sup-port himself five or six days without eating any thing else. The poor miners in the Peruvian mines are all " coqueros ; " and it is alleged that, without coca, they would be unable to undergo the painful toil to which their calling subjects them. When used to excess, the coca produces deleterious effects on the human system ; but, if moderately taken, it is far more innocent in its results than either opium or tobacco.

The coca leaf is not eaten alone. A certain prep- aration is necessary, and another substance is mixed with it, before it produces the proper effect. But let us watch the movements of Guapo, and we shall see how *he* does it; for Guapo is a confirmed coquero.

Guapo, true to his promise, does not sleep under the mollé trees. He leaves the party, and, with a melancholy air, has climbed up and seated himself upon a projecting rock, where he intends to pass the night. His last glance at Don Pablo and his family was one of foreboding. He had again remonstrated with his master, but to no purpose. The latter only laughed at the earnestness of the old Indian, and told him to go to his perch and leave the party to them- selves.

It was still gray light when Guapo climbed up to the rock. Against the sky his tall, lank form could be traced in all its outlines. For some moments he sat in a serious and reflective mood, evidently busy with thoughts about the " poison trees." His appe- tite, however, soon got the better of him, and he set to work to prepare his coca supper. It was a simple operation.

Around Guapo's neck there hung a small pouch made of the skin of the chinchilla, which beautiful little animal is a native of these parts. This pouch contained a quantity of the dry leaves of the coca. Having taken out some half dozen of these leaves, he put them into his mouth and commenced chewing them. In a short while, by the aid of tongue, teeth,

and lips, they were formed into a little ball of pulp,
that rolled about in his mouth. Another step in the
process now became necessary. A small gourd, that
hung around Guapo's neck by a thong, was laid hold
of. This was corked with a wooden stopper, in which
stopper a wire pin was fixed, long enough to reach
down to the bottom of the gourd. After taking out
the stopper, Guapo applied the lower part of the pin
to his lips, and then, plunging it once more into the
gourd, drew it out again. This time the pin came
out with a fine whitish powder adhering to the part
that had been wetted. Now, what was this powder?
It was nothing else than lime that had been burned
and then pulverized. Perhaps it was the ashes of
the mollé tree, of which we have already spoken,
and which, as we have said, possess a highly alkaline
property. The ashes of the musa, or plaintain, are
sometimes used ; but, after all, it is most likely that
it was the mollé ashes which Guapo carried ; for
these are most highly esteemed by the Indians of
southern Peru ; and Guapo was a connoisseur in
coca eating. Whichever of the three it was, — lime,
mollé, or musa, — Guapo carried the pin to his
mouth, and, without touching his lips, (it would have
burned him if he had,) he inserted it so as to penetrate the ball of chewed coca leaves that rested upon
the tip of his tongue. This was stabbed repeatedly
and adroitly by the pin, until all the powder remained
in the coca ball ; and then the pin was withdrawn,
wiped, and restored to its place along with the stopper
of the gourd.

Guapo now remained quietly " ruminating " for a

period of about forty minutes ; for this is about the time required for chewing a mess of coca leaves. Indeed, so exactly is this time observed that the Indians, when travelling, measure distances by it ; and one " coceada " is about equal to the time occupied in walking a couple of English miles.

The coceada of our old Indian being finished, he drew his lama-wool poncho around him, and, leaning back against the rock, was soon buried in a profound slumber.

/

CHAPTER V.

THE PUNA.

BY early dawn Guapo was awake, but he did not immediately awake the others. It was still too dark to follow the mountain road. His first care was to have his coca breakfast; and to this he applied himself at once.

Day was fairly broke when he had ended the process of mastication; and he bethought him of descending from the rock to arouse the sleepers. He knew they still slept, as no voice had yet issued from the grove of mollés. The mule and horse were heard cropping the grass, and the lamas were now feeding upon an open spot — the first they had eaten since their halt, as these creatures do not browse in the night.

Guapo descended with fear in his heart. How it would have joyed him to hear the voice of his master or of any of them! But no. Not a sound proceeded from any one of the party. He stole nimbly along the ledge, making his way through the mollé trees. At length he reached the spot. All asleep? Yes, all! "Are they dead?" thought Guapo, and his heart beat with anxiety. Indeed, they seemed so. The fatigue of travel had cast a sickly paleness over the faces of all, and one might easily have fancied they no longer lived ; but they breathed. " Yes, they breathe ! " ejaculated the old Indian, half aloud. " They live ! " Guapo bent down, and, seizing Don Pablo by the arm, shook him — at first gently, utter· ing, at the same time, some words to awake him But neither the shaking nor the voice had any effect Guapo shook more violently, and shouted louder Still Don Pablo slept. None of the others moved — none of them heard him. It was strange ; for the Indian knew that Don Pablo himself, as well as the others, were easily awaked on ordinary occasions. Guapo, becoming alarmed, now raised his voice to its loudest pitch, at the same time dragging Don Pablo's shoulder in a still more violent manner. This had the desired effect. The sleeper awoke, but so slow- ly, and evidently with such exertion, that there was something mysterious in it.

" What is it ? " he inquired, with half-opened eyes. " Is it morning already ? "

" The sun is up. Rouse, my master ! It is time we were on the road," replied the Indian.

" I feel very drowsy — I am heavy — I can scarce keep my eyes open. What can be the cause of this ? "

" The poison trees, master," answered Guapo.

The answer seemed to impress Don Pablo. He made a violent effort, and rose to his feet. When up he could scarcely stand. He felt as though he had swallowed a powerful opiate.

" It must be so, good Guapo. Perhaps there is

some truth in what you have said. O Heavens!"
exclaimed he, suddenly recollecting himself — "the
others — my wife and children!"

This thought had fully awakened Don Pablo; and
Guapo and he proceeded at once to arouse the others,
which they effected after much shouting and shaking.
All were still heavy with sleep, and felt as did Don
Pablo himself.

"Surely there is some narcotic power in the aroma
of these trees," muttered Don Pablo. "Come, wife,
let us be gone! We must remain under its influence
no longer, else what Guapo has said may prove too
true. Saddle up — we must eat our breakfasts farther
on. To the road! — to the road!"

Guapo soon had the horses ready, and all hurried
from the spot, and were once more climbing up the
mountain path. Even the animals seemed to move
slowly and lazily, as though they, too, had been under the influence of some soporific. But the pure
cold air of the mountain soon produced its effect.
All gradually recovered; and after cooking some
charqui and ocas in the ravine, and making their
breakfast upon these, they again felt light and fresh,
and pursued their journey with renewed vigor.

The road kept on up the ravine, and in some
places the banks rose almost perpendicularly from
the bed of the dry torrent, presenting on both sides
vast walls of black porphyry — for this is the princi
pal rock composing the giant chain of the Andes.
Above their heads screamed small parrots of rich
plumage of the species *Conurus rupicola*, which
make their nestling-places and dwell upon these

rocky cliffs. This is a singular fact, as all other parrots known are dwellers among trees, and are found in the forest at all times, except when on their passage from place to place. But even the squirrel, which is an animal peculiarly delighting in tree life, has its representative in several species of ground squirrels, that never ascend a tree ; and, among the monkeys, there exists the troglodyte, or cave-dwelling chimpanzee. No doubt squirrels or monkeys of any kind, transported to an open or treeless country, would soon habituate themselves to their new situation — for Nature affords many illustrations of this power of adaptation on the part of her creatures.

It was near sunset when our travellers reached the highest point of their route, nearly fourteen thousand feet above the level of the sea ! Here they emerged upon an open plain which stretched far before them. Above this plain towered mountains of all shapes to a height of many thousand feet from the level of the plain itself. Some of these mountains carried their covering of eternal snow, which, as the evening sun glanced upon it, exhibited the most beautiful tints of rose, and purple, and gold. The plain looked bleak and barren, and the cold which our travellers now felt added to the desolateness of the scene. No trees were in sight. Dry yellow grass covered the ground, and the rocks stood out naked and shaggy. They had reached one of those elevated tables of the Andes known as the *Puna*.

These singular tracts, elevated above the level of cultivation, are almost uninhabited. Their only inhabitants are a few poor Indians, who are employed by

the rich proprietors of the lower valleys as shepherds ; for upon those cold uplands thrive sheep, and
cattle, and lamas, and flocks of the wool-bearing alpaco. Through this wild region, however, you may
travel for days without encountering even a single
one of the wretched and isolated inhabitants who
watch over these flocks and herds.

On reaching the Puna, our party had made their
day's journey, and would have halted. The lamas
already showed signs of giving out by stopping and
uttering their strange booming note. But Guapo
knew these parts — for, though a descendant of the
incas, he had originally come from the great forest
beyond the eastern slope of the Andes, where many
of the Peruvian Indians had retired after the cruel
massacres of Pizarro. He now remembered that
not far from where they were was a shepherd's hut
and that the shepherd himself was an old friend of
his   That would be the place to stop for the night;
and, by Guapo's advice, Don Pablo resolved to continue on to the hut.   Guapo fell upon his knees before the lamas, and, after caressing and kissing them
and using a great variety of endearing expressions,
he at last coaxed these animals to proceed. No other
means would have availed, as beating would not make
either lama budge an inch. The leader, who was a
fine large animal and a great favorite with its master,
at length stepped boldly out ; and the other, encour-
aged by the sound of the small bells that tinkled
around the head of the leader, followed after, and
so the travellers moved on.

"Come, papa !" cried Leon ; " you are tired

yourself — mount this horse — I can walk a bit : " at the same instant the boy flung himself from the back of the horse, and led him up to where his father stood. Then, handing the bridle to the latter, he struck off along the plain, following Guapo and his lamas.

The road skirted round the rocks, where the mountain came down to meet the plain. The walk was not a long one, for the hut of which Guapo spoke became visible at less than a quarter of a mile's distance. An odd-looking hut it was — more like an ill-built stack of bean straw than a house. It had been built in the following manner : —

First, a round ring of large stones had been laid, then a row of turf, then another tier of stones, and so on, until the circular wall had reached the height of about four or five feet, the diameter being not more than eight or nine. On the top of the wall a number of poles had been set, so as to meet above where they were tied together. These poles were nothing else than the long flower stalks of the *maguey* or American aloe, (*Agave Americana*,) as no other wood of sufficient length grew in the vicinity. These poles served for rafters, and across them laths had been laid, and made fast. Over all this was placed a thatch of the long coarse Puna grass, which was tied in its place by grass ropes that were stretched from side to side over the top. This was the hut of Guapo's friend, and similar to all others that may be encountered in the wild region of the Puna. A door was left in the side, not over two feet high, so that it was necessary to crawl upon the hands and knees before any one could reach the interior.

As our travellers approached, they saw that the entrance was closed by an oxhide, which covered the whole of the opening.

Whether the shepherd was at home, was the next question ; but, as they got near to the house, Guapo suggested that Don Pablo should dismount and let Leon get upon horseback. This suggestion was made on account of the Puna dogs — of which creatures Guapo had a previous knowledge. These dogs, known by the name of inca dogs, (*Canis Ingæ*,) are, perhaps, the fiercest animals of their species. They are small, with pointed muzzles, tails curling upward, and long shaggy hair. They are half wild, snappish and surly as it is possible for dogs to be. They at-tack strangers with fury, and it is as much as their masters can do to rescue even a friend from their attack. Even when wounded, and unable any longer to keep their feet, they will crawl along the ground and bite the legs of those who have wounded them. They are even more hostile to white people than to Indians, and it is sometimes dangerous to approach an Indian hut where three or four of these fierce creatures are kept, as they will jump up against the side of a horse, and bite the legs of the rider. Their masters often use the stick before they can get obedi-ence from them. In every Indian hut several of these animals may be found, as they are extremely useful to the shepherds in guarding their flocks and for hunting. They are much employed throughout the Puna to hunt the "yútu," a species of partridge, which inhabits the rushy grass. This bird is traced by the dogs, seized before it can take to flight, and killed by a single bite of its fierce pursuer. Considering the savage nature of the inca dogs, Guapo showed great caution in approaching the hut of his friend. He first called loudly, but there was no reply. He then stole forward with his long knife, or "macheté," in his hand, and, having lifted the skin that covered the low doorway, peeped in. The hut was empty.

CHAPTER VI.

THE WILD BULL OF THE PUNA.

GUAPO was not much troubled at this. He knew he could take the liberty of using his friend's roof for the night, even should the latter not return to grant it. He crawled in. Of course his friend was only temporarily absent — no doubt looking after his flocks of sheep and alpacos ; and as he was a bache-lor there was no wife at home, but there were his furniture and utensils. Furniture ! No — there was none. There never is in the hut of a Puna shepherd. Utensils ! Yes — there was an earthen " olla," or pot to cook soup in, another to boil or roast maize, a jar to hold water, a few split gourd shells for plates, two or three others for cups — that was all. This was the catalogue of utensils. Two stones set a little apart formed the fireplace, in which the shepherd, when he makes a fire to cook with, makes it out of dry dung, (*taquia.*) A couple of dirty sheepskins lay upon the ground. These were the bed. Nothing more was to be seen. Yes, there was one thing more, and this gladdened the eyes of Guapo. In a bag that hung against the wall, and on which he soon laid his hands, he felt something — a collection of hard, round objects, about as big as large chestnuts. Guapo knew very well what these were. He knew they were " macas."

What are *macas* ? you will ask. Macas, then, are tuberous roots that grow in the elevated regions of the Puna, where neither ocas, ullucas, nor pota-toes will thrive. They are cultivated by the inhab-itants, and in many parts constitute almost the only food of these wretched people. They have an agree-able and rather sweetish flavor, and, when boiled in milk, taste somewhat like boiled chestnuts. They can be preserved for more than a year by simply drying them in the sun, and then exposing them to the cold air, when they become hard and shrivelled. They thrive best in this high region, for although they will grow in the lower valleys, they are there very insipid and worthless. The Indians prepare them for food by boiling them into a soup, or sirup, which is taken with parched maize corn.

Guapo knew that he had got his hands upon a bag of dried macas, and, although their owner was ab-sent, he had already. come to the determination to appropriate them for himself and party. His joy at the discovery had not subsided when another bag drew his attention, and this was the signal for another delightful surprise. His hand touched the new bag in a trice. There was a rattling sound within. Peas ? No — maize.

" Good ! " ejaculated Guapo ; " maize and macas ! That with what is left of the charqui — we shall not fast to-night."

Guapo now backed himself out of the hut, and joy-fully announced the discoveries he had made. The travellers dismounted. The horse and mule were picketed on lassoes on the plain. The lamas were left to go at will. They would not stray far from their owner.

It was piercing cold in this highland region. Doña Isidora and the children entered the hut, while Don Pablo and Guapo remained without for the purpose of collecting fuel. There was not a stick of wood, as no trees of any sort grew near. Both strayed off upon the plain to gather the *taquia*, or ordure of the cattle, though no cattle were in sight. Their tracks, however, were visible all around.

While engaged thus, the old Indian suddenly raised himself from his stooping position with an exclamation that betokened alarm. What had startled him ? A loud bellowing was heard — it was the bellowing of a bull. But what was there in that sound to alarm two fullgrown men ? Ah, you know not the bulls of the Puna.

Coming around a promontory of rocks, a large black bull was in sight. He was approaching them in full run, his head thrown down, his eyes glaring fiercely. At every spring he uttered a roar which was terrific to hear. A more horrid object it would be difficult to conceive. You may suppose that an adventure with an enraged bull is one of an ordinary character, and may occur any day, even in the green meadow pastures of Old England. So it is, if the animal were only an English bull. But it is a far different affair with the bulls of the Puna. Through-out all Spanish America animals of this kind are of a fiercer nature than elsewhere. It is from them the bulls used in the celebrated fights are obtained; and, perhaps, the race has been made fiercer by the treat- ment they receive on such occasions — for many of those that exhibit in the arena are afterwards used to breed from. But, in general, the Spanish American " vaqueros," or cattle herds, treat the cattle under their charge with much cruelty, and this has the effect of rendering them savage. Even in herds of cattle where there are no bulls, there are cows so danger- ous to approach that the vaqueros never attempt driving them unless when well mounted. A Mexican or South American cattle herd is, therefore, always a mounted man. There is a difference, too, among the bulls in different parts of these countries. On the llanos of Venezuela they are not so fierce as those of the Puna, and they are more and less so in dif- ferent parts of Mexico and the pampas of Buenos Ayres.

The Puna bulls are, perhaps, the fiercest and most dangerous of all. They are more than half wild. They scarcely ever see a human being, and they will attack one upon sight. To a mounted man there is little danger, unless by the stumbling or falling of his horse; but many a poor Indian, crossing these high plains afoot, has fallen a sacrifice to these vengeful brutes.

Both Don Pablo and Guapo knew all this, and therefore were aware of their own danger. Neither had a weapon — not so much as a stick. They had laid aside their knives and other arms, which had been carried inside the hut. To reach the hut before the bull reached *them* would be impossible; the brute

4

was coming nearly from it — for he had issued from
some shelter in the rocks not far off. They were full
two hundred yards out upon the plain, and to run in
the direction of the rocks would have been to run
counter to the bull and meet him face to face. Their
danger was imminent. What was to be done ?

There was not much time left them for considera-
tion. The furious animal was within thirty paces
distance, roaring loudly, shaking his head and brand-
ishing his long sharp horns. At this moment a happy
thought occurred almost simultaneously to Don Pablo
and the Indian. The evening, as we have already
said, was piercing cold, and both, in going out to
collect the fuel, had worn their ponchos. The trick
of the matadore with his red cloak suggested itself in
this moment of peril. Both had seen it performed
— Don Pablo often — and knew something of the
" way." In a moment both had stripped the ponchos
from their shoulders, and, placing themselves à la
matadore, awaited the onset of the bull. It was agreed
that, as soon as the bull was " hooded " by either
both should run at all speed to the rocks, where they
could easily climb out of reach of the animal.

Don Pablo happened to be more in the way, and
perhaps his more showy poncho attracted the brute
but whether or not, he was the first to receive the
charge. With the adroitness of a practised matadore
he flung his poncho on the horns of the animal, and
then both ran in the direction of the rocks. As they
faced towards the hut, however, to the horror of Don
Pablo he saw the Doña Isidora, with Leon and the
little Leona, all outside, and even at some distance

from the entrance. Attracted by the bellowing of the bull and the shouts of the men, they had rushed out of the hut.

Don Pablo, in wild accents, shouted to them to make for the door ; but, paralyzed by terror, they were for some moments unable to move. At length Doña Isidora, recovering herself, ran for the entrance pushing the children before her. But the low door-way was difficult of access ; they were slow in get ting under it ; and they would have been too late, as the bull, after shaking off the poncho, had turned and made directly for the hut.

" O God, preserve her ! " cried Don Pablo, as he saw the enraged animal within a few paces of where his wife had knelt to enter the doorway. " She is lost ! she is lost ! "

In fact, the bull was making directly towards her, and it seemed as if nothing could then have inter-posed to save her.

At that moment the tramp of a horse in full gallop sounded on their ears. Don Pablo looked up. A strange horseman was near the spot — an Indian. Over his head a singular instrument was revolving. There were three thongs fastened at one end, while at the other end of each was a ball. These balls were whirling and gyrating in the air. The next moment both thongs and balls were seen to part from the hands of the rider and warp themselves around the legs of the bull. The latter made an awkward spring forward, and then fell upon the plain, where he lay kicking and helpless. The horseman uttered a yell of triumph, sprang from his horse, and, running up to the prostrate animal, thrust the blade of his long macheté into its throat. The red stream gushed forth, and in a few seconds the black monster lay motionless upon the plain.

The new comer quietly unwound the thongs — the *bolas* — from the legs of the dead bull, and then addressed himself to our travellers.

CHAPTER VII.

THE "VAQUERO."

WHO was this deliverer? No other than the vaquero, the friend of Guapo, who now welcomed Guapo and his companions, telling them, in the polite phraseology of all Spanish Americans, that his *house (!)* was at their service; they were welcome to all it contained.

The macas, and maize, and a fresh steak from the wild bull enabled them to make a most excellent supper. In return for this hospitality, Don Pablo made the vaquero a handsome present out of his purse; but what gratified him still more was a supply of coca which his friend Guapo was enabled to bestow upon him, for his own stock had been exhausted for some days. Guapo, on leaving Cuzco, had spent his last *peseta* in buying this luxury, and therefore was well provided for weeks to come.

After they had had supper, he and his friend seated themselves on one side and quietly chewed for a good half hour; when at length Guapo, who knew he could trust the vaquero, because the latter, like himself, was one of the " patriotas," communicated to him the object of their journey through that desolate region. The vaquero not only promised secrecy, but bound himself to put any party of pursuers completely off the trail. The vaquero, even in his remote mountain home, had heard of Don Pablo, knew that he was a good patriot and friend of the Indians; and he would therefore have risked his life to serve such a man; for no people have proved more devoted to the friends of their race than these simple and faithful Indians of the Andes. How many instances of noble self-sacrifice — even of life itself — occurred during the painful history of their conquest by the cruel and sanguinary followers of Pizarro!

The vaquero, therefore, did all in his power to make his guests comfortable for the night. His dogs — there were four of them — were not so hospitably inclined, for they did not seem to know friends from enemies. They had come up shortly after their master himself arrived, and had made a desperate attack upon every body. The vaquero, however, assisted by Guapo, — who, being an Indian, was less troubled with them, — gave them a very rough handling with a large whip which he carried, and then, securing the whole of them, tied them together in a bunch, and left them at the back of the hut to snap and growl at each other, which they did throughout the livelong night. Supper over, all the travellers would have retired to rest; but the vaquero having announced that he was going out to set snares for the chinchillas and viscachas, Leon could not rest, but asked permission to accompany him. This was granted both by Don Pablo and the vaquero himself.

The chinchilla, and its near relative, the viscacha, are two little animals of the rodent, or grass-eating, kmd that inhabit the very highest mountains of Peru and Chili. They are nearly of the same size, and each about as big as a rabbit, which in habits they very much resemble. They have long tails, how-ever, which the rabbit has not, though the latter beats them in the length of his ears. The color of the chinchilla is known to every body, since its soft, vel-vety fur is highly prized by ladies as an article of dress, and may be seen in every London fur shop. The animal is of a beautiful marbled gray, white and black, with pure white feet. The fur of the viscacha is not so pretty, being of a brownish and white mix-ture. Its cheeks are black, with long, bristly mus-taches like those of a cat, while its head resembles that of the hare or rabbit. Both these innocent little creatures live upon the high declivities of the Andes, in holes and crevices among the rocks, where they remain concealed during the day, but steal out to feed twice in the twenty-four hours — that is, during the evening twilight and in the early morning. The mode of capturing them is by snares made of horse-hair, which are set in front of their caves, just as we snare rabbits in a warren, except that for the rab-bits we make use of light, elastic wire instead of the horsehair.

Leon was delighted with the excursion, as the vaquero showed him how to set the snares, and told him a great many curious stories of Puna life and habits. Some of these stories were about the great condor vulture, which the narrator of course described as a much bigger bird than it really is; for the condor, after all, is not so much bigger than the griffon vulture, or even the vulture of California. But you, young reader, have already had a full account of the vultures of America, the condor among the rest, therefore we shall not repeat what was said by the vaquero about this interesting bird.

On the way to the place where the snares were to bo set they passed a lagoon, or marshy lake, in which were many kinds of birds peculiar to these high regions. Out on the open water they saw a wild goose of a very beautiful species. It is called the " huachua " goose. Its plumage is of a snowy whiteness, all except the wings, which are bright green and violet, while the beak, legs, and feet are scarlet. They also saw two species of ibis wading about in the marsh, and a gigantic water hen (*Fulica gigantea*) almost as big as a turkey. This last is of a dark-gray color, with a red beak, at the base of which is a large yellow knob of the shape of a bean. On this account it is called by the Indians "bean nose." Upon the plain, near the border of the marsh, they noticed a beautiful plover, (*Charadrius*,) having plumage marked very much like that of the " huachua " goose, with green wings shining in the sun like polished metal. Another curious bird also sat upon the plain, or flew around their heads. This was a bird of prey of the species of jerfalcons, (*Polyborus*.) The vaquero called it the " huarahua." He told Leon it preyed only on carrion, and never killed its own food; that it was very harmless and tame; which was evidently true, as, shortly after, one of them, seated upon a stone, allowed the Indian to approach and knock it over with a stick. Such a silly bird Leon had never seen.

The vaquero was quite a naturalist in his way — that is, he knew all the animals of the Puna and their habits, just as you will sometimes find a gamekeeper in our own country, or often a shepherd or farm servant. He pointed out a rock woodpecker, which he called a " pito," (*Colaptes rupicola,*) that was fluttering about and flying from rock to rock. Like the cliff parrots we have already mentioned, this rock woodpecker was a curious phenomenon; for, as their very name implies, the woodpeckers are all tree-dwelling birds; yet here was one of the genus living among rocks where not a tree was to be seen, and scarcely a plant except the thorny cactuses and magueys, with which succulent vegetables the wood-pecker has nothing to do. The " pito " is a small, brown, speckled bird, with yellow belly; and there were great numbers of them flying about.

But the bird which most fixed the attention of Leon was a little bird about the size of a starling. Its plumage was rather pretty. It was brown, with black stripes on the back, and white breasted. But it was not the plumage of the bird that interested Leon. It was what his companion told him of a singular habit which it had — that of repeating, at the end of every hour during the night, its melancholy and monotonous note. The Indians call this bird the ' cock of the inca," and they moreover regard it with a sort of superstitious reverence.

Having placed his snares, the vaquero set out to

return with his youthful companion. As they walked back along the mountain foot, a fox stole out from the rocks and skulked towards the marshy lake, no doubt in search of prey. This fox was the *Canis azaræ*, a most troublesome species, found all through South America. He is the great pest of the Puna shepherds, as he is a fierce hunter, and kills many of the young lambs and alpacos. The vaquero was sorry he had not his dogs with him, as, from the route the fox had taken, he would have been certain to have captured him; and that would have been worth something; for the great sheep owners give their shepherds a sheep for every old fox that they can kill, and for every young one a lamb. But the dogs, on this occasion, had been left behind, lest they should have bitten Leon, and the vaquero was compelled to let "Renard" go his way. It was night when they returned to the hut; and then, after Leon had related the details of their excursion, all retired to rest.

CHAPTER VIII.

LAMAS, ALPACOS, VICUÑAS, AND GUANACOS.

Our travellers were stirring by early break of day. As they issued from the hut, a singular and interest-ing scene presented itself to their eyes. At one view — one *coup d'œil* — they beheld the whole four species of the celebrated camel sheep of the Andes, — for there are four of them, — lama, guanaco, alpaco, and vicuña. This was a rare sight indeed. They were all browsing upon the open plain ; first, the lamas near the hut ; then a flock of tame al-pacos out upon the plain ; thirdly, a herd of seven guanacos farther off ; and, still more distant, a larger herd of the shy vicuñas. The guanacos and vicuñas were of uniform colors, — that is, in each flock, the color of the individuals was the same, — while among the lamas and alpacos there were many varieties of color. The latter two kinds were tame ; in fact, they were under the charge of Guapo's friend the shep-herd ; whereas the herds of vicuñas and guanacos consisted of wild animals.

Perhaps no animal of South America has attracted so much attention as the lama, as it was the only beast of burden the Indians had trained to their use on the arrival of Europeans in that country. So many strange stories were told by the earlier Spanish travellers regarding this "camel sheep" that it was natural that great interest should attach to it. These reported that the lama was used for riding. Such, however, is not the case. It is only trained to carry burdens ; although an Indian boy may be sometimes seen on the back of a lama for mischief, or when crossing a stream and the lad does not wish to get his feet wet.

The lama is three feet high from hoof to shoulder, though his long neck makes him look taller. His color is generally brown, with black and yellow shades, sometimes speckled or spotted ; and there are black and white lamas ; but these are rare. His wool is long and coarse ; though the females, which are smaller, have a finer and better wool. The latter are never used to carry burdens, but only kept for breeding. They are fed in flocks upon the Puna heights ; and it was a flock of these that our travellers saw near the hut.

The males are trained to carry burdens at the age of four years. A pack saddle, called *yergua*, woven out of coarse wool, is fastened on the back, and upon this the goods are placed. The burden never exceeds one hundred and twenty or one hundred and thirty pounds. Should a heavier one be put on, the lama, like the camel, quite understands that he is "overweighted," and neither coaxing nor beat· ing will induce him to move a step. He will lie down, or, if much vexed, spit angrily at his driver ; and this spittle has a highly acrid property, and will cause blisters on the skin where it touches. Some· times a lama, overvexed by ill treatment, has been known, in despair, to dash his brains out against a rock.

The lamas are used much in the mines of Peru for carrying the ore. They frequently serve better than either asses or mules, as they can pass up and down declivities where neither ass nor mule can travel. They are sometimes taken in long trains from the mountains down to the coast region for salt and other goods; but on such occasions many of them die, as they cannot bear the warm climate of the lowlands. Their proper and native place is on the higher plains of the Andes.

A string of lamas, when on a journey, is a very interesting spectacle. One of the largest is usually the leader. The rest follow in single file, at a slow, measured pace, their heads ornamented tastefully with ribbons, while small bells, hanging around their necks, tinkle as they go. They throw their high heads from side to side, gazing around them, and when frightened at any thing will " break ranks " and scamper out of their path, to be collected again with some trouble. When resting, they utter a low, humming noise, which has been compared to the sound of an Æolian harp. They crouch down on their breast — where there is a callosity — when about to receive their burdens, and also sleep resting in the same attitude. A halt during the day is neces-sary, in order that they may be fed, as these animals will not eat by night. In consequence of this they make but short journeys, — ten to fifteen miles, — although they will travel for a long time, allowing them a day's rest out of every five or six. Like the

camels of the East, they can go days without water ·
and Buffon knew one that went *eighteen months* without it ; but Buffon is very poor authority. When one
of them becomes wearied and does not wish to proceed, it is exceedingly difficult to coax him onward.

These animals were at one time very valuable.
On the discovery of America a lama cost as much as
eighteen or twenty dollars ; but the introduction of
mules and other beasts of burden has considerably
cheapened them. At present they are sold for about
four dollars in the mining districts, but can be
bought where they are bred and reared for half that
amount. In the days of the incas their flesh was
much used as food. It is still eaten ; but for this
purpose the common sheep is preferred, as the flesh
of the lama is spongy and not very well flavored. The
wool is used for many sorts of coarse manufacture.
So much for lamas. Now the " guanaco."

This animal (whose name is sometimes written
" huanaca," though the pronunciation is the same with
" guanaco," or " guanaca ") is larger than the lama,
and for a long time was considered merely as the
wild lama, or the lama *run wild*, in which you will
perceive an essential distinction. It is neither, but
an animal of specific difference. It exists in a wild
state in the high mountains, though with great care
and trouble it can be domesticated and trained to
carry burdens as well as its congener the lama. In
form it resembles the latter ; but, as is the case with
most wild animals, the guanacos are all alike in
color. The upper parts of the body are of a reddish
brown, while underneath it is a dirty white. The

lips are white and the face of a dark gray. The wool is shorter than that of the lama, and of the same length all over the body. The guanaco lives in herds of five or seven individuals; and these are very shy, fleeing to the most inaccessible cliffs when any one approaches them. Like the chamois of Switzerland and the " bighorn" of the Rocky Mountains, they can glide along steep ledges where neither men nor dogs can find footing.

The " alpaco," or " paco," as it is sometimes called, is one of the most useful of the ' Peruvian sheep, and is more like the common sheep than the others. This arises from its bulkier shape, caused by its thick fleece of long wool. The latter is soft, fine, and often five inches in length, and, as is well known, has become an important article in the manufacture of cloth. Its color is usually either white or black, though there are some of the alpacos speckled or spotted. Ponchos are woven out of alpaco wool by the Indians of the Andes.

The alpaco is a domesticated animal, like the lama; but it is not used for carrying burdens. It is kept in large flocks, and regularly shorn as sheep are. If one of the alpacos gets separated from the flock, it will lie down and suffer itself to be beaten to death rather than go the way its driver wishes. You have no doubt sometimes seen a common sheep exhibit similar obstinacy.

Of all the Peruvian sheep the vicuña is certainly the prettiest and most graceful. It has more the form cf the deer or antelope than of the sheep ; and its color is so striking that it has obtained among the Peruvians the name of the animal itself — *color de vicuña*, (vicuña color.) It is of a reddish yellow, not unlike that of our domestic red cat, although the breast and under parts of the body are white. The flesh of the vicuña is excellent eating, and its wool is of more value than even that of the alpaco. Where a pound of the former sells for one dollar, — which is the usual price, — the pound of alpaco will fetch only a quarter of that sum. Hats and the finest fabrics can be woven from the fleece of the vicuña, and the incas used to clothe themselves in rich stuffs manufactured from it. In the present day the " ricos," or rich proprietors of Peru, pride themselves in possessing ponchos of vicuña wool.

The vicuña inhabits the high plains of the Andes, though, unlike the guanaco, it rarely ventures up the rocky cliffs, as its hoofs are only calculated for the soft turf of the plains. It roams about in larger herds than the other — eighteen or twenty in the herd ; and these are usually females under the protection and guidance of one polygamous old male. While feeding, the latter keeps watch over the flock, usually posting himself at some distance, so that he may have a better opportunity of seeing and hearing any danger that may approach. When any is perceived, a shrill whistle from the leader and a quick stroke of his hoof on the turf warn the flock, and all draw closely together, each stretching out its head in the direction of the danger. They then take to flight, at first slowly, but afterwards with the swift·

ness of the roe ; while the male, true to his trust, hangs in the rear and halts at intervals, as if to cover the retreat of the herd.

The lama, guanaco, alpaco, and vicuña, although different species, will breed with each other ; and it is certain that some of their hybrids will again produce young. There exist, therefore, many intermediate varieties, or " mules," throughout the countries of the Andes, some of which have been mistaken for separate species.

5

CHAPTER IX.

A VICUÑA HUNT.

THE vicuña, being of such value both inside and out, both in flesh and wool, is hunted by the mountain Indians with great assiduity. It is an animal most difficult to approach, and there is rarely any cover on these naked plains by which to approach it.

The chief mode of capturing it is by the " chacu." This cannot be effected by a single hunter. A great number is required. Usually the whole population of one of the villages of the " Sierras" lower down turns out for this sport, or rather business; for it is an animal source of profit. Even the women go along, to cook and perform other offices, as the hunt of the *chacu* sometimes lasts a week or more.

A hunting party will number from fifty to one hundred persons. They climb up to the *altos*, or high and secluded plains, where the vicuña dwells in greatest numbers. They carry with them immense coils of ropes and a large quantity of colored rags, together with bundles of stakes three or four feet in length. When a proper part of the plain has been chosen they drive in the stakes four or five yards apart and running in the circumference of a circle, sometimes nearly a mile in diameter. A rope is then stretched from stake to stake, at the height of between two and three feet from the ground, and over this rope are hung the colored rags provided for the occasion, and which keep fluttering in the wind. A sort of scarecrow fence is thus constructed in the form of a ring, except that on one side a space of about two hundred yards is left open to serve as an entrance for the game. The Indians then, most of them on horseback, make a grand detour, extending for miles over the country, and, having got behind the herds of vicuñas, drive them within the circle, and close up the entrance by completing the ring. The hunters then go inside, and, using the *bolas*, or even seizing the animals by their hind legs, soon capture the whole. Strange to say, these silly creatures make no attempt to break through the sham fence, nor even to leap over it. Not so with the guanacos when so enclosed. The latter spring against the fence at once ; and if, by chance, a party of guanacos be driven in along with the vicuñas, they not only break open the rope enclosure and free themselves, but also the whole herd of their cousins the vicuñas. It is, therefore, not considered any gain to get a flock of guanacos into the trap.

The hunt usually lasts several days; but during that time the enclosure of ropes is flitted from place to place until no more vicuñas can be found. Then the ropes, stakes, &c., are collected, and the produce of the hunt distributed among the hunters. But the church levies its tax upon the " chacu," and the skins — worth a dollar each — have to be given up to the priest of the village. A good round sum this amounts to, as frequently four or five hundred vicuñas are taken at a single *chacu*.

A good hunter is sometimes able to "approach" the vicuña. Guapo's friend was esteemed one of the best in all the Puna. The sight of the herd out on the plain, with their graceful forms and beautiful red-dish-orange bodies, was too much for him; and he resolved to try his skill upon them. He said he had a plan of his own, which he intended to practise on this occasion.

Don Pablo and his party — even Doña Isidora and the little Leona — were all outside the hut, although the morning air was raw and chill. But the domicile of the worthy vaquero was not empty for all that It was peopled by a very large colony of very small animals, and a night in their society had proved enough for the travellers. The chill air of the Puna was even more endurable than such company.

The vaquero crawled back into the hut, and in a few minutes returned, but so metamorphosed that had the party not seen him come out of the doorway they would have mistaken him for a lama. He was completely disguised in the skin of one of these ani-mals. His face only was partly visible, and his eyes looked out of the breast. The head and neck of the skin, stuffed with some light substance, stood up and forward after the manner of the living animal; and although the legs were a little clumsy, yet it would have required a more intelligent creature than the vicuña to have observed this defect.

All hands, even the saturnine Guapo, laughed loudly at the counterfeit; and the vaquero himself was heard to chuckle through the long wool upon the breast. He did not lose time, however, but instantly prepared to set off. He needed no other preparation than to get hold of his *bolas*—that was his favorite weapon. Before going farther, I shall tell you what sort of weapon it is.

The bolas consists of three balls—hence the name —of lead or stone, two of them heavier than the third. Each ball is fastened to the end of a stout thong made of twisted sinews of the vicuña itself, and the other ends of the three thongs are joined together. In using them the hunter holds the lightest ball in his hand, and twirls the other two in circles around his head until they have attained the proper velocity, when he takes aim and launches them forth. Through the air fly the thongs and balls, and all whirling round in circles, until they strike some object; and if that object be the legs of an animal, the thongs become immediately warped around them, until the animal is regularly hoppled, and in attempting to escape comes at once to the ground. Of course great practice is required before such an instrument can be used skilfully ; and to the novice there is some danger of one of the balls hitting him a crack on the head, and knocking over himself instead of the game. But there was no danger of Guapo's friend the vaquero committing this blunder. He had been swinging the bolas around his head for more than forty years !

Without more ado, then, he seized the weapon; and, having gathered it with his *fore feet* into a portable shape, he proceeded in the direction of the vicuñas.

The travellers remained by the hut, watching him with interest; but his movements were particularly interesting to Leon, who, like all boys, was naturally fond of such enterprises.

The herd of vicuñas was not more than three quarters of a mile off. For the first half of this distance the vaquero shambled along right speedily; but as he drew nearer to the animals he proceeded slower and with more caution.

The pretty creatures were busily browsing, and had no fear. They knew they were well guarded by their faithful sentinel, in whom they had every confidence — the lord and leader of the herd. Even from the hut, this one could be seen standing some distance apart from the rest. He was easily recognized by his greater bulk and prouder bearing.

The false lama has passed near the guanacos, and they have taken no heed of him. This is a good omen; for the guanacos are quite as sharp and shy as their smaller cousins, and since he has succeeded in deceiving them, he will likely do the same for the vicuñas. Already he approaches them. He does not make for the herd, but directly for the leader. Surely he is near enough; from the hut he seems close up to the creature. See! the vicuña tosses his head and strikes the ground with his hoof. Listen! it is his shrill whistle. The scattered herd suddenly start and flock together; but look! the *lama* stands erect on his hind legs; the bolas whirl around his head — they are launched out. Ha! the vicuña is down!

Where is the female drove? Have they scampered off and forsaken their lord? No! faithful as a loving wife, they run up to share his danger. With shrill cries they gather around him, moving to and fro. The lama is in their midst. See! he is deal-ing blows with some weapon — it is a knife! his vic-tims fall around him — one at every blow; one by one they are falling. At last, at last they are all down — yes, the whole herd are stretched, dead or dying, upon the plain!

The struggle is over; no sound is heard, save the hoof stroke of the guanacos, lamas, and alpacos, that cover the plain in their wild flight.

Leon could no longer restrain his curiosity, but ran off to the scene of the slaughter. There he counted no less than nineteen vicuñas lying dead, each one stabbed in the ribs! The Indian assured him that it was not the first *battue* of the kind he had made. A whole herd of vicuñas is often taken in this way. When the male is wounded or killed, the females will not leave him; but, as if out of gratitude for the protection he has during life afforded them, they share his fate without making an effort to escape!

CHAPTER X.

CAPTURING A CONDOR.

THE vaquero with his horse soon dragged the
vicuñas to the hut. Guapo gave him a help with the
mule, and in a few minutes they were all brought up.
One of them was immediately skinned, and part of
it prepared for breakfast, and our travellers ate heartily of it, as the cold Puna air had given an edge to
their appetites.

The new-killed animals, along with the red skin
of the bull, which had been spread out on the ground
at some distance from the hut, had already attracted
the condors; and four or five of these great birds
were now seen hovering in the air, evidently with
the intention of alighting at the first opportunity.

An idea seemed to enter the head of the vaquero,
while his guests were still at breakfast, and he asked
Leon if he would like to see a condor caught. Of
course Leon replied in the affirmative. What boy
wouldn't like to see a condor caught ?

The vaquero said he would gratify him with the
sight, and without staying to finish his breakfast —
indeed he had had his " coceada," and didn't care
for any — he started to his feet, and began to make
preparations for the capture.

How he was to catch one of these great birds,

Leon had not the slightest idea. Perhaps with the "bolas," thought he. That would have done well enough if he could only get near them ; but the condors were sufficiently shy not to let any man come within reach either with bolas or guns. It is only when they have been feasting on carrion, and have gorged themselves to repletion, that they can be thus approached; and then they may be even knocked over with sticks.

At other times the condor is a shy and wary bird No wonder either that he is so ; for, unlike most other vultures, he is hunted and killed at all times. The vultures of most countries are respected by the people, because they perform a valuable service in clearing away carrion ; and in many parts these birds are protected by statute. There are laws in the Southern United States, and in several of the Spanish American republics, which impose fines and penalties for killing the black vultures, (*Cathartes aura* and *C. atratus.*) In some Oriental countries, too, similar laws exist. But no statute protects the condor. On the contrary, he is a proscribed bird, and there is a bounty on his head, because he does great damage to the proprietors of sheep, and lamas, and alpacos, killing and devouring the young of these animals. His large quills, moreover, are much prized in the South American cities, and the killing of a condor is worth something. All this will account for the shyness of this great bird, while other vultures are usually so tame that you may approach within a few paces of them.

As yet the half dozen condors hovering about kept

well off from the hut; and Leon could not understand how any one of them was to be caught.

The vaquero, however, had a good many " dodges," and after the *ruse* he had just practised upon the vicuñas, Leon suspected he would employ some similar artifice with the condors. Leon was right. It was by a stratagem the bird was to be taken.

The vaquero laid hold of a long rope, and lifting the bull's hide upon his shoulders, asked Guapo to follow him with the two horses. When he had got out some four or five hundred yards from the hut, he simply spread himself flat upon the ground, and drew the skin over him, the fleshy side turned upward. There was a hollow in the ground about as big as his body — in fact, a trench he had himself made for a former occasion — and when lying in this on his back, his breast was about on a level with the surrounding turf. His object in asking Guapo to accompany him with the horses was simply a *ruse* to deceive the condors, who from their high elevation were all the while looking down upon the plain. But the vaquero covered himself so adroitly with his red blanket, that even their keen eyes could scarcely have noticed him; and as Guapo afterwards left the ground with the led horses, the vultures supposed that nothing remained but the skin, which from its sanguinary color to them appeared to be flesh.

The birds had now nothing to fear from the propinquity of the hut. There the party were all seated quietly eating their breakfast, and apparently taking no notice of them. In a few minutes' time, therefore, they descended lower, and lower, — and thei one of the very largest dropped upon the ground within a few feet of the hide. After surveying it for a moment, he appeared to see nothing suspicious about it, and hopped a little closer. Another at this moment came to the ground — which gave courage to the first — and this at length stalked boldly on the hide, and began to tear at it with his great beak.

A movement was now perceived on the part of the vaquero — the hide " lumped " up, and at the same time the wings of the condor were seen to play and flap about as if he wanted to rise into the air, but could not. He was evidently held by the legs !

The other bird had flown off at the first alarm, and the whole band were soon soaring far upward into the blue heavens.

Leon now expected to see the vaquero uncover himself. Not so, however, as yet. That wily hunter had no such intention; and although he was now in a sitting posture, grasping the legs of the condor, yet his head and shoulders were still enveloped in the bull's hide. He knew better than to show his naked face to the giant vulture, that at a single " peck " of his powerful beak would have deprived him of an eye, or otherwise injured him severely. The vaquero was aware of all this, and therefore did not leave his hiding-place until he had firmly knotted one end of the long cord around the shank of the bird — then slipping out at one side, he ran off to some distance before stopping. The condor, apparently relieved of his disagreeable company, made a sudden effort, and rose into the air, carrying the hide after him. Leon shouted out, for he thought the vulture had es-

caped ; but the vaquero knew better, as he held the
other end of the cord in his hand ; and the bird, partly from the weight of the skin, and partly from a
slight tug given by the hunter, soon came heavily to
the ground again. The vaquero was now joined by
Guapo ; and, after some sharp manœuvring, they
succeeded between them in passing the string through
the nostrils of the condor, by which means it was
quietly conducted to the hut, and staked on the ground
in the rear — to be disposed of whenever its captor
should think fit.

CHAPTER XI.

THE PERILS OF A PERUVIAN ROAD.

IT was as yet only an hour or so after daybreak —
for the vicuña hunt had occupied but a very short
time, and the capture of the condor a still shorter.
Don Pablo was anxious to be gone, as he knew he
was not beyond the reach of pursuit. A pair of the
vicuñas were hastily prepared, and packed upon a
lama for use upon their journey. Thus furnished,
the party resumed their route.

The vaquero did not accompany them. He had
an office to perform of far more importance to their
welfare and safety. As soon as they were gone he
let loose his four snarling curs, and taking them out
to where the pile of dead vicuñas lay upon the plain,
he left them there with instructions to guard the carcasses from foxes, condors, or whatever else might
wish to make a meal off them. Then mounting, he
rode off to the place where the road leading from
Cuzco ascended upon the table land, and having tied
his horse to a bush, he climbed upon a projecting
rock and sat down. From this point he commanded
a view of the winding road to the distance of miles
below him. No traveller — much less a party of
soldiers — could approach without his seeing them,
even many hours before they could get up to where

he sat; and it was for that reason he had stationed himself there. Had Don Pablo been pursued, the faithful Indian would have galloped after and given him warning, long before his pursuers could have reached the plain.

He sat until sunset — contenting himself with a few leaves of coca. No pursuer appeared in sight. He then mounted his horse, and rode back to his solitary hut.

Let us follow our travellers.

They crossed the table plain during the day, and rested that night under the shelter of some overhanging rocks on the other side. They supped upon part of the vicuñas, and felt more cheerful, as they widened the distance between themselves and danger. But in the morning they did not remain longer by their camp than was necessary to get breakfast. Half an hour after sunrise saw them once more on their route.

Their road led through a pass in the mountains. At first it ascended, and then began to go downward. They had crossed the last ridge of the Andes, and were now descending the eastern slopes. Another day's journey, or two at most, would bring them to the borders of that wild forest, which stretches from the foot hills of the Andes to the shores of the Atlantic Ocean — that forest with scarcely a civilized settlement throughout all its wide extent — where no roads exist — whose only paths are rivers — whose dark jungles are in places so impenetrable that the Indian cannot enter them, and even the fierce jaguar, embarrassed by the thick underwood, has to take to

the tree tops in pursuit of his prey. Another day's
journey or so would bring them to the borders of the
" Montaña " — for such is the name which, by a
strange misapplication of terms, has been given to
this primeval wood. Yes, the Montaña was before
them, and although yet distant, it could now and then
be seen as the road wound among the rocks, stretching far towards the sky like a green and misty ocean.

In that almost boundless region there dwelt none
but the aborigines of the soil — the wild Indians —
and these only in sparse and distant bands. Even
the Spaniards in their day of glory had failed to conquer it ; and the Portuguese from the other side were
not more successful. Here and there a lone missionary attempted to wheedle the simple natives into a
belief in his monkish religion, or, when able to do so,
forced it upon them by fire and sword. But most of
these efforts, both of conquest and conversion, had
failed ; and now, with the exception of some isolated
trading post, or decayed mission station, on the banks
of the great rivers, the whole " Montaña " was as
wild and savage as when the keels of Columbus first
ploughed the waters of the Carib Sea.

The Spanish colonists, on the Peruvian or western
border of this immense forest, had never been able
to penetrate it as colonists or settlers. Expeditions
from time to time had passed along its rivers in search
of the fabled gold country of *Manoa*, whose king
each morning gave himself a coating of gold dust,
and was hence called El Dorado, (the gilded ;) but
all these expeditions ended in mortification and de-
feat. The settlements never extended beyond the

sierras, or foot hills of the Andes, which stretch only
a few days' journey (in some places but a score of
leagues) from the populous cities on the mountain
heights.   Even at this present time, if you travel
thirty leagues eastward of the large town of Cuzco,
in the direction taken by Don Pablo, you will pass
the boundaries of civilization, and enter a country
unexplored and altogether unknown to the people of
Cuzco themselves.   About the " Montaña " very little
is known in the settlements of the Andes.   Fierce
tribes of Indians, the jaguar, the vampire bat, swarms
of mosquitoes, and the hot atmosphere, have kept
the settler, as well as the curious traveller, out of
these wooded plains.

Don Pablo had already passed the outskirts of
civilization.   Any settlement he might find beyond
would be the hut of some half-wild Indian.   There
was no fear of his encountering a white face upor
the unfrequented path he had chosen, though had he
gone by some other route he might have found white
settlements extending farther to the eastward.   As it
was, the wilderness lay before him, and he would
soon enter it.

And what was he to do in the wilderness ?   He
knew not.   He had never reflected on that.   He only
knew that behind him was a relentless foe thirsting
for his life.   To go back was to march to certain
death.   He had no thoughts of returning.   That
would have been madness.   His property was already confiscated — his death decreed by the vengeful viceroy, whose soldiers had orders to capture or
slay, wherever they should find him.   His only hope,

then, was to escape beyond the borders of civilization — to hide himself in the great " Montaña." Beyond this he had formed no plan. He had scarcely
thought about the future. Forward, then, for the
" Montaña."

The road which our travellers followed was nothing more than a narrow path, or " trail " formed by
cattle, or by some party of Indians occasionally passing up from the lower valleys to the mountain heights.
It lay along the edge of a torrent that leaped and
foamed over its rocky bed. The torrent was no
doubt on its way to join the greatest of rivers, the
mighty Amazon — the head waters of which spring
from all parts of the Andes, draining the slopes of
these mountains through more than twenty degrees
of latitude.

Towards evening the little party were beginning to
enter among the mountain spurs, or foot hills. Here
the travelling grew exceedingly difficult, the path
sometimes running up a steep acclivity, and then descending into deep ravines — so deep and dark that
the sun's rays seemed hardly to enter them. The
road was what Spanish Americans term " *Cuesta
arriba, cuesta abajo*," (up hill, down hill.)

In no part of the world are such roads to be met
with as among the Andes Mountains, both in South
America and in their Mexican continuation through
the northern division of the continent. This arises
from the peculiar geological structure of these mountains. Vast clefts traverse them, yawning far into the
earth. In South America these are called *quebradas*.
You may stand on the edge of one of them and look

6

sheer down a precipice two thousand feet. You may
fancy a whole mountain scooped out and carried
away, and yet you may have to reach the bottom of
this yawning gulf by a road which seems cut out of
the face of the cliff, or rather has been formed by a
freak of Nature — for in these countries the hand of
man has done but little for the roads. Sometimes
the path traverses a ledge so narrow that scarce room
is found for the feet of your trusty mule. Sometimes
a hanging bridge has to be crossed, spanning a horrid chasm, at the bottom of which roars a foaming
torrent — the bridge itself, composed of ropes and
brambles, all the while swinging like a hammock
under the tread of the affrighted traveller.

He who journeys through the tame scenery of European countries can form but little idea of the wild
and dangerous highways of the Andes. Even the
passes of the Alps or Carpathians are safe in comparison. On the Peruvian road the lives of men and
animals are often sacrificed. Mules slide from the
narrow ledges, or break through the frail " soga "
bridges, carrying their riders along with them, whirling through empty air to be plunged into foaming
waters or dashed on sharp rocks below. These are
accidents of continual occurrence; and yet, on account of the apathy of the Spano-Indian races that inhabit these countries, little is done for either roads or
bridges. Every one is left to take care of himself,
and get over them as he best may. It is only now
and then that positive necessity prompts to a great
effort, and then a road is repaired or a broken bridge
patched with new ropes.

But the road that was travelled by Don Pablo had seen no repairs — there were no bridges.   It was, in fact, a mere pathway, where the traveller scrambled over rocks, or plunged into the stream, and forded or swam across it as he best could.   Sometimes it lay along the water's edge, keeping in the bottom of the ravine ; at other places no space was left by the water, and then the path ascended and ran along some ledge perhaps for miles, at the end of which it would again descend to the bed of the stream.

CHAPTER XII.

ENCOUNTER UPON A CLIFF.

THAT night they encamped in the bottom of the ravine, close to the water's edge. They found just enough of level ground to enable them to stretch themselves ; but they were contented with that. There was nothing for the animals to eat except the succulent but thorny leaves of the *Cactus opuntia*, or the more fibrous blades of the wild agave. This evening there were no quiñoa seeds to be had, for none of these trees grew near. Even the botanist, Don Pablo, could find no vegetable substance that was eatable ; and they would have to sup upon the vicuña meat, without bread, potatoes, or other vegetables. Their stock of ocas, ullucas, and macas was quite out. They had cooked the last of the macas for that morning's meal.

Guapo here came to their relief. Guapo's experience went beyond the theoretical knowledge of the botanist. Guapo knew a vegetable which was good to eat — in fact, a most delicious vegetable when cooked with meat. This was no other than the fleshy heart of the wild maguey, (*agave*,) with part of the adhering roots. Among naked rocks, in the most barren parts of the desert wilderness, the wild agave may be found growing in luxuriance. Its thick, succulent blades, when split open, exude a cool liquid that often gives considerable relief to the thirsty traveller ; while the heart or egg-shaped nu-cleus from which spring the sheathing leaves, and even parts of the leaves themselves, when cooked with any sort of meat, become an excellent and nour-ishing food. The Indians make this use of the aloe on the high plains of Northern Mexico, among the roving bands of the Apaché, Navajo, and Comanché. These people cook them along with horse's flesh ; for there the wild horse is the principal food of whole tribes. Their mode of cooking both the flesh and the aloe is by baking them together in little ovens of stones sunk in the ground, and then heated by fire until they are nearly redhot. The ashes are then cleared out, the meat and vegetables placed in the ovens, and then buried until both are sufficiently done. In fact there is one tribe of the Apachés who have obtained the name of " Mezcaleros," from the fact of their eating the wild aloe, which in those countries goes under the name of " mezcal " plant.

In many parts of the Andes, where the soil is barren, the wild maguey is almost the only vegeta-tion to be seen, and in such places the Indians use it as food. It seems to be a gift of Nature to the des-ert ; so that even there man may find something on which to subsist.

Guapo with his knife had soon cleared off several large pieces of the maguey ; and these, fried along with the vicuña meat, enabled the party to make a supper sufficiently palatable. A cup of pure water from the cold mountain stream, sweeter than all the

wine in the world, washed it down, and they went to
rest with hearts full of contentment and gratitude.

They rose at an early hour, and, breakfasting as
they had supped, once more took the road.

After travelling a mile or two, the path gradually
ascended along one of those narrow ledges that shelve
out from the cliff of which we have already spoken.
They soon found themselves hundreds of feet above
the bed of the torrent; yet still hundreds of feet
above them rose the wall of dark porphyry, seamed,
and scarred, and frowning. The ledge, or path, was
of unequal breadth, here and there forming little
tables, or platforms. At other places, however, it
it was so narrow that those who were mounted could
look over the brink of the precipice into the frothing
water below — so narrow that no two animals could
have passed each other. These terrible passes were
sometimes more than a hundred yards in length,
and not straight, but winding around buttresses of
the rock, so that one end was not visible from the
other.

On frequented roads, where such places occur, it
is usual for travellers entering upon them to shout,
so that any one who chances to be coming from the
opposite side may have warning, and halt. Sometimes this warning is neglected, and two trains of
mules or lamas meet upon the ledge. Then there
is a terrible scene. The drivers quarrel ; one
party has to submit ; their animals have to be unloaded and dragged back by the heels to some wider
part of the path, so that each party can get past in
its turn.

Near the highest part of the road our travellers nad entered upon one of these narrow ledges, and were proceeding along it with caution. The trusty mule that carried Doña Isidora and Leona was in front; the horse followed, and then the lamas. It is safer to ride than walk on such occasions, especially upon mules; for these animals are more surefooted than the traveller himself. The horse that carried Leon, however, was as safe as any mule. He was one of the small Spanish American breed almost as surefooted as a chamois.

The torrent rushed and thundered beneath. It was fearful to listen and look downward. The heads of all were giddy, and their hearts full of fear. Guapo alone, accustomed to such dangers, was of steady nerve. He and Don Pablo, afoot, were in the rear.

They had neared the highest point of the road, where a jutting rock hid all beyond from their view They were already within a few paces of this rock when the mule — which, as we have stated, was in the front — suddenly stopped, showing such symptoms of terror that Doña Isidora and the little Leona both shrieked.

Of course all the rest came to a halt behind the terrified and trembling mule. Don Pablo, from behind, shouted out, inquiring the cause of the alarm; but before any answer could be given the cause became apparent to all. Around the rock suddenly appeared the head and horns of a fierce bull, and the next moment his whole body had come into view; while another pair of horns and another head were seen close behind him.

It would be difficult to describe the feelings of our travellers at that moment. The bull came on, with a determined and sullen look, until he stood nearly head to head with the mule. The smoke of his wide, steaming nostrils was mingled with the breath of the terrified mule, and he held his head downward, evidently with the intention of rushing forward upon the latter. Neither could have gone back ; and of course the fierce bull would drive the mule into the abyss. The other bull stood close behind, ready to continue the work if the first one failed ; and perhaps there were many others behind.

The mule was sensible of her danger ; and, planting her hoofs firmly on the hard rock, she clung closely to the precipice. But this would not have served her had not a hand interposed in her behalf. Amidst the terrified cries of the children the voice of Guapo was heard calling to Don Pablo, —

" Your pistols, master ! Give me your pistols ! "

Something glided quickly among the legs of the animals. It was the lithe body of the Indian. In a second's time he appeared in front of the mule. The bull was just lowering his head to charge forward ; his horns were set, the foam fell from his lips, and his eyes glanced fire out of their dark orbs. Before he could make the rush there came the loud report of a pistol, a cloud of sulphury smoke, a short struggle on the cliff, and then a dead plunge in the torrent below.

The smoke partially cleared away ; then came another crack, another cloud, another short struggle, and another distant plash in the water.

The smoke cleared away a second time. The two bulls were no longer to be seen.

Guapo, in front of the mule, now ran forward upon the ledge and looked round the buttress of rock ; then, turning suddenly, he waved his hand and shouted back, —

" No more, master. You may come on ; the road is clear."

CHAPTER XIII.

THE LONE CROSS IN THE FOREST.

AFTER two more days of fatiguing travel, the road parted from the bank of the river, and ran along the ridge of a high mountain spur in a direction at right angles to that of the Andes themselves. This spur continued for several miles, and then ended abruptly. At the point where it ended, the path, which for the whole of the day had been scarcely traceable, also came to an end. They were now of course in a forest-covered country — in the *Ceja de la Montaña* — that is, the forest that covers the foot hills of the mountains. The forest of the plains, which were yet lower down, is known as the " Montaña " proper.

During that day they had found the road in several places choked up with underwood, and Guapo had to clear it with his *macheté* — a sort of half sword, half knife, used throughout all Spanish America, partly to cut brushwood and partly as a weapon of defence. Where the ridge ended, however, what had once been a road was now entirely overgrown — vines and llianas of large size crossed the path. Evidently no one had passed for years. A road existed no longer ; the luxuriant vegetation had effaced it.

This is no unusual thing on the borders of the Montaña. Many a settlement had existed there in former times, and had been abandoned. No doubt the road they had been following once led to some such set-tlement that had long since fallen into ruin.

It is a melancholy fact that the Spanish Americans — including the Mexican nation — have been retro-grading for the last hundred years. Settlements which they have made, and even large cities built by them, are now deserted and in ruins; and extensive tracts of country, once occupied by them, have be-come uninhabited, and have gone. back to a state of nature. Whole provinces, conquered and peopled by the followers of Cortez and Pizarro, have within the last fifty years been retaken from them *by the In-dians:* and it would be very easy to prove that, had the descendants of the Spanish conquerors been left to themselves, another half century would have seen them driven from that very continent which their forefathers so easily conquered and so cruelly kept. This reconquest on the part of the Indian races was going on in a wholesale way in the northern prov inces of Mexico. But it is now interrupted by the approach of another and stronger race from the east — the Anglo-American.

To return to our travellers. Don Pablo was not surprised that the road had run out. He had been expecting this for miles back. What was to be done? Of course they must halt for that night at least. In-deed it was already near camping time. The sun was low in the sky, and the animals were all much jaded. The lamas could not have gone much far-ther. They looked as if they should never go far-ther. The heat of the climate — it had been getting warmer every hour — was too much for them. These animals, whose native home is among the high, cool mountain valleys, as already observed, cannot live in the low tropical plains. Even as they descended the Sierras, they had shown symptoms of suffering from the heat during all that day. Their strength was now fairly exhausted.

The party halted. A little open space was chosen for the camp. The animals were relieved of their burdens and tied to the trees, lest they might stray off and be lost in the thick woods. A fire was kindled, and part of the vicuña meat cooked for supper.

It was not yet night when they had finished eating, and all were seated on the ground. The countenance of the father was clouded with a melancholy expression. Doña Isidora sat by his side and tried to cheer him, endeavoring to force a smile into her large black eyes. The little Leona, with her head resting on her mother's lap, overcome with the heat and fatigue, had fallen asleep. Leon, seeing the dejected look of his father, was silent and thoughtful. Guapo was busy with his lamas.

"Come, dear husband!" said the lady, trying to assume a cheerful tone, "do not be so sad. We are now safe. Surely they will never pursue us here."

"They may not," mechanically replied Don Pablo; "but what then? We have escaped death, for what purpose? Either to live like savages in these wild woods — perhaps to be killed by savages — perhaps to die of hunger!"

"Do not say so, Don Pablo. I have never heard that the Indians of these parts were cruel. They

will not injure poor harmless people such as we are.
And as for starving, are not these luxuriant woods
filled with roots and fruits that will sustain life a long
while ? You, too, know so well what they are. Dear
husband, do not despond; God will not forsake us.
He has enabled us to escape from our enemies, from
fearful dangers on our journey. Fear not ! He will
not leave us to perish now."

The cheering words of his beautiful wife had their
effect upon Don Pablo. He embraced and kissed her
in a transport of love and gratitude. He felt inspired
with new hope. The vigor of mind and body, that
for days had deserted him, now suddenly returned;
and he sprang to his feet evidently with some newly-
formed resolution.

The country both before and behind them was shut
out from their view by the thick foliage and underwood. A tall tree grew by the spot, with branches
down to the level of a man's head. Don Pablo approached this tree, and, seizing the branches, drew
himself up, and then climbed on towards its top.
When he had reached a sufficient height to overlook
the surrounding woods he stopped, and, resting himself upon one of the branches, looked abroad towards
the east. All the rest stood watching him from below.

He had been gazing but a few seconds when his
face brightened up, and a smile of satisfaction was
seen to play upon his countenance. He evidently
saw something that pleased him. Isidora, impatient,
called out to him from below ; but Don Pablo waved
his hand to her, as if admonishing her to be silent

" Have patience, love," he cried down. " I shall
descend presently and tell you all. I have good news ;
but be patient."

It required a good share of patience, for Don Pablo after this remained a full half hour upon the tree.
He was not all the time looking abroad, however.
Part of it he sat upon his perch — his head leaning
forward, and his eyes not appearing to be particularly
engaged with any thing. He was busy with his
thoughts, and evidently meditating on some great
project. Perhaps the going down of the sun admon-
ished him, as much as the desire of satisfying his
wife's curiosity ; but just as the bright orb was sinking among the far tree tops he descended.

" Now, Don Pablo," said the fair Isidora, pretend-
ing to frown and look angry, " you have tried our
patience, have you not ? Come, then, no more mystery, but tell us all. What have you seen ? "

" Forgive me, wife ; you shall know all."

Both sat down upon the trunk of a dead tree that
Guapo had felled and was cutting up for firewood :
not that it was at all cold, but they had now arrived
in the country of the terrible *jaguar*, and it would be
necessary to keep up a blazing fire throughout the
night.

" Your words were true, love," began Don Pablo.
" God has not forsaken us. I have seen three things
that have inspired me with fresh life and hope.

" First, I looked out upon the Montaña, which I
expected to see stretching away to the horizon like a
green ocean. I saw this in fact ; but, to my surprise,
I saw more. I beheld a broad river winding like an

immense serpent through the distant forest. It ran in a direction north-east as far as the eye could reach. Even upon the horizon I could distinguish spots of its bright water glancing like silver under the rays of the setting sun. My heart leaped with joy, for I recognized a river whose existence has been doubted. It can be no other, thought I, than the *Madre de Dios.* I have often heard that there existed such a river in these parts, that runs on to the Amazon. A missionary is said to have visited it; but with the destruction of the missions the record has been lost. I have no doubt the river I have seen is the *Madre de Dios* of that missionary.

" The thought of being so near the banks of this river suggested other thoughts. At once a design entered into my mind. ' We can build a raft,' thought I, ' launch it upon this noble river, and float down to the Amazon, and thence to the mouth of the great stream itself. There is a Portuguese settlement there — the town of Grand Para. There we shall be safe from our foes.'

" Such were my first thoughts on beholding the new river. I reflected further. ' Our fortune is gone,' I reflected ; ' we have nothing in the wide world — what should we do at Para, even if we arrived there in safety ? How could we attempt such a journey without provisions? It would be impossible.'

" My hopes fell as quickly as they had sprung up."

" I noticed your countenance change as you sat upon the tree."

" True, you might easily have done so : the prospect of reaching Para penniless, and becoming a beggar in the streets — the nearer prospect of starv-ing in the wilderness of the Amazon — were before my mind.

" My eyes for a while were bent mechanically upon the green ocean of tree tops. All at once an object arrested them. It was a patch of bright rose-colored foliage, easily distinguishable amid the green leaves that surrounded it. It was not down in the Montaña — for that is a thousand feet below us. It was upon the side of the Sierra. My eyes glanced quickly around. I beheld other patches of similar foliage, some of them nearly an acre in breadth. My heart again leaped with joy. I knew well what these red spots of the forest were. They were clumps of *cinchona* trees — those trees that yield the cele-brated febrifuge — the Peruvian bark.

" New ideas passed rapidly through my mind. ' Our fortune is gone,' thought I. ' Here is a fortune in these valuable trees. Here is a mine that only re-quires to be worked. I shall turn *cascarillero* — I shall be a *bark hunter.*'

" At first I thought that we might gather the bark, and send Guapo to sell it in the towns of the Sierra. Then the idea came into my mind that it might be possible to collect an immense quantity, store it up, build a great raft, float it down the rivers, and dispose of it in Para. I knew that in this way it would more than quadruple its price — for the traders of the Sierra purchase it from the poor cascarilleros, and have enormous profits upon it from the larger mer-chants.

" But how to live while making this store ? Yes, how to live even on the morrow ? Could we support ourselves by hunting, or find sustenance from fruits and roots, as you have suggested ? This was the most important question of all, for our present neces- sities far outweighed our future prospects.

" The very thought of our necessity caused me once more to glance over the forest, and I continued to scan it on all sides. My eye was again arrested, and fixed upon a point where I saw there existed a different vegetation from any that could be seen else- where. There is a small valley about five hundred feet below us. It is a sort of table valley, and the stream along which we have been travelling runs through it, afterwards dashing over a fall to join the river below. In this valley I saw huge broad leaves of a brilliant yellowish green. I knew them at once to be the leaves of the great *musaceæ*, either plantains or bananas. I thought, too, I could distinguish the form of the *yucca* plant. These are the certain signs of some settlement, or. where one has existed. 1 fancy the latter is the correct idea, as I could distin- guish neither house nor smoke. It may be some de- serted Indian ' chacra,' or it may be the grounds of an old mission. In either case, we shall be likely to find those useful plants from which we may obtain food."

" O papa ! mamma ! " cried Leon, running up and interrupting the conversation. " See what is here among the trees ! I declare, it is a great cross ! "

Don Pablo and Isidora walked towards the spot. There, sure enough, was a large wooden cross plant-

7

ed in the ground, and leaning to one side. The wood
was much decayed, but the inscription that had been
deeply cut in the transverse beam was still legible
It was simply the Spanish phrase, —

"BRAZOS DE DIOS," (The arm of God.)

Isidora took Don Pablo by the hand, and, looking
steadfastly in his face, pointed to the inscription.
" It *is* true," said she ; " God protects us ! "

CHAPTER XIV.

THE DESERTED MISSION.

THAT night all went to rest with hope in their hearts, though still not without some anxiety. If you reflect upon the situation in which they were placed, you will not wonder that they were anxious about the future. Their first care had been to fly into the wilderness, without thinking upon the neces- sities they might encounter there — without reflecting that they had made no provision of food to sustain them. It is true that in the great Montaña there are many plants and trees whose roots and fruits can be eaten ; but a traveller may go for days without find- ing one of these. Indeed, to pass through this great forest, in most places, is impossible, so completely are the creeping parasites matted and laced together. It is necessary to keep along the rivers in a canoe or raft, else you cannot get from place to place. You cannot even walk along the banks of many of these rivers, as the underwood hangs into the very water. For the same reason game is hard to be procured ; and neither Don Pablo nor Guapo were provided with proper weapons to hunt with. Don Pablo's pistols were all the firearms they had, and Guapo had no other weapon than his macheté. With their present means, then, there was very little chance of their killing any game, even should they have fallen in with it. But they saw none as yet, except some birds, such as parrots, macaws, and toucans, that fluttered among the leaves. No wonder, then, they were anxious about what they should find to eat, or whether they should find any thing at all.

Don Pablo considered the cross a good omen, or rather a good *sign*. Some missionary must have planted it in years gone by. No doubt a missionary station must have been near ; and it was highly probable that what he had seen in the little valley below would turn out to be the very place where it had stood.

As soon as it became day, therefore, Don Pablo again ascended the tree to take the bearings of the valley, so that they should proceed towards it. Guapo also climbed up, so that both might make sure of the route they ought to take — for in the tangled forests of South America it is no easy matter to reach any object which you may have only seen at a distance from the top of a tree. Without a compass, the traveller soon loses his direction, and, after hours of vain exertion and devious wandering, often finds himself at the very place from which he had started.

After carefully noting the direction of the valley, Don Pablo and Guapo came down from the tree ; and while the former, assisted by Leon, packed and saddled the animals, Guapo was busy with his macheté in clearing away the brushwood that obstructed the path. This did not turn out such a task after all. It was only at the brow of the ridge where the un dergrowth had choked up the way. A little farther down it was quite passable; and the party, animals and all, were soon winding down the Sierra towards the valley. Half an hour's travelling brought them to their destination; and then a shout of joy, coming simultaneously from all of them, announced their arrival upon the spot.

What was it that caused them to utter this shout of joy? Before them towered the great *musaceæ* — plantains and bananas, *(Musa paradisiaca* and *Sapientum.)* There were both — their broad yellow-green and waxlike leaves sheathing their succulent stems, and bending gracefully over to a length of twenty feet. But beautiful as were the leaves of these giant plants, more attractive still to the eyes of our travellers were the huge clusters of fruit pods that hung from beneath them. Each of these would have weighed nearly a hundred weight! There was food for hundreds. These plants grew by the water's edge, in a damp soil — their natural habitat. Their leaves drooped over the stream. Another plant, equally interesting, was seen farther back, in a dry place. There were many of these ten or fifteen feet high, and as thick as a man's wrist. This was the *yucca* plant, *(Jatropha manihot.)* All of them knew it. They knew that its roots produced the far-famed cassava. Cassava is bread. Hurrah! the staff of life was secure!

But, more than this, there were fruits in abundance: there were mangoes and guavas, oranges, and the celebrated cherimoya — the favorite of Peru. There were shaddocks and sweet limes; and see! yonder is a clump of sugar canes, with their thin silken leaves and yellow tassels waving in the wind. O, look here ! Here is a coffee shrub, with its ripe, aromatic berries ; and here is the cacao tree, *(Theobroma cacao.)* Coffee and chocolate — there was a choice of beverages ! Ha ! what have we here — this plant like an orange tree ? It is a species of holly. As I live, it is the *yerba maté*, the " Paraguay tea," *(Ilex Paraguensis.)* What shall we light upon next ?

And so the delighted travellers went on over the ground, through the thick-tangled weeds and convolvuli, making new discoveries at every step. Even Guapo's favorite, the coca shrub, was found growing among the rest ; and the eyes of the old Indian sparkled at the sight of it.

Don Pablo's first conjecture had been right. They had arrived at the ruin of some old missionary station long since deserted. Some zealous monk had planted all these plants and trees ; had for years, no doubt, tended them with care ; had dreamed of establishing around this lonely spot a great hierarchy, and making the " wilderness blossom as the rose." An evil day had come — perhaps during the revolt of Juan Santos, or may be in the later revolution of Tupac Amaru. The hand of the savage had been turned against the priest, who had fallen a victim ; and his roof — the mission house — had been given to the flames. Not a vestige of building was to be seen — neither stick nor stone ; and, had it not been for the curious variety of vegetation collected on the spot, this once cultivated and flourishing garden might have been taken for part of the primeval forest.

It must have been a long time since the place was

inhabited; for great trees and parasites had grown up in the midst of the cultivated plants.

After the first transports of delight had to some ex tent subsided, a consultation was held as to future pro ceedings. They were not long in coming to a con clusion. It was resolved that a house should be buit in the middle of this wild garden, which should be for a time at least, their home.

The poor lamas had made their last journey. They were to be killed. Guapo, although reluctant to part with his old favorites, knew that they could not live in the warm climate of the valley, and therefore consented. Their flesh, it is true, is none of the best; but it would taste the better that no other was to bo had; and their wool and skins would be found useful. The lamas were killed.

CHAPTER XV.

THE GUACO AND THE CORAL SNAKE.

IT was Guapo himself that killed the lamas; and, having skinned them, he cut the flesh into thin strips and hung it upon the branches to dry in the sun. This, of course, was necessary, as they had no salt to cure it with; but meat well dried under a hot sun will keep good for a long time. It is curious that in all Spanish American countries they preserve most of their meat in this way; whereas in North America, among the people of our own race, "jerked beef" (for that is the name we give it) is very rare. Now, in Spanish America there are vast depositories of salt, both in mines and on plains, with salt lakes, called *salinas;* yet, for want of a proper commercial activity existing among these people, in many places the valuable article (salt) is both scarce and dear. In Mexico dried or "jerked" beef is called "tasajo." In Peru, as we have stated, it is "charqui;" but mutton cured in this way is distinguished by the name "chalona." Now, as the lamas are a species of sheep, it was "chalona" that Guapo was making out of their mutton.

The others were not idle. Don Pablo, assisted by Leon, was clearing a place on which they intended to build the house; while the Doña Isidora, with her soft, slender fingers, (for the first time in her life, perhaps,) was acting as laundress ; and the little Leona assisted her as much as she was able. Where did they get their soap ? for they had not brought so much as a single cake along with them. But Don Pablo was too good a botanist not to know the nature of the trees that grew around and the uses to which they could be applied. Near by grew a curious tree, which is known among the Indians as the *parapara*. It was the soap berry of botanists, (*Sapindus saponaria ;*) and Don Pablo knew that the bark of the berries, when rubbed, produces a lather that will wash linen equal to the best " Castile." Doña Isidora was not long in making a trial of it, and found this to be true. The little round stones of the berries, when cleared of the pulp, are very pretty, and are much used by the missionaries in making rosaries. Leon found, dropping one of them on a stone, that it was as elastic as a ball of India rubber, for it rebounded several times to the height of a man's head.

In the evening they all rested from their various occupations, and seated themselves upon the new-cleared ground, upon the trunk of a tree that had been felled. They were one and all quite cheerful. They felt no more apprehension of pursuit. It would have been a very revengeful enemy indeed who would have followed them so far into the wilderness ; they had no fear of that. Doña Isidora had just cooked a kettle of coffee. They had both pots and kettles ; for these were some of the utensils with which Guapo, even in the hurry of flight, had taken the precaution to load his lamas. This coffee turned out to be of the finest quality. It was of a peculiar species, which has long been cultivated by the mis-sionaries of Peru, and which yields a very high price. It used to be sent by the viceroys as a valued present to the kings of Spain. To sweeten the coffee some joints of sugar cane had been crushed and boiled in a rough manner; and for bread they had roasted plain-tains. During the repast they were all quite merry, and pleasant jokes were passed for the first time in many days.

While thus engaged a singular sound fell upon their ears. It was like a voice repeating the word " Guaco." They all listened. " Guaco — Guaco ! " again came the voice.

" Hola ! " cried Leon. " Guapo — Guapo ! There's some one calling you, Guapo. There again ! No, it's ' Guaco.' Listen ! ' Guaco — Guaco ! ' What is it, I wonder ? "

" That's the snake bird," quietly answered Guapo, who, it must be remembered, was a native of the Montaña, and knew a great deal both about the birds and beasts of these regions.

" The snake bird ! " exclaimed Leon, evidently in-terested in the name.

" Yes, young master," replied Guapo. " Look ! yonder it goes."

The eyes of all were instantly turned in the direc-tion pointed out by Guapo. There, sure enough, was a bird not much larger than a common pigeon; but which had all the appearance of a sparrow hawk. It was " swallow tailed," however; and this, with its peculiar form and the manner of its flight, showed that it was one of the kite hawks. When first noticed it was perched upon the top of a high tree; but it soon flew to another not so high, uttering as it went the " Guaco — Guaco ! " It then pitched itself to a still lower branch, and was evidently after something which none of the party could see. That something, however, soon became apparent. The ground had been cleared in a broad track down to the water's edge; and near the middle of the open space an object was observed in motion, making towards the weeds. That object was a snake. It was not a large one — not more than three feet in length; and its beautiful body, variegated with bands of black, red, and bright yellow, glistened as it moved. Its predominating color was a fleshy red, or coral, from whence it has its name; for both Don Pablo and Guapo, as soon as they saw it, pronounced it the " coral snake." Beautiful as it appeared, all knew that it was one of the most poisonous of serpents — one of the most dreaded of South American reptiles.

The first thought of Guapo and Leon was to spring up, seize upon some weapon, and kill the creature. Don Pablo, however, restrained them.

" Stay where you are," said he; " be patient. We shall have a scene. Look at the hawk — see ! "

As Don Pablo spoke, the guaco, which had hopped down to the lowest branches of a neighboring tree, swooped suddenly at the snake, evidently aiming to clutch it around the neck. The latter, however, had been too quick, and, coiling itself like a flash of lightning, darted its head out towards the bird in a threatening manner. Its eyes sparkled with rage, and their fiery glitter could be seen even at many yards' distance.

The bird diverged from its course, and, after passing the snake, turned and swooped again from the opposite direction. But the reptile had shifted its body so as to meet the attack, and its threatening head once more was reared high above its coiled body. The guaco was foiled a second time.

This second failure seemed to enrage the bird, as it turned at shorter intervals, and, apparently losing all fear, fluttered over the reptile, striking both with beak and claws. The latter still kept in its coil; but its head moved hastily from side to side, so as always to " show front " to its active antagonist.

After this play had continued for some time the snake was seen to draw in its head farther than usual; and the hawk, evidently somewhat off his guard, deeming this a fair opportunity, pounced forward to seize it. But he was met half way. The head of the serpent shot forward like a rapier, and reached his breast. The hawk felt that he was wounded; and, uttering a wild scream, he flew suddenly away. All eyes watched him as he flew off, expecting that he would fall; for the bite of the coral snake will kill even a man in a few minutes, and a bird or small animal in much less time. It is not correct to say that all of them expected to see him fall. Guapo, from experience, knew better; and even Don Pablo, as a naturalist, had heard a strange account of this singular bird, and was curious to witness the result. The hawk, therefore, was narrowly watched.

It flew directly for a tree, up against the trunk of which, and clinging to its branches, grew a parasite, or creeping plant. The latter was of the thickness of a willow rod, with long, slender leaves, of a dark-green color. The bird did not alight upon the top of the tree, but on a branch where it could reach the leaves of the creeper, which it began immediate'y to pluck and devour. In a short while it had eaten as many as a dozen of these long leaves, when it again took to wing, and flew back in the direction of the snake.

All had, for the moment, forgotten the snake in their eagerness to watch the movements of the bird. To their astonishment the reptile was still in the same place, and coiled up as when last seen. This was easily explained, however, as snakes who defend themselves in that attitude usually remain coiled until they are certain that their enemy has gone away and will not return to the attack.

The contest was now renewed with redoubled fury. The bird fought with fresh courage, knowing that he had taken precautions against a fatal result, while the snake defended itself with the energy of despair. This time the battle was a short one. The guaco, using its wings, succeeded in striking its antagonist upon the upraised head, and, quickly following up the blow, planted his talons so as to encircle the throat of his victim. The effect of his gripe was instantly apparent. The reptile unfolded itself, and the slender coral body was seen writhing and twisting along the ground. But it did not remain long upon the ground ; for in a few moments the guaco rose

into the air, and carried the struggling victim into
the woods to devour it at his leisure.

Now, Guapo was exceedingly pleased at what had
occurred. Why? It was not because such a scene
was at all new to him. No; he had often witnessed
such, and was no longer curious upon that head. It
was something more than mere curiosity that moved
Guapo. When the affair was over he rose from his
seat, and, stalking off to the place where the bird had
been seen to eat the leaves, he gathered a quantity
of them, and then returned to the fire. Don Pablo
recognized them as the leaves of a plant of the genus
Mikania, and known popularly as the " vejuco de
guaco." Guapo knew nothing of the scientific designation of the plant ; but he had long ago been
taught the valuable properties of its leaves as an antidote against the bite of the most poisonous snakes.
He had known them to cure the bite of the cascabel,
(*rattlesnake*,) and even of the small spotted viper,
(*Echidna ocellata*,) the most poisonous of all the
American snakes.

What, then, did Guapo with the leaves of the
vejuco? First he chopped them up as fine as he
could ; and then, tying them tightly in a piece of
cotton cloth, he expressed from them a quantity of
juice, enough for his purpose. That done, with the
point of a knife he made small incisions between his
toes, and also upon his breast and fingers. Into each
of these incisions, even while the blood was flowing
from them, he dropped the juice of the mikania, and
rubbed it in with fresh leaves of the plant itself,
and then, with some tufts of the soft floss of the silk

cotton tree, (*Bombax ceiba*,) he covered the incisions so as to stop the bleeding. He wound up this strange performance by chewing some of the leaves and swallowing about a spoonful of the juice. This made the " inoculation " complete ; and Guapo, as he him-self declared, was now invulnerable to the bite of the most venomous serpent.

He offered to " inoculate " the others in the same way. They at first refused, Don Pablo among the rest ; but after a day or two, when each of the party had met with several narrow escapes from vipers, coral snakes, and the much-dreaded " jararaca," (*craspedocephalus*,) Don Pablo thought it prudent that all should submit to the operation ; and accord-ingly Guapo " doctored " the party without more ado.

CHAPTER XVI.

THE PALM WOODS.

It happened that upon the opposite side of the stream there was a broad track covered with palm trees, while not one was to be seen on that side where they intended building their house. As these are the most convenient trees for constructing a house to suit the hot climate of the Montaña, it appeared necessary that they should use them. But how were they to get at them? The stream flowed between them and the camp; and although not a large river, yet at that place it was very wide and deep, for in the flat table valley it expanded to the dimensions of a little lake. Below, where it issued out of the valley, it ran for some distance in a deep cleft between rocky banks almost or quite perpendicular, and above the valley it came dashing through an impassable ravine. If they could only get over to cut the palms, they knew they could roll them to the bank and float them across the stretch of still water. But how to get over required some consideration. Guapo could swim like a water dog, but Don Pablo could not; and Leon, having been brought up as a town boy, had had but little practice, and consequently was but a poor swimmer. What, then, was to be done, as Guapo could not well manage the palms without help?

After examining the stream, both above and below, no crossing place could be found ; but just at the point where it ran out of the valley the space between the high banks was very narrow. A good long plank would have reached across it, had they only had one — but that they had not. Now, upon the opposite bank there grew a tall tree. It was one of the beautiful silk-cotton trees already mentioned. It stood upon the very edge of the chasm. Both Don Pablo and Guapo saw at a glance that this tree could be felled and made to fall across the stream so as to form the very bridge they wanted.

Not much time was lost about it. Guapo, tying his axe upon his shoulders, ran up the near side un-til he was opposite the still running water, and then, plunging in, swam across in a few seconds. He soon after appeared on the opposite bank, at the root of the bombax, which he attacked in such a manner that one who did not know what he was about might have fancied he was angry at it. In a few minutes a great notch appeared in the side of the tree ; and Guapo, continuing his sturdy blows, made the yellow chips fly out in showers. Of course the notch was cut on the side next the stream, so that the tree would fall in that direction. The beaver understands that much ; and Guapo had considerably more intelligence than any beaver.

In about half an hour the bombax began to creak and lean a little. Then Don Pablo threw over a lasso which had been brought along. Guapo noosed one end over a high limb, and, tying a stone to the other, pitched it back to Don Pablo, who hauled it taut.

R

Then a few cuts of the axe broke the skin of the tree on the other side. Don Pablo pulled by the rope ; and with a loud tear and a crash, and a vast deal of crackling among the branches, the great bombax settled into a horizontal position across the chasm. The bridge was built.

After all it was no slight adventure to cross it. The rounded trunk was any thing but sure footing ; and even had it been a flat plank, the depth of the chasm — nearly a hundred feet clear — and the white roaring torrent below were enough to shake the stoutest nerves. All, however, got over in safety and proceeded up to the palm woods. I say all — but I mean only the male population of the new settlement. Doña Isidora and the little Leona remained by the camp, both of them busy scraping *yucca* roots, to be manufactured into cassava, and then into bread.

On arriving among the palm trees, Don Pablo was struck with a singular fact. He observed (indeed he had already noticed as much from the opposite side of the river) that, instead of one species of palm, there were not less than a dozen kinds growing in this wood. This was a very unusual circumstance ; as, although two or three species are often found together, such a varied collection as were there could only have been made by human hands. Here, again, was recognized the work of the missionary monk, who had no doubt planted most of the species, having received them very likely from many distant stations of his fellow-laborers in other parts of the Amazon valley.

Whether Franciscan, Jesuit, or Dominican, (for all

three have had their missions in this part of the world,) the holy father who resided here, thought Don Pablo, must have been an ardent horticulturist. Whether or not he converted many Indians to his faith, he seemed to have exerted himself to provide for their temporal necessities; for there was hardly a useful plant or tree suitable to the climate that was not to be found growing near the spot. Such were the reflections of Don Pablo.

" What a variety of beautiful palms ! " said he, looking around upon these by far the fairest forms of the vegetable creation.

Now, my boy reader, I have not the slightest doubt but that you, too, think the palms the fairest forms of the vegetable creation. I have not the shadow of a doubt that your heart beats joyfully at the very word " palm ; " that you love to gaze at one of these state- ly trees; and that you would give all your pocket money for an afternoon's ramble through a real palm wood. Would you not ? Yes ; I am sure of it. Now, I could tell you a great deal about palms if I *would ;* and I would, too, if my space and time allowed me ; but neither will, alas ! Why, if I were only to give you even the shortest and dryest botanic description of all the different palms that are known to us, that mere dry catalogue would fill a book as big as this one.

How many species do you think there are ? Up to this time you have thought, perhaps, there was only one, and that was the *palm tree itself.* May be you had heard of more, such as the sago palm, the cocoa-nut palm, the date palm, or the cabbage palm and you fancied there might be others — perhaps as many as a dozen. Now, you will hardly credit me when I tell you that we know of no less than *six hundred species of palms*, all differing from each other. I may add, further, that it is my belief that there exist on the earth as many more — that is, the enormous number of twelve hundred. The reason why I entertain this belief is, that in all cases where similar guesses have been hazarded — whether with regard to plants, or birds, or *mammalia* — they have eventually proved far below the mark; and as the palm countries are the very regions of the earth least known and least explored by botanists, it is but reasonable to conclude that great numbers of species have never yet been described, nor even seen. Another fact which strengthens this probability is, that peculiar species of palms are sometimes found only in a limited district, and nowhere else in the same country. A small river even sometimes forms the boundary line of a species ; and although whole groves may be seen on the one side, not a tree of the same sort grows on the other. Some botanists even prognosticate that more than two thousand species of palms will yet become known. Of the six hundred species known, about half belong to the old world, and half to America. In America they are chiefly found growing on the continent, although several species are natives of the West India islands — while on the eastern hemisphere the greatest number of species belong to the islands.

I might tell you a great deal of the importance of these noble trees to the human race, for they are as useful as they are beautiful. Almost every sort has its particular use in the economy of human life. Not only do they serve certain purposes in Africa, Asia, America, and Oceanica, but in all these divisions of the earth there are whole nations who *live almost exclusively* upon one or another species of palm.

A discovery has lately been made in regard to an African species, which it is to be hoped will have an important influence in doing away with the infamous slave traffic so long existing in that unhappy country. You have heard of *palm oil.* Well, it is extracted from the nuts of a species of palm. The oil is no new discovery; but it is only lately that it has been found to be quite as good for the manufacture of candles as either spermaceti or wax. The consequence has been a great increase in the traffic of this article on the western coast of Africa ; and the native princes, finding that it is more profitable than slave selling, have in many parts given up the last-named atrocious commerce, and have taken to gathering palm oil. If a palm tree can effect what has baffled the skill of the combined philanthropists and powers of Europe, then, indeed, we shall say, " All honor to the noble palms."

But I might go on talking of palms until our little volume came to an end. I must, therefore, no longer speak generally of these beautiful trees, but confine myself to such species as came under the observa-tion, and ministered to the wants, of the new settlers.

CHAPTER XVII.

A HOUSE OF PALMS.

THE first species of palms that attracted the observation of Don Pablo and his party was that known as the " patawa." palm. It belongs to the genus *Œnocarpus*. There are several species of this genus in South America, but none more beautiful than the " patawa." It is a palm with a straight, smooth stem and pinnate leaves — the stem being sixty feet in height and about a foot in diameter. The stem becomes smooth only in old trees. In the young ones, and even in those that stand in a thick shady forest, it presents a very shaggy appearance, and is completely hidden by the bases of the old leaves that have decayed and fallen off. From the margins of these bases grow spinous processes of nearly three feet in length, which point upward. These are used by the Indians to make the arrows of their " blow guns," of which more hereafter. From the fruits of this palm a most delicious drink is manufactured with very little trouble. The fruit itself is about the size of a plum, but of an oval shape and deep violet color. It grows in large clusters just under the leaves. To make the drink, the fruits are .hrown into a vessel of hot water, where they remain for a few minutes, until the pulp becomes soft. The

hot water is next poured off, and cold water is substi‹
tuted. In this the fruits are crushed and rubbed with
the hands until all the pulp is washed from the stones.
The liquid is then strained, so as to separate the stones
and other substances, when it is ready for use ; and a
most luxurious beverage it is — in its taste bearing
some resemblance to filberts and cream.

A palm called the "assái" has a small sloelike
fruit, which produces a similar beverage — thick and
creamy, and of a fine plum color. In all the Portuguese settlements the "assái" is a favorite drink,
and is taken along with cassava bread, as we use
milk or coffee.

It was not on account of its fruit, however, that
Don Pablo rejoiced at beholding the "patawa" palms.
Perhaps Leon thought more about the rich clusters
of oval plums; but his father looked only to the
straight, smooth stems, which were designed for
corner posts, beams, and the heavier wood work of
the house.

In a few minutes Guapo was busy with his axe,
and one after another fell the princely trunks of the
"patawa," until enough were cut down for their
purpose.

Don Pablo next looked out for some palm of a
more slender trunk for the rafters and joists.

This was soon found in the "catinga," which is a
species of the "assái" palm, (*Euterpe*,) the one of
which we have just spoken as producing the "assái
wine." The catinga was the very thing for the
rafters. It is tall, nearly forty feet high, but quite
slender. It is one of the smooth palms, with pinnate

leaves not unlike those of the " patawa." There is a peculiarity about its top; that is, there is a column or sheath of several feet in length, out of which the leaves spring; and at the lower end of this column, and not immediately at the root of the leaves, the fruit clusters grow. This sheathing column is of a red color, which gives the tree a strange look. Another peculiarity of the catinga is, that its roots grow out of the ground, and from a little cone from the top of which rises the stem. The fruits of this sort are smaller than the true assái; but a drink is also made from them, which some people consider more delicious than that either of the assái or patawa. The rafters, then, were got from the catinga.

Now for the thatch; that was the next considera-tion.

" Master ! " cried Guapo, pointing off into the woods ; " yonder's ' bussu' — very thing for thatch ! "

Guapo indicated a very singular-looking tree, with a thick, clumsy, crooked, and deeply-ringed stem. It was not a bit like either of the palm trees they had already cut down. Its trunk was not over ten or a dozen feet high; but then such leaves! They were not pinnated, like those already described, but what is termed " entire ;" that is, all in one piece, and thirty feet in length by full five in width! Fancy two or three dozen of these gigantic leaves standing up almost erect from the top of the thick trunk, and you may form some idea of the " bussu " palm. There are many palm trees whose leaves are used for thatching houses; but of all others for that purpose the bussu is the best. These great fronds have a midrib; and from this, on both sides, run veins in a diagonal direction to the edge. When they are used for thatch the leaf is split up the midrib, and then each half is laid upon the rafters, not straight, but in such a way that the veins of the leaf will lie in a ver‑ tical direction, and thus serve as gutters to guide the rain water down the roof. A very few leaves will thatch a house; and a covering of this kind, when properly laid on, will last for ten or twelve years. So much are the bussu leaves prized for thatch, that the Indians, in parts where this palm does not grow, often make a canoe voyage of a week to procure them.

The spathe which contains the flowers is also put to many uses. It is of a long spindle shape, of fibrous, clothlike texture, and brown color. The Indians use it as cloth. It makes an excellent bag, in which the native carries his paints or other arti‑ cles; and a large one, stretched out, makes a very comfortable cap. Indeed Guapo used the first spathe he laid his hands upon for this very purpose.

There remained now to be found some palm tree that would split easily, and make laths for the roof, as well as planks for the door, shelves, and benches. They soon discovered the very palm for these pur‑ poses. It was one of the genus *Iriartea*, and known as the " pashiuba " palm. It was a tree that differed from all the others in its aspect. It was a noble‑look‑ .ng tree, rising, with a smooth stem, to the height of seventy feet. At its top there was a sheathing col‑ umn, swollen larger than the stem, and not unlike the sheathing column of the catinga, already mentioned, except that that of the pashiuba was of a deep‑green

color. Its leaves, however, differed materially from
those of the catinga. It is true that, like them, they
were pinnate ; but the leaflets, instead of being slender and tapering, were of a triangular shape, notched
along the edges, and not growing very regularly out
from the midrib. Their general arrangement as
well as the form, therefore, gave the tree a different,
and perhaps more beautiful, aspect. But the most
singular characteristic of the pashiuba was its roots.
I have said that the roots of the catinga rose above
the surface of the soil. So did they, but only to a
limited height, forming a little cone. Now, the roots
of the pashiuba stood up to the height of ten or a
dozen feet! Each root was nearly straight in itself;
but there were a number of them, and they sloped
upwards, so as to make a sort of pyramid, out of the
apex of which grew the stem. There were wide
spaces between the roots — so wide that you could
easily pass through ; and a fullgrown man might
stand upright, with his head under the very base of
the stem. Fancy a man standing under the trunk of
a tree that rose seventy feet above his head!

There were young trees of the same species growing around, and these were miniature models of the
older ones. Sometimes these lesser ones are supported on three roots, like the tripod of a surveyor's
compass, and this gives them a somewhat ludicrous
appearance. There are many species of this sort
of palms, which are classed under the genus *Iriartea.*
In most of them, the fruit, which is small, oval, and
red, or yellow, is bitter and uneatable ; but their wood
is prized for many purposes. The wood of the

species which Don Pablo had found is hard on the outside, but soft within, and splits readier into laths and planks than any other kind of palm.

Guapo attacked the roots with his axe; and enough trunks were soon felled to make laths, doors, and all sorts of benches.

The different kinds were now collected on the edge of the stream, and were tied together by a ropelike, creeping plant called a " sipo," so that they formed a rude raft. The leaves of the " bussu," with great clusters of the fruits of the catinga and patawa, were laid upon the raft; and then Guapo, mounting himself on top of all, pushed out with his long pole, and ferried the whole across. The others walked round by the bridge, and were just in time to assist Guapo in mooring his somewhat unwieldy craft.

Next day the framework of the house was put up, and, on the day after, the walls. These were made of bamboo canes, (*Bambusa guadua*,) plenty of which grew near the bottom of the valley. They grew wild; for the slopes of the Andes are the favorite soil of these gigantic grasses. They were set on end, side by side, and then tied to each other and to the beams of palm trees. On the third day the " bussu" leaves were laid on, and the house was finished.

CHAPTER XVIII.

TRACKING THE TAPIR.

It has been already mentioned that the stream in front of the house was wider than at other parts, forming a sort of lake. There was a slow current down the middle, but at the sides the water was near-ly stagnant ; and there grew in some places bunches of flags, interspersed with beautiful white lilies. Among these could be distinguished that gigantic *nympha* so celebrated under the name of *Victoria regia* — for South America is the native country of this rare plant.

Every night, as our party were resting from their labors, they heard strange noises proceeding from the water. There was plunging and plashing, and now and then a snorting sound like that sometimes uttered by frightened swine. Perhaps it would have puzzled any of them to tell whence these sounds pro-ceeded or what animal gave utterance to them ; for there could be no doubt they were caused by an animal. Some of them guessed " alligators ; " but that was not a correct guess ; for, although there are plenty of alligators in all the rivers of tropical America, there seemed to be none in that particular place. In truth, they might have remained long in the dark about what creature they thus heard sweltering about nightly; for they could neither see nor hear any thing of it in the day. But Guapo, who knew every sound of the Montaña, enlightened them at once. Guapo had been a keen *tapir hunter* in his time, and understood all the habits of that strange animal. It was a tapir, then, which they had heard taking his regular nightly bath and regaling himself on the roots of the flags and *nymphæ*.

Have you ever seen a tapir? Not a living one, I fancy; perhaps the skin of one in a museum. He is an interesting creature, for this reason — that he is the largest land animal indigenous to South America. The lama and guanaco stand higher, because their legs are longer; but they are far inferior to the tapir in bulk and weight; while the bears of South America, of which there are two or three species, are small-sized bears, and therefore less than the tapir. In fact, no very large land animals were found indigenous in the southern division of the American continent. There were none of the *bovine* tribe, as the buffalo and muskox of North America; and no large deer, as the elk and moose of the northern latitudes. The deer of South America, of which there are several undescribed species, are all small animals. The tapir, then, in point of size, takes precedence in the South America *fauna*.

His rounded body gives him some resemblance to a great hog, or a donkey with its hair shaved off; but, in fact, he is not very like either; he is more like a *tapir* than any thing else — that is, he is a creature *sui generis*. Perhaps, if you were to shave a large donkey, cut off most part of his ears and tail,

shoiten his limbs,—and, if possible, make them
stouter and clumsier,—lengthen his upper jaw so
that it should protrude over the under one into a pro-
longed curving snout, and then give him a coat of
blackish-brown paint, you would get something not
unlike a tapir. To complete the resemblance, however, you would have to continue the erect mane over
the forehead, between the ears, and down to the level
of the eyes, which would give that crested appearance that characterizes the tapir. Instead of hoofs,
moreover, you would give your donkey large toes —
four upon the fore feet, and upon the hind ones three.
A little silky hair upon the stumped tail, and a few
thinly-scattered hairs of a brown color over the body,
would make the likeness still more striking; and it
would be necessary, too, that the donkey be one of
the very biggest kind to be as big as a big tapir.

The tapir is a harmless creature ; and although it
has a good set of teeth, it never uses them for the
purpose of defending itself. When attacked by
either men or fierce animals, it tries to escape by
flight, and if that fails, submits to be killed; but
there is no " fight " to be got out of a tapir.

The tapir leads a very solitary life, being met with
alone, or sometimes in the company of the female.
The latter has but one young at a birth, which follows
her until able to provide for itself; when they associate no longer together, but part company, each taking
its own way.

This animal is called amphibious, because it spends
part of its time in the water ; but, although it has
been called the American representative of the

rhinoceros and hippopotamus, it is not so much a
water animal as either of these. It seeks its food in
the river, or the marshes that border it, and can remain for several minutes under water; but, for all
that, most of its time is passed on dry land. It
sleeps during the day in some dry spot upon a
bed of withered leaves, from whence it sallies every
evening, and makes to the marshy banks of some
well-known stream. It frequently leaves its lair
during rain, and goes in search of food. Like hogs,
it is very fond of wallowing in a muddy place; but,
unlike these slovenly animals, it does not return to its
bed until it has plunged into the clear water and thoroughly purified itself of the mud.

One habit of the tapir — and an unfortunate one
for itself — is, that in going its rounds it always follows the old track. In this way a path is soon
formed from its lair to its feeding-place, so conspicuous that a hunter might trail it upon the run. It is
easy, therefore, to " waylay " a tapir. Guapo knew
this well, and had already, while over among the
palms, marked the track of one that came nightly to
the stream, and had settled it in his mind that that
particular tapir had not many days to live. In fact
Leon coaxed him to fix the tapir hunt for the next
morning; which Guapo, with Don Pablo's permission,
accordingly did. Guapo was anxious as any of them
to kill the tapir; for, like many Indians, he was fond
of its flesh, though that is by no means a palatable
article of food. On the contrary, it is dry, and to
most people tastes disagreeably. Guapo, however,
liked it exceedingly; and, moreover, he wanted the

tough skin for some purpose of his own. The wild
Indians value the skin highly, as it is the best thing
they can procure for " viches," or shields, to ward
off the poisoned arrows of their enemies.

Next morning, an hour or so after daybreak, Guapo
started for the hunt, accompanied by Leon. Don
Pablo remained at home with his wife and the little
Leona. Now, had the tapir hunter possessed a gun,
or even a bow and arrows, his plan of proceeding
would have been different, and he would no doubt
have chosen a different hour for the hunt. He would
have chosen the twilight of the evening or morning,
and would have hid himself in the bushes, so as to
command a view of the track which the tapir would
be certain to take on his way to or from the water.
He would then have simply shot the creature as it
was going past. But this is not so easy a matter
neither ; for the tapir, fearful of enemies while on
land, always travels at a trot. As Guapo had neither
bow nor gun, — nothing, in fact, but his *macheté*, —
how was he to get near enough to use this weapon ?
Clumsy looking as the tapir certainly is, he can
shuffle over the ground faster than the fastest Indian.

Guapo knew all this ; but he also knew a stratagem by which the amphibious brute could be out-
witted ; and this stratagem he designed putting in
practice. For the purpose he carried another weapon
besides the *macheté*. That weapon was a very pacific
one ; it was a *spade*. Fortunately he had one which
he had brought with him from the mountains.

Now, what did Guapo mean to do with the spade ?
The tapir is not a burrowing animal, and therefore

would not require to be " dug out." We shall presently see what use was made of the spade.

After crossing the bridge and getting well round
among the palms, the hunter came upon a path well
tracked into the mud. It was the path of the tapir —
that could be easily seen. There were the broad
footmarks, some with three and others with four toes ;
and there, too, were places where the animal had
" wallowed." The tracks were quite fresh, and
made, as Guapo said, not an hour before they had
arrived on the spot.

This was just what the tapir hunter wanted ; and,
choosing a place where the track ran between two
palm trees, and could not well have gone round
either of them, he halted, rested his *macheté* against
a tree, and took a determined hold of the spade.
Leon now began to see what use he intended to make
of the spade. He was *going to dig a pit*.

That was, in fact, the very thing he was going to
do ; and in less than an hour, with the help of Leon,
it was done — the latter carrying away the earth
upon " bussu " leaves as fast as Guapo shovelled it
out. When the pit was sunk to what Guapo considered a sufficient depth, he came out of it ; and then,
choosing some slender poles, with palm leaves,
branches, and grass, he covered it in such a manner
that a fox himself would not have known it to be
a pit trap. But such it was — wide enough and
deep enough, as Guapo deemed, to entrap the largest
tapir.

It now only remained to get the tapir into it ; but
therein lay the difficulty. Leon could not understand

9

how this was to be managed. He knew that at night, as the animal was on its way to the water, it might step on the covering and fall in. But Guapo had promised him that he should see the tapir trapped in an hour's time. Guapo had a plan of his own for bringing it that way; and he at once proceeded to put his plan into execution.

They started along the trail going *from* the water, and towards the lair of the beast. The hunter knew it would not be very distant; perhaps a quarter or half a mile — perhaps less. Before starting he cautioned Leon to keep close behind him, and not to make the least noise. So little as a whisper or the rustling of the brush, he alleged, might spoil all his plans. Guapo marched, or rather crouched, along, at first freely; but after some time his step grew more stealthy and cautious. He knew that he was getting near to the sleeping victim. After stopping and repeating his caution to his companion, he proceeded as before until they had got better than a quarter of a mile from the water. Here they began to ascend a gentle hill, where the ground was dry and strewed with fallen trees. At some places the trail was difficult to make out; and Leon would soon have lost it had he been left to himself; but there was no fear of Guapo losing it. A hound could not have followed it more surely.

Suddenly Guapo stopped, then went on a few steps, then stopped a second time, and made a sign for Leon to come up. Without speaking, he pointed to a little thicket of scrubby bushes, through the leaves of which they could just make out some large brown object perfectly at rest. That was the tapir himself, sound asleep.

Guapo had already instructed his companion that, when they should arrive near the den of the animal, they were to make a wide circuit around — Leon going one way, while he himself took the other. Both now drew back a little, and then parted — the hunter going to one side, and Leon in the opposite direction. After making their circuit, they met at some distance beyond the back of the den ; and then Guapo, telling the other to follow him, and without observing any further caution, walked straight towards where the tapir lay. The Indian knew by experience that the latter, when roused, would make directly along its accustomed trail to the water; for to the water it always flies when alarmed by an enemy. When they had got within a few paces of the den a movement was seen among the leaves ; then a crackling noise was heard, as the huge body of the animal broke through the bushes and took to flight. He did not trot, according to his usual gait, but went off in a gallop, with his head carried in a singular and awkward manner between his fore legs. You have no doubt seen a donkey sometimes gallop in a similar style.

Guapo bounded after, followed by Leon, who kept close at his heels. Of course the tapir was in sight only a few seconds ; but the hunter knew that he would take the beaten track, and therefore was at no loss. They made no unnecessary noise, lest the tapir might be frightened from its path, but ran on in silence.

They soon got back to the pitfall, Guapo of course leading the way.

"Hola!" cried the latter, when he came in sight of it — "hola, young master! He's in the trap!"

Sure enough, he was; and the next moment they stood upon the edge of the p'.t, and beheld the great brown body struggling and tumbling about at the bottom.

Guapo did not pause a moment, but leaped in, *macheté* in hand. He had no fear of the animal biting him, for he knew it would not do so; but Guapo, in his hurry, had leaped carelessly, and, his foot slipping, he fell over the smooth body of the tapir. The latter, in its fright, jumped upward; and the next moment Guapo was *undermost* at the bottom of the pit.

The animal had no design of trampling the hunter; but, seeing that it could easily leap out, — the pit being shallowed for it by Guapo's body and the fallen branches, — it made a spring, and came out on the edge. Leon had got round upon the side next the river; but he chanced to be on the wrong side just then; for the heavy tapir, dashing past, knocked against him, and sent him sprawling among the trees. Before he could recover himself or Guapo climb out of the pit, a loud plunge in the water announced that the animal had escaped to an element where it might defy their pursuit.

Both were quite crestfallen and disappointed, but Guapo especially so. He had prided himself very much on his skill as a tapir hunter, and his pride was mortified at the result. He seemed very much cha-

grined ; and, as he and Leon returned towards the
house, he stopped at intervals and looked into the
water ; then, shaking his macheté in a threatening
manner, cried out, —

"Dive away, old thickskin ! Dive deep as you
will, I'll have your hide yet."

CHAPTER XIX.

THE POISONED ARROWS.

T**HE** result of the tapir chase determined Guapo to have himself better armed. There was one weapon — and a very efficient one too — which he knew how both to make and use. That weapon was a " gravatána," or blow gun, sometimes called " pocuna." He had had an eye to this weapon all along, and had already provided the materials necessary for making it. These materials were of a varied character, and had cost him some trouble in getting them together.

First, then, for the blow tube itself he had cut stems of a slender palm tree — a species of *Iriartea*, but not that sort already described. It was the *Pashiuba miri* of the Indians. This little palm grows to the height of from twelve to twenty feet, and is never thicker than a man's wrist. Its roots, like the others of its genus, rise above the ground, but only a few inches. The stems which Guapo had chosen were of different sizes. One was about the thickness of the handle of a garden rake, while the other was not over the diameter of a walking cane. Both were hollow in the heart, or rather they contained pith like the alder tree, which when forced out left a smooth bore.

Having cut these stems to a length of about ten

feet, and pushed out the pith, Guapo inserted the smaller one into the bore of the larger, which fitted tightly all the way — for he had chosen it of the proper thickness to this end. The object of thus using two stems instead of one will not, at first, be understood. It was for the purpose of making the tube perfectly straight, as this is a most important consideration in the gravatána. The outer and stronger stem corrected any bend that there might be in the inner one, and they were carefully arranged so that the one should straighten the other. Had it not been perfectly straight, Guapo would have bound it to a post and made it so; but it happened to come quite right without further trouble. The tube of the lesser one was now cleaned out thoroughly, and polished by a little bunch of the roots of a tree fern until it was as smooth and hard as ebony. A mouthpiece of wood was placed at the smaller end of the tube, and a sight was glued on the outside. This " sight " was the tooth of an animal — one of the long, curving incisors of a rodent animal called the " paca," which is found in most parts of tropical America. To make the instrument look neater, Guapo had procured the, tough, shining bark of a creeping plant, which he wound spirally around the outside from the mouthpiece to the muzzle ; and then the gravatána was finished.

There was yet much to be done before it could be used. Arrows were to be made, and a quiver in which to carry them, and poison to dip their points in — for the arrows of the blow gun do not kill by

the wound they inflict, but by the poison with which
they are charged.

The next thing, then, to which Guapo turned his
attention was the manufacture of the arrows. These
can be made of cane, reeds, and other kinds of
wood ; but the best materials for the purpose are the
long spines of the patawa palm, of which I have
already spoken. These spines grow out from the
lower part of the leaf petioles, and, in young trees
and those much sheltered, remain upon the trunk,
giving it a very shaggy appearance. They are often
three feet in length, about as thick as large wire,
rather flattish, and of a black color. To make the
arrows, Guapo cut them to the length of fifteen or
eighteen inches, and then pointed them sharply at
one end. About three inches from the points he
notched them all, so that they would break in the
wound rather than drop out again, in consequence of
the struggles of the animal. About two or three inches
from the thick end of the arrow Guapo wrapped lightly around the shaft some strands of the soft silky
cotton, which he had procured from the pods of the
great " ceiba," or silk-cotton tree, already mentioned.
This he fastened on with a fibre of an aloe plant —
one of the *bromelias ;* and the cotton, when thus
secured, assumed a conical or spindle shape, having
its larger end towards the but of the arrow. When
inserted into the gravatána, the swell of the cotton
filled the tube exactly — not so tightly as to impede
the passage of the arrow, nor so loosely as to allow
of " windage " when blown upon through the mouthpiece.

The arrows were now ready, with the exception of the poison for their tips ; and this was the most important of all, for without it both blow gun and arrows would have been useless weapons indeed. But Guapo was just the man who knew how to make this poison ; and that is more than could be said of every Indian, for it is only the " piaches " (priests, or " medicine men ") who understand the process. Nay, more : there are even some tribes where not an individual knows how the arrow poison is made ; and these have to procure it by barter from others, paying a high price, and sometimes going a great distance for it.

This celebrated poison is known under different names ; but those of " curare," " ticuna," and " wouraly," are the principal.

It is one of the most deadly poisons yet discovered — as much so as the *upastiente* of Java or the bean of St. Ignatius ; but it is perfectly harmless when swallowed, and indeed it is often taken by the Indians as an excellent stomachic. Should it get into the blood, however, by means of an arrow wound or a sore, no remedy has yet been discovered that will cure it. Death is certain, and a death similar to that caused by the bite of a venomous serpent. So say those who have suffered from it, but recovered on account of their having been only slightly wounded or lightly inoculated with it. Let us see, then, how Guapo prepared this deadly mixture.

He had gone out to the forest, and returned carrying a bundle of slender rods. They were pieces of a lliana, or creeping plant. It was the *bejuco de curare*, or "mavacure," as it is sometimes called. The leaves he had stripped off and left behind as useless. Had he brought them with him, they would have been seen to be small leaves of an oblong-oval shape, sharp at the points, and of a whitish-green color. Don Pablo knew the plant to be a species of *Strychnos*.

Guapo with his knife first scraped all the bark, as well as the alburnum or white coating, from the rods, which last he flung away. The mixture of bark and alburnum was next placed upon a smooth stone and mashed into a fibre of a yellowish color. This done, it was gathered into a heap, and placed within a funnel which had already been made out of a plantain leaf. The funnel was a long, narrow cone; and to strengthen it, it was set within another funnel made of the thick leaf of the " bussu " palm, and then both were supported by a framework of palm fibres. Underneath the apex was placed a small pan, — which could afterwards be put over the fire, — and then cold water was thrown into the funnel along with the bark. A yellowish liquid soon commenced to filter and drip into the pan ; and this liquid was the *curare*, the arrow poison. It still required, however, to be concentrated by evaporation ; and for this purpose the pan was transferred to a slow fire, where it was kept until the liquid became thickened by the heat.

Another process was yet required before the curare was ready for the arrows. It was sufficiently concentrated and deadly, but still too thin to adhere properly to their tips ; and for this purpose a mixture of some gummy juice was necessary. This Guapo soon pre-

pared from the large leaves of a tree called the
" kiracaguero " and poured it into the infusion ; and
then the curare turned from its yellow color to black,
and was ready for use. The change of color was
produced by the decomposition of a hydruret of carbon ; the hydrogen was burned and the carbon set
free.

Guapo now dipped a few of his arrows, and carefully deposited them in a large joint of bamboo, which
served as a quiver. I say *carefully ;* for, had one of
these arrows dropped with its poisoned point upon his
naked foot, or wounded him elsewhere, he never
would have prepared any more curare. But he
handled them with care, and the remainder of the
liquid he poured into a small gourd, (similar to that
in which he carried his coca lime,) which he closely
corked up with a piece of the pith from a palm.

Don Pablo, with Doña Isidora and the children, had
watched with interest all this process. At first they
were afraid to go near, believing that the fumes of
the liquid might be injurious. This was long believed
to be the case, in consequence of the absurd tales
spread abroad by the old missionaries, and even at a
later period by the traveller La Condamine. These
asserted that, when the Indians wished to make the
curare poison, they selected for this purpose the old
women of the tribe, whose lives were not deemed of
any value, and that several of these always fell a
sacrifice while " cooking " the curare. This silly
story is now refuted ; and Guapo not only assured
his companions that there was no danger, but even
tasted the curare from time to time while in the pan,

in order to judge when it was sufficiently concentrated. This he could tell by its taste, as it grew more
and more bitter as the evaporation proceeded. The
arrow poisons of South America are not all made
from the creeping plant, the mavacure. Among
some Indian tribes a root is used called " curare de
raiz ; " and with others the poison is produced by a
mixture of several species of juices from the plant
Ambihuasca, tobacco, red pepper, a bark called " barbasco," from a tree of the genus *Jacquinia*, and a
plant of the name "sarnango." Of all these the
juice of the *Ambihuasca* is the most powerful ingre-
dient ; but the making of this species of poison is a
most complicated process.

Guapo was not long in having an opportunity to
test his gravatána ; and this was just what he desired ;
for the old Indian was not a little vain of his skill,
and he wished to make a show of it in the eyes of
his companions. His vanity, however, was the more
pardonable, as he was in reality a first-rate shot,
which he proved to the satisfaction of every body within half an hour. The instrument had scarcely been
finished and laid aside when a loud screaming and
chattering was heard in the air ; and on looking up, a
flock of large birds was seen flying over the heavens.
They were still high up ; but all of a sudden they
darted down together and alit on a tall tree that stood
nearly alone. Here they continued their chattering,
only in a lower and more confidential tone ; and they
could be seen, not hopping, but climbing about, sometimes with their backs and heads turned downwards,
and, in short, clinging to the branches in every imagi-

nable way. These birds were all of one kind, each of them full eighteen inches in length, and of a uni-form color over the body, which was a purple, or deep indigo — their beaks only being white. In the sun their plumage glistened with a metallic lustre. They were, in fact, a rare species — the *ana*, or *purple macaw.*

Without saying a word, Guapo seized his gravatá-na and arrows and stole off through the underwood towards the tree upon which the macaws had perched. In a few minutes he stood under it, screened from the view of the birds by the broad leaves of a plantain that happened to grow beneath. This cover was necessary; else the macaws, which are shy birds, might have uttered one of their wild, choral screams, and flown off. They did not, however; and Guapo had a fair chance at them. All his movements could be observed by the party at the house, as he was on that side of the plantain.

He was seen to adjust an arrow into the tube, and then raise the gravatána to his lips. Strange to say, he did not hold it as we do a common gun — that is, with the left hand advanced along the tube. On the contrary, both hands were held nearly together, at the lower end, and close to his mouth. Now, you will wonder how he could hold such a long tube steady in this way. It is, indeed, a very difficult thing, and much practice alone can accomplish it. As they watched him narrowly, his chest was seen to expand, his cheeks rose with a strong " puff," and some of them thought they could perceive the passage of the little arrow out of the tube. However this might be, they soon after saw something sticking in the side of one of the macaws, and could see the bird pecking at it with its great beak and trying to pull it out. In this it appeared to have succeeded after a short while, for something fell from the tree. It was the shaft, with its cotton " boss," that fell down. The point, broken off where it had been notched, was still in the body of the bird, and was infusing the deadly venom into its veins. In about two minutes' time the wound-ed bird seemed to grow giddy, and began to stagger. It then fell over, still clutching the branch with its strong, prehensile claws; but after hanging a mo-ment, these, too, relaxed, and the body fell heavily to the ground. It was quite dead.

Long before it came down Guapo had pushed a fresh arrow into the tube and given a fresh puff through it, wounding a second of the macaws. Then another arrow was chosen, and another victim, until several had been shot, and the creatures upon the tree could be seen in all stages of dying. Some, on re-ceiving the wound, uttered a cry and flew off; but the poison soon brought them down, and they invariably fell at no great distance from the tree.

At length Guapo was seen to desist and walk bold-ly out from his ambush. To the surprise of all, the remaining macaws, of which there were still six or seven upon the tree, showed no fear of him, nor did they attempt to fly away. This was explained, how-ever, by their subsequent conduct; for in a few sec-onds more they were seen, one by one, falling to the ground, until not a single bird was left upon the tree. All of them had been killed by the arrows of the blow gun.

Leon now run out to assist Guapo in gathering his game. There were no less than eight couple of them in all, and they were all quite dead — some of them shot in the thigh, some in the neck or wing, and others through the body. None of them had lived over two minutes after receiving the wound. Such is the quickness with which the " curare " does its work.

As a hunting instrument for most species of game, the South American Indian prefers the gravatána to any other; and with good reason. Had Guapo been armed with a rifle or fowling piece he would have shot one macaw, or perhaps a pair, and then the rest would have uttered a tantalizing scream and winged their way out of his reach. He might have missed the whole flock, too; for on a high tree, such as that on which they had alit, it is no easy matter to kill a macaw with a shot gun. Now the gravatána throws its arrow to a height of from thirty to forty yards, and the least touch is sufficient to do the business. Its silence, moreover, enables the hunter to repeat the shot until several head of game reward his skill. The Indians use it with most effect in a vertical or upward direction; and they are always surer to kill a bird with it when perched on a high tree than when seated on a low shrub or on the ground.

As we have observed that the curare can be taken inwardly without any danger, it will be evident to all

that game killed by the poisoned arrows may be
eaten with safety. Indeed there are many epicures
in South America who prefer it in this way ; and
when a chicken is wanted for the table, these people
require that it should be killed by an arrow dipped in
curare.

CHAPTER XX.

THE MILK TREE.

GUAPO kept his promise with the tapir, and on that very same day. Shortly after the macaws had been brought in, little Leona, who had been straying down by the water's edge, came running back to the house, and in breathless haste cried out, " Mamma ! mamma ! what a big hog !"

" Where, my pet?" inquired her mother, with a degree of anxiety; for she fancied that the child might have seen some fierce beast of prey instead of a hog.

" In the water," replied Leona ; " among the great lilies."

" It's the tapir !" cried Leon. " Carrambo ! it's our tapir !"

Guapo was busy plucking his macaws; but at the word tapir he sprang to his feet, making the feathers fly in all directions.

" Where, señorita ?" he asked, addressing little Leona.

" Down below," replied the child ; " near the edge of the river."

Guapo seized his gravatána and crouched down towards the bank, with Leon at his heels. On near-ing the water he stopped, and, with his body half

10

bent, looked down stream. There, sure enough, was the huge brown beast, standing with his body half out of the water, and pulling up the roots of the flags with his great teeth, and long, movable snout. It was not likely he would return to his former den after the chase he had had; and fancying, no doubt, that all the danger lay upon the opposite shore, he had come to this side to browse a while.

Guapo cautioned Leon to remain where he was, while he himself, almost crawling upon his belly, proceeded along the bank. In a few minutes he was out of sight; and Leon, seeing nothing more of him, kept his eyes sharply fixed upon the tapir.

The latter remained quietly feeding for about ten minutes, when the boy saw him give a little start. Perhaps, thought he, he has heard Guapo among the weeds, — for the tapir has good ears, — and that was what caused him to make the motion. The tapir stopped feeding for a moment, but then recommenced, though evidently not with as much eagerness as before. Presently he stopped a second time, and seemed undetermined as to whether he should not turn and take to the clear water. In this way he hesitated for several minutes; then, to the astonishment of Leon, his body began to rock from side to side; and the next moment, with a plunge, he fell heavily backward, making the waves undulate on all sides of him. The arrow had done its work — he was dead!

A loud shout from Guapo echoed along the river, and the Indian was seen plunging forward to the dead tapir, which the next moment he had seized by the leg, and was dragging towards the bank. He was here met by the whole party, all of whom were anxious to see this rare and singular creature. Ropes were soon attached to the legs; and Guapo, assisted by Don Pablo and Leon, drew the huge carcass out upon the shore and dragged it up to the house.

Guapo at once skinned it, carefully preserving the hide, to make soles for his sandals and other pur-poses; and that night all of them tried a "tapir steak" for supper. All, however, Guapo alone excepted, preferred the flesh of the purple macaws, which, cooked as they were with onions and red pepper, were excellent eating, particularly for Span-ish American palates. Guapo had all the tapir to himself.   *   *   *   *   *

The bamboo palm house was now quite finished, and several articles of furniture too; for during the nights both Don Pablo and his trusty man Guapo had worked at many things. You will, no doubt, be ask-ing where they procured lights, will you not? I shall tell you. One of the loftiest and most beautiful of the palm trees — *the wax palm* (*Ceroxylon Andicola*) — grew in these very parts ; for the lower slopes of the Andes are its favorite habitat. Out of its trunk exudes wax, which has only to be scraped off and made into candles, that burn as well as those made of the wax of bees. Indeed the missionaries, in their various religious ceremonies, — or " mummeries," as they might be better styled, — have always made large use of these palm candles. Another " wax palm," called " Carnáuba," (*Copernicia cerifera*,) is found in South America. In this one the wax — of a

pure white color, and without any admixture of resin
— collects upon the under side of the leaves, and
can be had in large quantities by merely stripping it
off. But, even had neither of these palms been found,
they needed not to have gone without lights; for the
fruits of the "patawa," already described, when sub-
mitted to pressure, yield a pure liquid oil, without
any disagreeable smell, and most excellent for burning in lamps. So you see there was no lack of light
in the cheerful cottage.

But there were two things, you will say, still want-
ing, — one of them a necessary article, and the other
almost so, — and which could not possibly be procured
in such a place. These two things were *salt* and
milk. Now, there was neither a salt mine, nor a
lake, nor a drop of salt water, nor yet either cow,
goat, or ass, within scores of miles of the place; and
still they had both salt and milk.

The milk they procured from a tree which grew
in the woods close by, and a tree so singular and
celebrated that you have no doubt heard of it before
now. It was the *palo de vaca*, or " cow tree," called
sometimes by an equally appropriate name — *arbol
del leche*, or " milk tree." It is one of the noblest
trees of the forest, rising, with its tall, straight stem,
tc a great height, and adorned with large, oblong,
pointed leaves, some of which are nearly a foot in
length. It carries fruit which is eatable, about the
size of a peach, and containing one or two stones;
and the wood itself is valuable, being hard, fine
grained, and durable. But it is the sap which gives
celebrity to the tree. This is neither more nor less

than milk, of a thick creamy kind, and most agreeable in flavor. Indeed there are many persons who prefer it to the milk of cows; and it has been proved to be equally nutritious, the people fattening upon it in districts where it grows. It is collected, as the sugar water is from the maple, simply by making a notch, or incision, in the bark, and placing a vessel underneath, into which the sap runs abundantly. It runs most freely at the hour of sunrise; and this is also true as regards the sap of the sugar tree and many other trees of that kind. Sometimes it is drank pure as it flows from the tree; but there are some people who, not relishing it in its thick, gummy state, dilute it with water and strain it before using it. It is excellent for tea or coffee, quite equal to the best cream, and of a richer color. When left to stand in an open vessel, a thick coagulum forms on the top, which the natives term cheese, and which they eat in a similar manner, and with equal relish. Another virtue of this extraordinary tree is that the cream, without any preparation, makes a glue for all purposes as good as that used by cabinet makers; and indeed Don Pablo and Guapo had already availed themselves of it in this way.

So much for the *palo de vaca*.

It still remains for me to tell you where the *salt* came from; and although the milk tree was ever so welcome, yet the salt was a thing of still greater necessity. Indeed the latter might be looked upon as an indispensable article in household economy. You, my young reader, know not what it is to be without salt. With whole sacks of this beautiful mineral within your reach, almost as cheap as sand, you cannot fancy the longing — the absolute craving — for it which they feel who are for a period deprived of it. Even the wild animals will make long journeys in search of those salt springs — or, as they are called, " licks " — which exist in many places in the wilderness of America. For salt, Don Pablo and his companions would have exchanged any thing they had — their sugar, plantains, cocoa, coffee, or even the cassava, which was their bread. They longed for salt, and knew not how they could get on without it. The only substitute was the " aji," or capsicum, of which several species grew around; and almost every dish they ate was strongly spiced with it. But still this was not salt, and they were not contented with it.

It was now that they found a friend in Guapo. Guapo knew that among many of the Indian tribes the fruit of a certain species of palm was manufactured into salt; and he knew the palm, too, if he could only get his eyes upon it. Seeing his master and the rest so troubled upon this head, Guapo rose one morning early and stole off among the groves of palm on the other side of the river. There, in a marshy place, with its roots even growing in the water, stood the very tree — a small palm of about four inches in diameter and twenty to thirty feet high. It was thicker at the base than the top; and the top itself rose several feet above the tuft of pinnate, feathery fronds, ending in a pointed spike. It was the " jara " palm, of the genus *Leopoldinia*.

It was the fruits upon which Guapo bent his eyes

with earnestness. Each one was as large as a peach, of an oval shape, slightly flattened, and of a yellow-ish-green color. They grew in large clusters among the bases of the leaves; and Guapo was not long in ascending several trees — for the jara is a smooth-skinned palm, and can be climbed — and breaking off the spadices and flinging them to the ground. He had soon collected a bag full, with which he hurried back to the house.

All wondered what Guapo meant to do with these fruits; for they tasted them and found them very bitter. Guapo soon showed them his intention. Hav-ing prepared a sort of furnace, he set the nuts on fire; and when they were thoroughly reduced to ashes, to the great joy and astonishment of all, these ashes, which were as white as flour, had the taste of salt! It is true it was not equal to " Turk's Island," nor yet to " Bay " salt; but it proved to be good enough for cooking purposes, and satisfied the craving which all had felt for this indispensable article.

CHAPTER XXI.

THE CANNIBAL FISH AND THE GYMNOTUS.

ABOUT this time an incident occurred that was very near having a fatal termination for one of the party — Leon. The day was a very hot one, and, as the cool water looked inviting, Leon could not resist the temptation of taking a bath. Having undressed himself, he plunged into the river, nearly in front of where the house stood, and began splashing about quite delighted. The rest were not heeding him, as each was engaged with some occupation within the house.

Leon at first kept wading about in a place that was not beyond his depth; but, by little and little, he took short swims, as he wished to practise, and become a good swimmer like Guapo. His father had not only given him permission, but had even advised him to do so. And it may be here remarked that all parents would do well to take the same course with their children and allow them to acquire this healthful and useful art. No one can deny that thousands of lives are annually sacrificed because so few have taken the trouble to learn swimming.

Well, Leon was determined to be a swimmer, and at each attempt he made a wider stretch into the deep water, swam around, and then back again to the bank.

In one of these excursions, just as he had got farthest out, all at once he felt a sharp pain as if from the bite of some animal, and then another, and another, upon different parts of the body, as if several sets of teeth were attacking him at once.

Leon screamed, — who wouldn't have done so? — and his scream brought the whole household to the edge of the water in less than a score of seconds. All of them believed that he was either drowning or attacked by a crocodile. On arriving at the bank, however, they saw that he was still above water and swimming boldly for the shore — no signs of a crocodile were to be seen.

What was the matter?

Of course that question was asked him by all of them in a breath. His reply was that " he could not tell — *something was biting him all over!* "

The quick eye of the mother now caught sight of blood — around the swimmer the water was tinged with it — her piercing shriek rent the air.

" O God ! my child — my child ! Save him — save him ! "

Both Don Pablo and Guapo dashed into the water and plunged forward to meet him. In the next moment he was raised in their arms; but the blood streamed down his body and limbs, apparently from a dozen wounds. As they lifted him out of the water they saw what had caused these wounds. A shoal of small fish, with ashy-green backs and bright orange bellies and fins, was seen below. With large, open mouths they had followed their victim to the very surface ; and, now that he was lifted out of their reach,

they shot forward and attacked the legs of his res-
cuers, causing Don Pablo and Guapo to dance up in
the water and make with all haste for the bank.   As
soon as they had reached it, they turned round and
looked into the water.   There were these blood-
thirsty pursuers, that had followed them up to the very
bank, and now swam about, darting from point to
point, and ready for a fresh attack on any one that
might enter the water.

" They are the ' cannibal fish ! ' " said Guapo, in
an angry tone, as he turned to attend to Leon.   " I
shall punish them yet for it.   Trust me, young master, you shall be revenged. "

Leon was now carried up to the house, and it was
found that in all he had received nearly a dozen
wounds.   Some of them were on the calves of his
legs, where the piece of flesh was actually taken out.
Had he been farther out in the river when first attacked, he might never have reached the shore alive,
as the fierce creatures were gathering in far greater
numbers when he was rescued, and would most un-
doubtedly have torn him to pieces and eaten him up.
Such has been the fate of many persons who have
fallen among the " cannibal fish " in the midst of
wide rivers where they had no chance of escape.
These ferocious little " caribes," or " caribitos," as
they are called, (for the word *carib* signifies cannibal,) lie at the bottom of rivers, and are not easily
seen ; but the moment an attack is made by one of
them, and a drop of blood stains the water, the whole
shoal rises to the surface ; and woe to the creature
that is assailed by their sharp triangular teeth !

Of course the wounds of Leon, although painful were not dangerous ; but the chief danger lay in the loss of blood which was pouring from so many veins. But Guapo found ready to his hand the best thing in the world for stopping it. On some mimosa trees, not far from the house, he had already observed — indeed so had all of them — a very singular species of ants' nests of a yellowish-brown color. The ants themselves were of a beautiful emerald green. They were the *Formica spinicollis*. These nests were composed of a soft cotton down, which the ants had collected from a species of *Melastoma*, a handsome shrub found growing in these regions ; and this down Guapo knew to be the best for blood stopping. Even Don Pablo had heard of its being used by the Indians for this purpose, and knew it by the name of " *yesca de hormigas*," or " touchwood of ants." He had heard, moreover, that it was far superior even to the ants' nests of Cayenne, which form an article of commerce, and are highly prized in the hospitals of Europe. Guapo, therefore, ran off and robbed the green ants of their nests, and speedily returned with his hands full of the soft " yesca." This was applied to the wounds, and in a few minutes the bleeding was effectually stopped ; and Leon, although still suffering pain, had now only to be patient and get well.

Strange to say, another incident occurred that very evening, which taught our party a further lesson of the danger of taking to the water without knowing more of its inhabitants. Just as they had finished supper, and were seated in front of their new house,

the mule, that had been let loose, stepped into the
river to drink and cool its flanks. It was standing in
the water, which came up to its belly, and, having
finished its drink, was quietly gazing around it. All
at once it was observed to give a violent plunge and
make with hot haste for the bank. It snorted and looked
terrified ; while its red nostrils were wide open, and
its eyes appeared as if they would start from their
sockets. At length it reached the bank, and, stag-
gering forward, rolled over in the sand as if it was
going to die.

What could all this mean ? Had it, too, been
attacked by the " caribes " ? No ; that was not
likely, as the bite of these creatures upon the hard
shanks of the mule could not have produced such
an effect. They might have frightened it ; but
they could not have thrown it into " fits ; " for it
was evidently in some sort of a fit at that moment.

It might have been a puzzle to our party not easily
solved had Guapo not been upon the spot. But
Guapo had witnessed such an incident before. Just
before the mule gave the first plunge Guapo's eyes
had been wandering in that direction. He had noticed an odd-looking form glide near the mule and
pass under the animal's belly. This creature was of
a greenish-yellow color, about five feet in length, and
four or five inches thick. It resembled some kind of
water snake more than a fish ; but Guapo knew it
was not a snake, but an eel. It was the great *electric
eel* — the " temblador," or " gymnotus."

This explained the mystery. The gymnotus,

having placed itself under the belly of the unsus·
pecting mule, was able to bring its body in contact
at all points ; and hence the powerful shock that had
created such an effect.

The mule, however, soon recovered ; but, from
that time forward, no coaxing, nor leading, nor dri·
ving, nor whipping, nor pushing would induce that
same mule to go within twenty feet of the bank of
that same piece of water.

Guapo now bethought himself of the narrow escape
he himself had had while swimming across to the
palm woods; and the appearance of the gymnotus
only rendered him more determined to keep the
promise he had made to Leon — that is, that he
would revenge him of the caribes.

None of them could understand how Guapo was to
get this revenge without catching the fish ; and that
would. be difficult to do. Guapo, however, showed
them how on the very next day.

During that evening he made an excursion into the
wood, and returned home carrying with him a large
bundle of roots.

They were the roots of two species of plants —
one of the genus *Piscidea*, the other a *Jacquinia*.
Out of these, when properly pounded together, Guapo
intended to make the celebrated " barbasco," or fish
poison, which is used by all the Indians of South
America in capturing fish. Guapo knew that a suffi·
cient quantity of the barbasco thrown into the water
would kill either " temblador," caribe, or any fish
that ever swam with fins.

And so it proved. In the morning Guapo, having prepared his barbasco, proceeded to the upper end of the lakelike opening of the river, and there flung his poison into the stream. The slow current through the valley greatly favored him; and, from the large quantity of roots he had used, the whole pool was soon infected with it. This was seen from the whitish tinge which the water assumed. The barbasco had scarcely time to sink to the bottom when small fish were seen coming to the surface and turning " wrong side uppermost." Then larger ones appeared; and in a few minutes all the fish in that particular stretch of water, with several gymnoti, were seen floating on the surface quite dead. To the great joy of Guapo and Leon, who sat by the bank watching, hundreds of the little caribes, with their bronze gills quite open and their yellow bellies turned up, were seen among the rest.

But Guapo had not made this great slaughter purely out of revenge. He had another object. They were not too well off for meat; and a dish of fish would be welcome. Guapo and Don Pablo had already provided themselves with long-handled nets; and they soon scooped out several basketfuls of fish. Among others they netted numerous " caribes ; " for these little monsters, fierce as they are, are not surpassed for delicacy of flavor by any fish in the South American rivers. The gymnoti approached the bank, where Guapo fished them out, not to eat, although they are often eaten. There was not a spark of electricity in them now; the barbasco had cured them of that. Any one might have handled them with safety, as there was not a charge left in their whole battery.

The lake was quite cleared of all its dangerous denizens, and Leon might bathe with safety as soon as he got well ; and over the fish dinner they could now laugh at the adventures both of Leon and the electrified mule.

CHAPTER XXII.

THE CINCHONA TREES.

IN about two weeks from their arrival in the valley, the house, with a stable for the horse and mule, was completed, and all the necessary furniture as well. Had you entered the establishment about this time you would have observed many odd articles and implements, most of them quite new. You would have seen boxes woven out of palm leaves, and bags made of the fibrous, clothlike spathe of the " bussu," filled with the soft, silky cotton of the bombax, to be afterwards spun and woven for shirts and dresses. You would have seen baskets of various shapes and sizes, woven out of the rind of the leaf stalks of a singular palm called " Iú," (*Astrocaryum*,) which has no stem, but only leaves of ten feet long, growing directly out of the ground. You would have seen chairs made of split palms and bamboo, and a good-sized table, upon which, at meal time, might be noticed a tablecloth, not of diaper, but, what served equally well, the broad, smooth, silken leaves of the plantain. There were cups, too, and plates, and bowls, and dishes, and bottles of the light gourd shell, (*Crescentia cujete*,) some of the bottles holding useful liquids, and corked with the elastic pith of a palm. Other vessels of a boat shape might be noticed.

There were large wooden vessels pointed at the ends
like little canoes. They were nothing more than the
spathes or flower sheaths of one of the largest of
palms — the "*Inaga*," (*Maximiliana regia.*) This
noble tree rises to the height of one hundred feet,
and carries feathery fronds of more than fifty feet in
length. The spathes are so large that they are used
by the Indian women for cradles and baskets; and
their wood is so hard that hunters often cook meat
in them, hanging them over the fire when filled with
water.

Many other singular implements might have been
noticed in the new home. One, a cylinder of what
appeared to be wood, covered thickly with spinous
points, hung against the wall. That was a grater,
used for the manioc, or yucca roots; and it was a
grater of Nature's own making; for it was nothing
more than a piece of one of the air roots of the
" pashiuba " palm, already described. Another curious object hung near this last. It was a sort of
conical bag, woven out of palm fibre, with a loop at
the bottom, through which loop a strong pole was
passed, that acted as a lever when the article was in
use. This wicker-work bag was the "tipiti." Its
use was to compress the grated pulp of the manioc
roots so as to separate the juice from it, and thus
make " cassava." The roots of the yucca, or manioc
plant, grow in bunches like potatoes. Some of them
are oblong, the length of a man's arm, and more
than twenty pounds in weight. When required for
use, the bark is scraped off, and they are grated
down. They are then put into the tipiti already

11

mentioned, and the bag is hung up to a strong pin, while the lever is passed through the loop at the bottom. Its short end goes under a firm notch, and then some one usually sits upon the long end until the pulp is squeezed sufficiently dry. The bag is so formed that its extension, by the force of the lever, causes its sides to close upon the pulp, and thus press out the juice. The pulp is next dried in an oven, and becomes the famous " cassava," or " farinha," which, throughout the greater part of South America, is the only bread that is used. The juice of course runs through the wicker work of the *tipiti* into a vessel below, and there produces a sediment which is the well-known " tapioca."

There are two kinds of the yucca, or manioc root, — the *yucca dulce* and *yucca amarga*, — the sweet and bitter. One may be eaten raw without danger. The other, which very closely resembles it, if eaten raw, would produce almost instant death, as its juice is one of the deadliest of vegetable poisons. Even while it is dripping from the tipiti into the vessel placed below, great care is always taken lest children or other animals should drink of it.

There were no beds ; such things are hardly to be found in any part of tropical America — at least not in the low, hot countries. To sleep in a bed in these climates is far from being pleasant. The sleeper would be at the mercy of a thousand crawling things — insects and reptiles. Hammocks, or " redes," as they are there called, take the place of bedsteads ; and five hammocks, of different dimensions, could be seen about the new house. Some were strung up within, others in the porch in front; for, in building his house, Don Pablo had fashioned it so that the roof protruded in front, and formed a shaded veran-da — a pleasant place in which to enjoy the even-ings. Guapo had made the hammocks, having woven the cords out of the epidermis of the leaf of a noble palm called " tucum," (*Astrocaryum.*)

Their home being now sufficiently comfortable, Don Pablo began to turn his attention to the object for which he had settled on that spot. He had already examined the cinchona trees, and saw that they were of the finest species. They were, in fact, the same which have since become celebrated as producing the " Cuzconin," and known as "*Cascaril-la de Cuzco*," (Cuzco bark.)

Of the Peruvian bark trees there are many species — between twenty and thirty. Most of these are true cinchona trees; but there are also many kinds of the genus *Exostemma*, whose bark is collected as a febrifuge, and passes in commerce under the name of *Peruvian bark*. All these are of different quali-ties and value. Some are utterly worthless, and, like many other kinds of " goods," form a sad com-mentary on the honesty of commerce.

The species which grew on the sides of the adja-cent hills Don Pablo recognized as one of the most valuable. It was a nearly-allied species to the tree of Loxa, (*Cinchona condaminea*,) which produces the best bark. It was a tall, slender tree — when fullgrown, rising to the height of eighty feet; but there were some of every age and size. Its leaves were five inches long and about half that breadth, of a reddish color, and with a glistening surface, which rendered them easily distinguished from the foliage of the other trees. Now, it is a fortunate circumstance that the Peruvian bark trees differ from all others in the color of their leaves. Were this not the case, " bark hunting " would be a very troublesome operation. The labor of finding the trees would not be repaid with double the price obtained for the bark. You may be thinking, my young friend, that a " cascarillero," or " bark hunter," has nothing to do but find a wood of these trees, and then the trouble of searching is over, and nothing remains but to go to work and fell them. So it would be did the cinchona trees grow together in large numbers ; but they do not. Only a few — sometimes only a single tree — will be found in one place ; and I may here remark that the same is true of most of the trees of the great Montaña of South America. This is a curious fact, because it is a different arrangement from that made by Nature in the forests of North America. There a whole country will be covered with timber of a single, or at most two or three, species ; whereas in South America the forests are composed of an endless variety. Hence it has been found difficult to establish saw mills in these forests, as no one timber can be conveniently furnished in sufficient quantity to make it worth while. Some of the palms — as the great *morichi* — form an exception to this rule. These are found in vast *palmares*, or palm woods, extending over large tracts of country, and monopolizing the soil to themselves.

Don Pablo, having spent the whole of a day in ex

amining the cinchonas, returned home quite satisfied with them, both as regarded their quantity and value. He 'saw, from a high tree which he had climbed, " *manchas*," or spots of the glistening reddish leaves, nearly an acre in breadth. This was a fortune in itself. Could he only collect one hundred thousand pounds of this bark, and convey it down stream to the mouth of the Amazon, it would there yield him the handsome sum of forty thousand or fifty thousand dollars. How long before he could accomplish this task he had not yet calculated; but he resolved to set about it at once.

A large house had been already constructed for storing the bark; and in the dry, hot climate of the high Montaña, where they now were, Don Pablo knew it could be dried in the woods where it was stripped from the trees.

CHAPTER XXIII.

A PAIR OF SLOW GOERS

At length, all things being ready, Don Pablo and party set out for a day's work among the cinchonas. As it was the first day of bark gathering, all went along to enjoy the novelty of the thing. A " man-cha " of the cinchona trees was not far off; so their journey would be a short one. For this reason the horse and mule remained in the stable, eating the fruits of the " murumuru " palm, (another species of *Astrocaryum*,) of which all cattle are exceedingly fond. Even the hard, undigested stones or nuts, after passing through the bodies of horses and cattle, are eagerly devoured by wild or tame hogs; and the zamuros, or black vultures, *(Cathartes aura* and *atratus,)* when hungered, take to the pulpy fruit of this thorny palm tree.

It was a very early hour when they set out; for Don Pablo and his people were no sluggards. Indeed in that climate the early morning hours are the pleasantest; and they had made it a rule to be always up by daybreak. They could thus afford to take a *siesta* in their hammocks during the hot noontide — a custom very common, and almost necessary, in tropical countries. Their road to the cinchonas led up the stream, on the same side with the house.

After going a few hundred yards, they entered a grove of trees that had white trunks and leaves of a light silvery color. The straight, slender stems of these trees and the disposition of their branches — leaning over at the tops — gave them somewhat the appearance of palms. They were not palms, however, but "ambaïba" trees, *(Cecropia peltata.)* So said Don Pablo, as they passed under their shade.

"I shouldn't wonder," added he, "if we should see that strange animal, the aï. The leaves of these trees are its favorite food, and it lives altogether among their branches."

"You mean the 'nimble Peter,' do you not, papa?"

This inquiry was put by Leon, who had read about the animal under this name, and had read many false stories of it, even in the works of the great Buffon.

"Yes," replied Don Pablo; "it goes by that name sometimes, on account of its sluggish habits and slow motions. For the same reason the English call it 'sloth;' and it is known among naturalists as *brady-pus.* There are two or three species, but all with very similar habits; though, as usual, the French classifiers have separated them into distinct genera."

"Why, Buffon says," rejoined Leon, "that it is the most miserable creature in the world; that it can scarcely get from tree to tree; that some remain in the same tree all their lives, or that, when one has eaten all the leaves off a tree, it drops to the ground, to save itself the trouble of getting down by the trunk; and that when on the ground it cannot move a yard in an hour. Is all this true?"

"Totally untrue. It is true the aï does not move

rapidly over the ground; but the ground is not its
proper place, no more than it is that of the orang
outang, or other tree monkeys.   Its conformation
shows that Nature intended it for an inhabitant of the
trees, where it can move about with sufficient ease to
procure its food.   On the branches it is quite at
home ; or rather, I should say, *under* the branches ;
for, unlike the squirrels and monkeys, it travels along
the under sides of the horizontal limbs, with its back
downward.   This it can do with ease, by means of
its great curving claws, which are large enough to
span the thickest boughs.   In this position, with a
long neck of *nine vertebræ*, — the only animal which
has that number, — it can reach the leaves on all
sides of it ; and, when not feeding, this is its natural
position of repose.   Its remaining during its whole
life in one tree, or suffering itself to fall from the
branches, are romances of the early Spanish voyagers, to which M. Buffon gave too much credit.
The aï does not descend to the ground at all when it
can help it, but passes from one tree to another by
means of tne outspreading branches.   Sometimes,
when these do not meet, it has cunning enough to
wait for a windy day ; and then, taking advantage of
some branch blown nearer by the wind, it grasps it
and passes to the next tree.   As it requires no drink,
and can live without any other food than the leaves
of the cecropia, of course it remains on a single tree
so long as it has plenty of leaves.   See ! " exclaimed
Don Pablo, pointing up ; " here are several trees
stripped of their leaves !   I'll warrant that was done
by the aï."

"*A-ee!*" echoed a voice in the most lugubrious tones.

"I thought so," cried Don Pablo, laughing at the surprise which the voice had created among the rest of the party. "That's the very fellow himself; this way — here he is!"

All of them ran under the tree to which Don Pablo pointed, and looked up. There, sure enough, was an animal about the size of a cat, of a dark hay color, with a patch of dirty orange and black upon the back. This could be easily seen; for the creature was hanging along a horizontal branch, with its back downward; and its huge curving claws, all in a bunch, were hooked over the branch. Its hair was thick and rough, and no tail was visible; but its small, round head and flat face were almost as like the human face as is that of any monkey. Indeed the others would have taken it for a monkey — Guapo excepted — had they not been already talking about it.

"O, yonder's another!" cried Leon, pointing higher up in the tree; and, sure enough, there was; for the aï is usually found in company with its mate. The other was a copy of the one already observed, with some slight difference in size; no doubt it was the female one. Both had observed the approach of the party, and now uttered their melancholy "Ayee — a-ee!" that sounded any thing but agreeable. In fact, so very disagreeable is the voice of this creature that it has been considered its best weapon of defence. Besides the utterance of their cry, neither of them made any effort to escape or defend themselves.

Don Pablo and the rest were about to pass on and

leave the aïs to their leaf diet; but Guapo had other notions on that subject. Ugly as these creatures were, Guapo intended to have one of them for his dinner. He therefore begged Don Pablo to stop a moment until he should get them down. How was this to be done? Would he climb up and drag them from the tree? That is not so easily accomplished; for the aïs, with their crescent claws, can hold on with terrible force. Besides, they were out upon the slender branches, where it would have been difficut to get at them. But Guapo did not intend to climb. The tree was a slender one; he had his axe with him and the next moment its keen blade was crashing through the bark of the ambaïba wood. A few minutes served to bring the tree down; and down it came, the aïs screaming as it fell. Guapo now approached to seize them; but about this he used some caution. Both, finding themselves without hope of escape, prepared for defence. Buffon asserts that they make none. That is not true, as was seen by all the party. Throwing themselves on their backs, they struck out with their fore arms in a sort of mechanical manner. These, with the long horny claws, they kept playing in front of their bodies, striking alternately with them, and rapidly, as a dog will do when suddenly plunged into water. Guapo did not put his hands near them. He knew they would not bite, but he also knew that he might get a scratch with the sharp claws; and that he did not wish for. But Guapo had a way to take them; and that he now put in practice. Lopping a couple of branches from the tree, he held one out to each of the aïs, and touched them with it on the

breast. Each, as soon as it felt the branch, clutched it tightly between its powerful fore arms, and held on as if for life and death. It would have taken a stronger man than Guapo to have pulled either of the branches away again. The thing was now done. Giving his axe to Leon to carry for him, Guapo lifted an aï, still clinging to the branch, in each hand, and carried them off as if they had been a pair of water pots. He did not wish to kill them until he got them home, alleging that they were better for eating when freshly butchered.

The bark hunters now continued their route, and shortly after entered a little glade or opening in the forest, about an acre in size. When they had reached the middle of this, Guapo threw his aïs upon the ground and marched on.

" Why do you leave them ? " inquired the others.

" No fear for them," replied Guapo ; " they'll be there when we come back. If I carried them into the woods they might steal off while we were at work ; but it would take them six hours to get to the nearest tree."

All laughed at this and went on, leaving the aïs to themselves. Before passing out from the glade they stopped a moment to look at the great conical nests of the termites, or white ants, several of which, like soldiers' tents, stood near the edge of the glade. It was yet early ; the air was chilly, and the ants were not abroad ; so that, after gazing for a while on these singular habitations, the bark gatherers pursued their way, and were soon under the shadow of the cinchona trees.

CHAPTER XXIV.

THE BARK HUNTERS.

In a few minutes the work began — that work which was to occupy them, perhaps, for several years. The first blow of Guapo's axe was the signal to begin the making of a fortune. It was followed by many others, until one of the cinchonas lay along the sward. Then Guapo attacked another, as near the root as was convenient for chopping.

Don Pablo's part of the work now began. Armed with a sharp knife, he made circular incisions round the trunk, at the distance of several feet from each other, and a single longitudinal one intersecting all the others. The branches were also served in a similar way, and then the tree was left as it lay. In three or four days they would return to strip off the bark both from trunk and branches, and this would be spread out under the sun to dry. When light and dry it would be carried to the storehouse. So the work went merrily on. The trees were taken as they stood — the very young ones alone being left, as the bark of these is useless for commerce.

The Doña Isidora sat upon a fallen trunk, and, conversing with her husband, watched the proceedings with interest. A new and happy future seemed at no great distance off. Little Leona stood beside Guapo, watching the yellow chips as they flew, and listening to some very fine stories with which Guapo was regaling her. Guapo loved little Leona. He would have risked his life for her, would Guapo; and Leona knew it.

Leon was not particularly engaged on that day. When the bark was ready for peeling he intended to take a hand with the rest. He could then employ himself in spreading it, or could lead the mule in carrying it to the storehouse. Leon did not intend to be idle; but there happened to be no work for him just then; and, after watching the bark cutters for a while, he sauntered back along the path, in order to have a little fun with the aïs. Leon had no very great confidence that he would find them in the place where they had been left; and yet he believed in Guapo. But it was hard to understand that two animals, each endowed with a full set of legs and feet, should not be able to make their way for a distance of twenty paces and escape, after the rough handling they had had, too. He would have a peep at them, any how, to see how they were coming on. So back he went.

On getting near the glade their voices reached him. They were there, after all. He could hear them utter their pitiful " ay-ee — ay-ee ! " and, as he thought, in a louder and more distressing tone than ever. What could be the matter? They had been silent for some time, he was sure; for such cries as they now uttered could have been heard easily where the rest were. What could be the meaning of this fresh outburst ? Had some new enemy attacked them ? It seemed like enough.

Leon stole forward and peeped into the glade. No — there was nothing near them. But what was the matter with the creatures ? Instead of lying quietly, as they had done when left behind, they were now rolling and tumbling backward and forward, and pitching about, and dancing first on their feet and then on their heads, and cutting all sorts of strange capers. Could it be for their own amusement ? No; their lamentable cries precluded that supposition; besides, their odd attitudes and contortions bespoke terror and pain.

"Carrambo ! " muttered Leon. " What's the matter with them ? "

They seemed inclined to escape towards the trees; but, after making a few lengths, they would fall to the ground, tumble about, and then, getting up again, head in the opposite direction.

Leon was puzzled — no wonder. He looked around for a solution of this queer conduct on the part of the aïs. No explanation appeared. At length he bethought himself of going up to them. Perhaps, when nearer, he might learn what set them a-dancing.

" Ha ! " he ejaculated, struck with some sudden thought. " I know now ; there's a snake at them."

This conjecture — for it was only a conjecture — caused him to stop short. It might be some venomous snake, thought he. The grass was not long, and he could have seen a very large snake ; but still a small coral snake, or the little poisonous viper, might have been there. He fancied he saw something moving , but to get a better view he passed slowly around the edge of the glade, until he was nearly on the opposite side to that where he had entered. He still kept at a good distance from the aïs, but as yet discovered no snake.

To his great surprise the aïs now lay stretched along the grass; their struggles appeared each moment to grow less violent, and their melancholy cries became weaker and weaker. Their contortions at length came to an end. A feeble effort to raise themselves alone could be perceived, — then a spasmodic motion of their long, crooked limbs, — their cries became indistinct; and, after a while, both lay motionless and silent. Were they dead ? Surely so, thought Leon.

He stood gazing at them for some minutes. Not a motion of their bodies could be perceived. Surely they no longer lived. But, then, what could have killed them ? There was no snake to be seen ; no animal of any kind except themselves. Had they been taken with some sudden disease — some kind of convulsions that had ended fatally ? This seemed the most probable thing, judging from the odd manner in which they had acted. May be they had eaten some sort of plant that had poisoned them.

These conjectures passed rapidly through the mind of Leon. Of course he resolved to satisfy himself as to the cause of their death, if dead they actually were. He began to draw nearer, making his advances with stealth and caution, as he was still apprehensive about the snake.

After he had made a few paces in a forward direc-

tion, he began to perceive something moving around
the bodies of the animals. Snakes ? No. What
then ? A few paces nearer. See ! the whole ground
is in motion. The bodies of the aïs, though dead,
are covered with living, moving objects. Ha ! *it is
a " chacu " of the white ants.*

Leon now comprehended the whole affair. The
ground was literally alive with the terrible *termites.*
They had made their forray, or " chacu," as it is
called, from the neighboring cones; they had attacked the helpless aïs, and put them to death with
their poisonous stings. Already they were tearing
them to pieces and bearing them off to their dark
caves. So thick were they on the bodies of the animals that the latter had suddenly changed their color,
and now appeared to be nothing more than living
heaps of crawling insects.

It was a hideous sight to behold, and Leon felt his
flesh creep as he looked upon it. Still he felt a curiosity to witness the result; and he stood watching the
busy crowd that had gathered about the aïs. He had
heard strange accounts of these white ants; how that,
in a few minutes, they will tear the carcasses of large
animals to pieces and carry them away to their dens;
and he was determined to prove the truth of this by
observation. He did not go any nearer, for he was
not without some dread of these ugly creatures; but
happening to find himself beside a small tree, with
low, horizontal branches, he climbed up and sat down
upon one of the branches, resting his feet upon another. He was inclined to take the thing as easily as
possible.

His perch commanded a full view of the operations of the termites, and for a long time he sat watching them with interest. He could see that it was not the same set that were always on the carcasses of the aïs. On the contrary, one host were always leaving the spot, while another took their places, and from the great conical houses fresh bands appeared to issue. In fact, two great parallel belts of them, like army columns, stretched from the " hills " to the aïs, going in opposite directions. Those which travelled towards the cells presented a very different appearance to the others. These were loaded with pieces of torn flesh, or skin with tufts of hair adhering to it ; and each ant carried a piece by far larger than its own body. Their bodies, in fact, were quite hidden under their disproportionate burdens. The others — those which were coming from the conical hills — were empty handed, and presented the appearance of a whitish stream flowing along the surface of the ground.

It was a most singular sight ; and Leon sat watch-ing the creatures until his head was giddy, and he felt as though the ground itself was in motion.

12

,

CHAPTER XXV.

THE PUMA AND THE GREAT ANT BEAR.

ALL at once the attention of the boy was called
away from the crawling millions. A rustling among
some dead leaves was heard. It appeared to proceed
from the edge of the glade, not far from the ant hills.
The branches of the underwood were seen to move;
and the next moment a slender, cylindrical object,
about a foot and a half in length, was protruded out
from the leaves. Had there not been a pair of small
eyes and ears near the farther end of this cylindrical
object, no one would have taken it for the head and
snout of an animal. But Leon saw the little sparkling
black eyes, and he therefore conjectured that it was
some such creature. The next moment the body
came into view, and a singular creature it was. It
was about the size of a very large Newfoundland
dog, though of a different shape. It was covered all
over with long, brownish hair, part of which looked
so coarse as to resemble dry grass or bristles. On
each shoulder was a wide stripe of black, bordered
with whitish bands; and the tail, which was full three
feet long, was clothed with a thick growth of coarse
hair, several inches in length, that looked like strips
of whalebone. This was carried aloft, and curving
over the back. But the most curious feature of the

animal was its snout. Talk of the nose of a grey-
hound; it would be a " pug " in comparison! That
of this animal was full twice as long, and not half
so thick, with a little mouth not over an inch in size,
and without a single tooth ! It was certainly the oddest snout Leon had ever seen. The legs, too, were
remarkable. They were stout and thick, the hinder
ones appearing much shorter than the fore legs; but
this was because the creature in its hind feet was
plantigrade; that is, it walked with the whole of its
soles touching the surface, which only bears and a
few other sorts of quadrupeds do. Its fore feet, too,
were oddly placed upon the ground. They had four
long claws upon each; but these claws, instead of
being spread out as in the dog or cat, were all folded
backward along the sole ; and the creature, to avoid
treading on them, actually walked on the sides of its
feet. The claws were only used for scraping up the
ground, and then it could bring them forward in a
perpendicular position, like the blade of a hoe or the
teeth of a garden rake. Of course, with feet furnished in such an out-of-the-way fashion, the animal
moved but slowly over the ground. In fact it went
very slowly and with a stealthy pace.

Although Leon had never seen the creature before,
he had read about it, and had also seen pictures of
it. He knew it, therefore, at a glance. That pro-
boscis-looking snout was not to be mistaken. It could
belong to no other creature than the *tamanoir,* or
great ant eater, by the people of South America
called the *ant bear*, (*Myrmecophaga jubata*.) It was,
in fact, that very thing ; but to Leon's astonishment,

as soon as it got fairly out of the bushes, he noticed a singular-looking hunch upon its back, just over the shoulder. At first he could not make out what this was, as he had never heard of such a protuberance ; besides, the tail half hid it from his view. All of a sudden the animal turned its head backwards, touched the hunch with its snout, gave itself a shake, and then the odd excrescence fell to the ground, and proved to be a young ant eater, with bushy tail and long snout, the " very image of its mother." The large one was thus seen to be a female, that had been carrying her infant upon her shoulders.

It was close to one of the ant hills where the old tamanoir placed her young upon the ground ; and, turning away from it, she approached the great cone. Erecting herself upon her hind feet, she stood with the fore ones resting against the hill, apparently examining it and considering in what part of it the shell, or roof, was thinnest and weakest. These cones, composed of agglutinated sand and earth, are frequently so stoutly put together that it requires a pickaxe or crowbar to break them open. But the ant eater knew well that her fore feet were armed with an implement equal to either pick or crow ; and she would certainly have made a hole there and then had she not noticed, on looking around to the other side, that the inhabitants of the hill were all abroad upon one of their forrays. This seemed to bring about a sudden change in her determination ; and, dropping her fore feet to the ground, she once more threw up her great tail and returned to where she had left her young one. Partly pushing it before her with her snout, and partly lifting it between her strong fore arms, she succeeded in bringing the latter to the border of the path along which travelled the ants. Here she squatted down, and placed herself so that the point of her nose just touched the selvage of the swarming hosts, having caused the youngster by her side to do the same. Then, throwing out a long, wormlike tongue, which glittered with a viscous coating, she drew it back, again covered with ants. These passed into her mouth, and thence, of course, into her capacious stomach. The tongue, which was more than a foot in length, and nearly as thick as a quill, was again thrown out, and again drawn back; and this opera-tion she continued, the tongue making about two " hauls " to every second of time. Now and then she stopped eating, in order to give some instructions to the little one that was seen closely imitating her, and with its more slender tongue dealing death among the *termites*.

So very comic was the sight that Leon could not help laughing at it as he sat upon his perch.

An end, however, was put to his merriment by the sudden appearance of another animal — one of a dif-ferent character. It was a large, catlike creature, of a reddish yellow or tawny color, long body and tail, round head, with whiskers, and bright, gleaming eyes. Leon had seen that sort of animal before ; he had seen it led in strings by Indians through the streets of Cuzco, and he at once recognized it. It was the *puma* — the maneless lion of America.

The specimens which Leon had seen with the In-dians had been rendered tame and harmless. He

knew that ; but he had also been told that the animal
in its wild state is a savage and dangerous beast.
This is true of the puma in some districts ; while in
others the creature is cowardly, and will flee at the
sight-of man.   In all cases, however, when the puma
is brought to bay, it makes a desperate fight ; and
both dogs and men have been killed in the attack.

Leon had not been frightened at the tamanoir.
Even had it been a savage creature, he knew it
could not climb a tree, though there are two smaller
species of ant bears in South America that can ; and
he therefore knew he was quite safe on his perch.
But his feelings were very different when the red
body of the puma came in sight.   It could run up
the smoothest trunk in the forest with as much ease
and agility as a cat ; and there would be no chance
of escaping from it if it felt disposed to attack him.
Of this the boy was fully conscious ; and no wonder
he was alarmed.

His first thought was to leap down and make for
the cinchona trees, where the others were ; but the
puma had entered the glade from that side, and it
was therefore directly in his way ; he would have
run right in its teeth by going towards the cinchona
trees.   He next thought of slipping quietly down and
getting into the woods behind him.   Unfortunately
the tree on which he was stood out in the glade quite
apart from any others : the puma would see him go
off, and of course could overtake him in a dozen
leaps.   These thoughts passed through the boy's
mind in a few seconds of time ; and in a few seconds of time he was convinced that his best course

would be to remain where he was and keep quiet. Perhaps the puma would not notice him ; as yet he had not.

No doubt he would have done so had there been nothing else on the spot to take off his attention ; but just as he came into the open ground his eyes fell upon the ant eaters, where they lay squatted and licking up the termites. He had entered the glade in a sort of skulking trot; but the moment he saw the tamanoirs he halted, drew his body into a crouching attitude, and remained thus for some moments, while his long tail oscillated from side to side as that of a cat when about to spring upon a mouse or a sparrow. Just at this moment the tamanoir, having turned round to address some conversation to her young companion, espied him, and sprang to her feet. She recognized in the puma — as in others of his race — a deadly enemy. With one sweep of her fore arm she flung the young one behind her, until it rested against the wall of the ant hill, and then, following in all haste, threw herself into an erect attitude in front of her young, covering it with her body. She was now standing firm upon her hind feet, her back resting against the mud wall ; but her long snout had entirely disappeared. That was held close along her breast, and entirely concealed by the shaggy tail, which for this purpose had been brought up in front. Her defence rested in her strong fore arms, which, with the great claws standing at right angles, were now held out in a threatening manner. The young one, no doubt aware of some danger, had drawn itself into its smallest bulk and was clewed up behind her.

The puma dashed forward, open mouthed, and began the attack. He looked as though he would carry every thing by the first assault, but a sharp tear from the tamanoir's claws drew the blood from his cheek ; and, although it rendered him more furious, it seemed to increase his caution. In the two or three successive attempts he kept prudently out of reach of these terrible weapons. His adversary held her fore legs wide open, as though she was desirous of getting the other to rush between them, that she might clutch him, after the manner of the bears. This was exactly what she wanted; and in this consists the chief mode of defence adopted by these animals. The puma, however, seemed to be up to her trick.

This thrust-and-parry game continued for some minutes, and might have lasted longer had it not been for the young tamanoir. This foolish little creature, who up to that moment was not very sure what the fuss was all about, had the imprudent curiosity to thrust out its slender snout. The puma espied it, and making a dart forward, seized the snout in his great teeth, and jerked the animal from under. It uttered a low squall; but the next moment its head was "crunched" between the muscular jaws of the puma.

The old one now appeared to lose all fear and caution. Her tail fell down, her long snout was unsheathed from under its protection, and she seemed undecided what to do. But she was not allowed much time to reflect. The puma, seeing the snout, the most vulnerable part, uncovered, launched himself forward like an arrow, and caught hold of it in his bristling fangs.   Then, having dragged his victim forward, he flung her upon her breast, and, mounting rapidly on her back, proceeded to worry her at his pleasure.

Although Leon pitied the poor tamanoir, yet he dared not interfere, and would have permitted the puma to finish his work ; but at that moment a sharp pain, which he suddenly felt in his ankle, caused him to start upon his seat and utter an involuntary scream.

CHAPTER XXVI.

ATTACK OF THE WHITE ANTS.

LEON looked down to ascertain what had caused him such a sudden pain. The sight that met his eyes made his blood run cold. The ground below was alive and moving. A white stratum of ants covered it on all sides to the distance of several yards. *They were ascending the tree!* Nay, more: a string of them had already crawled up ; the trunk was crowded by others coming after; and several were upon his feet, and legs, and thighs. It was one of these that had stung him.

The fate of the aïs, which he had just witnessed, and the sight of the hideous host, caused him again to scream out. At the same time he had risen to his feet, and was pulling himself up among the upper branches. He soon reached the highest; but he had not been a moment there when he reflected that it would be no security. The creatures were crawling upwards as fast as they could come.

His next thought was to descend again, leap from the tree, and, crushing the vermin under his feet, make for the bark cutters. He had made up his mind to this course, and was already half down, when *he remembered the puma.* In his alarm at the approach of the ants he had quite forgotten this enemy ; and he now remembered that it was directly in the way of his intended escape. He turned his eyes in that direction. It was not there. The ant bears were still upon the ground, — the young one dead, and the mother struggling in her last agonies, — but no puma.

The boy began to hope that his cries had frightened him off. His hope was shortlived ; for, on glancing around the glade, he now beheld the fierce brute crouching among the grass, and evidently coming towards him. What was to be done ? Would the puma attack him in the tree ? Surely he would ; but what better would he be on the ground ? No better, but worse. At all events he had not time for much reflection, for before two seconds the fierce puma was close to the tree. Leon was helpless ; he gave himself up for lost. He could only cry for help ; and he raised his voice to its highest pitch.

The puma did not spring up the tree at once, as Leon had expected. On the contrary, it crouched round and round, with glaring eyes and wagging tail, as if calculating the mode of attack. Its lips were red, — stained with the blood of the ant eaters, — and this added to the hideousness of its appearance. But it needed not that ; for it was hideous enough at any time.

Leon kept his eyes upon it, every moment expecting it to spring up the tree. All at once he saw it give a sudden start ; and at the same instant he heard a hissing noise, as if something passed rapid.y through the air. Ha ! something sticking in the

body of the puma! It is an arrow — a poisoned
arrow! The puma utters a fierce growl; it turns
upon itself; the arrow is crushed between its teeth.
Another " hist " — another arrow! Hark! a well-
known voice — well-known voices — the voices of
Don Pablo and Guapo! See! they burst into the
glade — Don Pablo with his axe, and Guapo with
his unerring gravatána!

The puma turns to flee. He has already reachca
the border of the wood; he staggers; the poison is
doing its work. Hurrah! he is down; but the poison
does not kill him, for the axe of Don Pablo is crashing through his skull. Hurrah! the monster is dead,
and Leon is triumphantly borne off on the shoulders
of the faithful Guapo!

Don Pablo dragged the puma away, in order that
they might get his fine skin. The ant eaters —
both of which were now dead — he left behind, as he
saw that the termites were crawling thickly around
them and had already begun their work of devasta-
tion. Strange to say, as the party returned that way,
going to dinner, not a vestige remained either of the
aïs or the ant eaters except a few bones and some
portions of coarse hair. The rest of all these animals had been cleared off by the ants and carried
into the cells of their hollow cones.

It was no doubt the noise of the bark hunters that
had started the ant eaters abroad, for these creatures
usually prowl only in the night. The same may
have aroused the fierce puma from his lair, although
he is not strictly a nocturnal hunter.

A curious incident occurred as they approached

the glade on their way home. The male tamanoir was roused from his nest among the dry leaves; and Guapo, instead of running upon him and killing the creature, warned them all to keep a little back, and he would show them some fun. Guapo now commenced shaking the leaves, so that they rattled as if rain was falling upon them. At this the ant eater jerked up its broad tail, and appeared to shelter itself as with an umbrella. Guapo then went towards it and commenced driving it before him just as if it had been a sheep or goat; and in this manner he took it all the way to the house. Of course Guapo took care not to irritate it; for, when that is done, the ant eater will either turn out of his way or stop to defend itself.

The tamanoir is not so defenceless a creature as might at first sight be imagined by considering his small, toothless mouth and slow motions. His mode of defence is that which has been described, and which is quite sufficient against the tiger cat, the ocelot, and all the smaller species of feline animals. No doubt the old female would have proved a match for the puma had she not been thrown off her guard by his seizing upon her young. It is even asserted that the great ant bear sometimes hugs the jaguar to death; but this I believe to be a mistake, as the latter is far too powerful and active to be thus conquered. Doubtless the resemblance of the jaguar to some of the smaller spotted cats of these countries leads to a great many misconceptions concerning the prowess of the *American tiger.*

Besides the tamanoir, there are two, or perhaps

three, other species of *ant bears* in the forests of
South America. These, however, are so different in
habits and appearance that they might properly be
classed as a separate genus of animals. They are
tree climbers ; which the tamanoir is not, spite of his
great claws. They pursue the ants that build their
nests upon the high branches, as well as the wasps
and bees ; and, to befit them for this life, they are
furnished with *naked prehensile tails*, like the opos·
sums and monkeys. These are characteristics en·
tirely distinct from those of the *Myrmecophaga jubata*,
or *great* ant eater.

One of these species is the *tamandua*, called by
the Spano-Americans *Osso hormiguero*, (ant bear.)
The tamandua is much less than the tamanoir,
being only three and a half feet in length, while
the latter is over seven. The former is of a stouter
build, with neither so long a snout in proportion,
nor such claws. The claws, moreover, are made
for tree climbing, and are not so much in the way
when the animal walks on the ground. It is there·
fore a more active creature, and stands better upon
its limbs. Its fur is short and silky ; but the tail is
nearly naked, and, as already stated, highly prehen·
sile, although it does not sleep hanging by the tail as
some other animals do.

The tamandua is usually of a dull straw color ;
although it varies in this respect, so that several
species have been supposed to exist. It spends
most of its time upon the trees ; and, in addition to
its ant diet, it feeds upon wild honey, and bees,
too, whenever it can catch them. The female, 'ike

the tamanoir, produces only one young at a birth
and, like the other species, carries it upon her back
until it is able to provide for itself. The tamandua
has sometimes been called *tridactyla*, or the " three-
toed ant eater," because it has only three claws upon
each of its fore feet, whereas the tamanoir is provided with four.

Another species of " ant bear," differing from both
in size and in many of its habits, is the " little ant
eater," (*Myrmecophaga didactyla.*) This one has
only two claws on each fore foot; hence its specific
name. It is a very small creature, — not larger than
the common gray squirrel, — with a prehensile tail
like the tamandua. The tail, however, is not entirely
naked — only on the under side near the point. It
is not so good a walker as the three-toed kind, though
more active on its feet than the tamanoir. Standing
upon its hind feet, and supporting itself also by the
tail, — which it has already thrown around some
branch, — the little ant eater uses its fore feet as
hands to carry food to its mouth. It lives among
the trees, and feeds upon wasps, bees, and especially
the larvæ of both; but it does not use the tongue to
any great extent. It is on this account an essentially
different sort of animal.

The little ant eater is usually of a bright-yellow
color, brownish on the back; but there are many
varieties in this respect, and some are of a snowy
whiteness. Its fur is soft and silky, sometimes slightly curled or matted at the points ; and the tail fur is
annulated, or ringed, with the prevailing colors of the
body. So much for the ant bears of America.

CHAPTER XXVII.

THE ANT LION.

ANTS are disagreeable insects in any country, but especially so in warm, tropical climates. Their ugly appearance, their destructive habits, but, above all, the pain of their sting, or rather bite, — for ants do not sting as wasps, but bite with the jaws, and then infuse poison into the wound, — all these render them very unpopular creatures. A superficial thinker would suppose that such troublesome insects could be of no use, and would question the propriety of Nature in having created them. But, when we give the subject a little attention, we find that they were not created in vain. Were it not for these busy creatures, what would become of the vast quantities of decomposing substances found in some countries? What would be done with the decaying vegetation and the dead animal matter? Why, in many places, were it not consumed by these insects and reorganized into new forms of life, it would produce pestilence and death; and surely these are far more disagreeable things than ants.

Of ants there are many different kinds; but the greatest number of species belong to warm countries, where, indeed, they are most useful. Some of these species are so curious in their habits that whole vol-

THE ANT LION. 193

umes have been written about them, and naturalists
have spent a lifetime in their study and observation.
Their social and domestic economy is of the most
singular character, more so than that of the bees;
and I am afraid here to give a single trait of their
lives, lest I should be led on to talk too much about
them. I need only mention the wonderful nests or
hills which some species build — those great cones
of twenty feet in height, and so strong that wild bulls
run up their sides and stand upon their tops without
doing them the least injury! Others make their
houses of cylindrical form, rising several feet from
the surface. Others, again, prefer nesting in the
trees, where they construct large cellular masses of
many shapes, suspending them from the highest
branches; while many species make their waxen
dwellings in hollow trunks or beneath the surface of
the earth. There is not a species, however, whose
habits, fully observed and described, would not strike
you with astonishment. Indeed it is difficult to
believe all that is related about these insects by naturalists who have made them their study. One can
hardly understand how such little creatures can be
gifted with so much intelligence, or *instinct*, as some
choose to call it.

Man is not the only enemy of the ants. If he
were so, it is to be feared that these small, insignifi-
cant creatures would soon make the earth too hot for
him. So prolific are they, that if left to themselves
our whole planet would in a short period become a
gigantic ant's nest!

Nature has wisely provided against the over-increase

13

of the ant family. No living thing has a greater
variety of enemies than they. In all the divisions
of animated nature there are ant destroyers — *ant
eaters.* To begin with the mammalia: man himself
feeds upon them; for there are tribes of Indians in
South America the principal part of whose food consists of dried termites, which they bake into a kind
of " paste." There are quadrupeds that live exclusively on them; as the ant bear, already described;
and the *pangolins*, or scaly ant eaters, of the eastern
continent. There are birds, too, of many sorts that
devour the ants; and there are even some who make
them exclusively their food; as the genus *Myothera,*
or " ant catchers." Many kinds of reptiles, both
snakes and lizards, are ant eaters; and, what is
strangest of all, there are *insects* that prey upon
them !

No wonder, then, with such a variety of enemies,
that the ants are kept within proper limits, and are
not allowed to overrun the earth.

The observations just made are very similar to
those that were addressed by Doña Isidora to the
little Leona one day when they were left alone.
The others had gone about their usual occupation of
bark cutting; and these, of course, remained at home
to take care of the house and cook the dinner. That
was already hanging over a fire outside the house;
for in these hot countries it is often more convenient
to do the cooking out of doors.

Doña Isidora, busy with some sewing, was seated
under the shadow of the banana trees, and the pretty
little Leona was playing near her. Leona had been

abusing the ants, partly on account of their having so frightened Leon, and partly because one of the red species had bitten herself the day before; and it was for this reason that her mother had entered into such explanations regarding these creatures, with a view of exculpating them from the bitter accusations urged against them by Leona. Talking about ants very naturally led them to cast their eyes to the ground to see if any of the creatures were near; and sure enough there were several of the red ones wandering about. Just then the eyes of Doña Isidora rested upon a very different insect, and she drew the attention of her daughter to it. It was an insect of considerable size, being full an inch in length, with an elongated, oval body, and a small, flat head. From the head protruded two great horny jaws, that bore some resemblance to a pair of caliper compasses. Its legs were short and very unfitted for motion. Indeed they were not of much use for that purpose, as it could make very little way on them, but crawled only sideways or backwards, with great apparent difficulty. The creature was of a grayish or sand color; and in the sand, where it was seated, it might not have been observed at all had not the lady's eyes been directed upon the very spot. But Doña Isidora, who was a very good entomologist, recognized it, and, knowing that it was a very curious insect, on this account called the attention of her daughter to it.

"What is it, mamma?" inquired the little Leona bending forward to examine it.

"The *ant lion.*"

" The ant lion! Why, mamma, it is an insect
How, then, can it be called lion ? "

" It is a name given it," replied the lady, " on
account of its fierce habits, which, in that respect,
assimilate it to its powerful namesake, the king of
the beasts ; and indeed this little creature has more
strength and ferocity in proportion to its size than
even the lion himself."

" But why the *ant* lion, mamma ? "

" Because it preys principally on ants. I have
said there are insect ant eaters. This is one of
them."

" But how can such a slow creature as that get
hold of them ? Why, the ants could crawl out of
its way in a moment ! "

" That is true. Nevertheless it manages to capture as many as it requires. Remember ' the race is
not always to the swift.' It is by stratagem it succeeds in taking its prey — a very singular stratagem,
too. If you will sit back and not frighten it, I have
no doubt it will soon give you an opportunity of seeing how it manages the matter."

Leona took a seat by the side of her mother.
They were both at just such a distance from the ant
lion that they could observe every movement it made ;
but for a considerable time it remained quiet — no
doubt because they had alarmed it. In the interval
Doña Isidora imparted to her daughter some further
information about its natural history.

" The ant lion, (*Myrmeleon*,)" said she, " is not an
insect in its perfect state, but only the *larva* of one.
The perfect insect is a very different creature, hav-

ing wings and longer legs. It is one of the *neurop-terous* tribe, or those with nerved wings. The wings of this species rest against each other, forming a covering over its body like the roof upon a house. They are most beautifully reticulated like the finest lacework, and variegated with dark spots, that give the insect a very elegant appearance. Its habits are quite different to those which it follows when a larva, or in that state when it is the ant lion. It flies but little during the day, and is usually found quietly sitting amongst the leaves of plants, and seems to be one of the most pacific and harmless of insects. How very different with the larva! — the very reverse. See!"

Doña Isidora pointed to the ant lion, that was just then beginning to bestir itself; and both sat silent, regarding it attentively.

First, then, the little creature, going backwards and working with its calipers, traced a circle on the surface of the sand. This circle was between two and three inches in diameter. Having completed it, it now commenced to clear out all the sand within the circle. To accomplish this, it was seen to scrape up the sand with one of its fore feet and shovel a quantity of it upon its flat head; then, giving a sudden jerk of the neck, it pitched the sand several inches outside the traced circumference. This operation it repeated so often and so adroitly that in a very short time a round pit began to show itself in the surface of the ground. Wherever it encountered a stone, this was raised between its calipers and pitched out beyond the ring. Sometimes stones occurred that were too large to be thrown out in this way. These it managed to get upon its back; and then, crawling cautiously up the sides of the pit, it tumbled them upon the edge and rolled them away. Had it met with a stone so large as to render this impossible, it would have left the place and chosen another spot of ground. Fortunately this was not the case; and they had an opportunity of watching the labor to its conclusion.

For nearly an hour they sat watching it,—of course not neglecting their other affairs,—and at the end of that time the ant lion had jerked out so much sand that a little funnel-shaped pit was formed, nearly as deep as it was wide. This was its trap; and it was now finished and ready for action.

Having made all its arrangements, it had nothing more to do than remain at the bottom of the pit and wait patiently until some unfortunate ant should chance to come that way and fall in; and where these insects were constantly wandering over the ground, such an accident would, sooner or later, be certain to take place.

Lest the ant should peep into the pit, discover its hideous form below, and then retreat, this ant lion had actually the cunning to bury its body in the sand, leaving only a small portion of its head to be seen.

Both Doña Isidora and the little Leona remained watching with increased interest. They were very anxious to witness the result. They were not kept long in suspense. I have already stated that many ants were crawling about. There were dozens of them " quartering " the ground in every direction in

search of their own prey; and they left not an inch
of it unsearched. At last one was seen to approach
the trap of the ant lion. Curiosity brings it to the
very edge of that terrible pitfall. It protrudes its
head and part of its body over the brink; it is not
such a terrible gulf to look into; if it should slip
down, it could easily crawl out again. Ha! it little
knows the enemy that is ambushed there. It per-
ceives something singular — an odd something —
perhaps it might be something good to eat. It is half
resolved to slide down and make a closer examination
of this something. It is balancing on the brink, and
would, no doubt, have gone down voluntarily; but that
is no longer left to its own choice. The mysterious
object at the bottom of the funnel suddenly springs
up and shows itself. It is the ant lion, in all its hideous proportions; and before the little ant can draw
itself away, the other has flung around it a shower
of sand that brings it rolling down the side of the pit.
Then the sharp calipers are closed upon the victim;
all the moisture in his body is sucked out; and his
remains, now a dry and shapeless mass, are rested
for a moment upon the head of the destroyer, and
then jerked far outside the pit!

The ant lion now dresses his trap, and, again bury-
ing himself in the sand, awaits another victim.

CHAPTER XXVIII.

THE TATOU-POYOU AND THE DEER CARCASS.

DONA ISIDORA and Leona had watched all the manœuvres of the ant lion with great interest; and Leona, after the bite she had had, was not in any mood to sympathize with the ants. Indeed she felt rather grateful to the ant lion, ugly as he was, for killing them.

Presently Leon returned from the woods, and was shown the trap in full operation; but Leon upon this day was full of adventures that had occurred upon the hills to himself, Guapo, and Don Pablo. In fact he had hastened home before the others to tell his mamma of the odd incidents to which he had been a witness.

That morning they had discovered a new *mancha* of cinchona trees. When proceeding towards them they came upon the dead carcass of a deer. It was a large species, the *Cervus antisensis* ; but, as it had evidently been dead several days, it was swollen out to twice its original size, as is always the case with carcasses of animals left exposed in a warm climate. It was odd that some preying animals had not eaten it up. A clump of tall trees that shaded it, had, no doubt, concealed it from the sharp sight of the vul-tures ; and these birds, contrary to what has so often been alleged, can find no dead body by the smell. Neither ants nor animals that prey upon carrion had chanced to come that way; and there lay the deer intact.

So thought Don Pablo and Leon. Guapo, however, was of a different opinion; and, going up to the body, he struck it a blow with his axe. To the surprise of the others, instead of the dead sound which they expected to hear, a dry crash followed the blow, and a dark hole appeared where a piece of thin, shell-like substance had fallen off. Another blow from Guapo's axe, and the whole side went in. Not a bit of carcass was there; there were bones — clean bones — and dry hard skin, but no flesh, not an atom of flesh.

" Tatou-poyou ! " quietly remarked Guapo.

" What ! " said Don Pablo, " an armadillo, you think ? " recognizing in Guapo's words the Indian name for one of the large species of armadillos.

" Yes," replied Guapo. " All eaten by the tatou-poyou. See ! there's his hole."

Don Pablo and Leon bent over the sham carcass; and, sure enough, under where its body had been they could see a large hole in the ground. Outside the carcass, also, at the distance of several feet, was another.

" That is where he entered," said Guapo, pointing to the second. " He's not about here now," continued he ; " no, no — ate all the meat and gone long ago."

This was evident; as the hollow skeleton was quite dry, and had evidently been empty for a good while,

Don Pablo was pleased at this incident, as it gave him an opportunity of verifying a curious habit of the armadillos. These creatures are among the finest burrowers in the world, and can bury themselves in the earth in a few seconds' time; but, being badly toothed, — some of them altogether without teeth, — they can only feed upon very soft substances. Putrid flesh is with them a favorite " dish ;" and, in order to get at the softest side of a carcass, they burrow under and enter it from below, rarely leaving their horrid cave until they have thoroughly cleared it out.

The bark hunters now passed on, Don Pablo making many inquiries about the armadillos, and Guapo giving replies, while Leòn listened with interest. Guapo knew a good deal about these curious creatures ; for he had eaten many a dozen of them in his time, and as many different kinds of them too. Their feeding upon carrion had no effect on Guapo's stomach ; and, indeed, white people in South America relish them as much as Indians. The white people, however, make a distinction in the species, as they suppose some kinds to be more disposed to a vegetable diet than others. There are some in the neighborhood of the settlements that *occasionally pay a visit to the graveyards, or cemeteries*, and these kinds do not go down well. All of them will devour almost any sort of trash that is soft and pulpy, and they are more destructive to the ant than even the ant eaters themselves. How so ? Because, instead of making a nice little hole in the side of the ant hill, as the tamanoirs do, and through this hole eating the ants themselves, the armadillos break down a large part of the structure and devour the *larvæ.* Now, the ants love these *larvæ* more than their own lives ; and when these are destroyed they yield themselves up to de-spair, refuse to patch up the building, the rain gets in, and the colony is ruined and breaks up.

It does not follow, however, that the flesh of the armadillo should be "queer" because the animal itself eats queer substances. Among carnivorous creatures the very opposite is sometimes the truth ; and some animals, — as the tapir, for instance, — that feed exclusively on sweet and succulent vegetables, produce a most bitter flesh for themselves. About this there is no standing law either way.

The flesh of the armadillo is excellent eating, not unlike young pork ; and, when " roasted in the shell," (the Indian mode of cooking it,) it is quite equal, if not superior, to a baked " pig," a dish very much eaten in our own country.

Guapo did not call them armadillos ; he had sever-al Indian names for different kinds of them. "Ar-madillo" is the Spanish name, and signifies the " little armed one," the diminutive of " armado," or " armed." This name is peculiarly appropriate to these animals, as the hard, bony casing which covers the whole upper parts of their bodies bears an exceeding resemblance to the suits of armor worn in the days of Cortez and chivalry.

On the head there is the helmet; the back is shielded by a corselet ; and even the limbs are covered with greaves. Of course this armor is arranged dif-ferently in the different species, and there is more or less hair upon all between the joinings of the plates.

These points were not touched upon by Guapo, but others of equal interest were. He went on to say that he knew many different kinds of them; some not bigger than a rat, and some as large as a full-grown sheep; some that were slow in their paces, and others that could outrun a man ; some that were flat and could squat so close as hardly to be seen against the ground, — (these were *tatou-poyous*, the sort that had hollowed out the deer,)— and some again that were highbacked and nearly globe shaped. Such was Guapo's account of these curious animals, which are found only in the warmer regions of North and South America.

CHAPTER XXIX.

AN ARMADILLO HUNT.

CONVERSING in this way, the bark hunters at length reached the cinchona trees, and then all talk about armadillos was at an end. They went lustily to their work, — which was of more importance, — and, under Guapo's axe, several of the cinchonas soon "bit the dust."

There was a spot of open ground just a little to one side of where these trees stood. They had noticed, on coming up, a flock of zamuros, or black vultures, out upon this ground, clustered around some object. It was the carcass of another deer. The first blow of the axe startled the birds, and they flapped a short way off. They soon returned, how-ever, not being shy birds, but the contrary.

There was nothing in all this to create surprise, except, perhaps, the dead deer. What had been killing these animals ? Not a beast of prey, for that would have devoured them ; unless, indeed, it might be the puma, that often kills more than he can eat.

The thought had occurred to Don Pablo that they might have died from the poisoned arrows of an In-dian. This thought somewhat disquieted him ; for he knew not what kind of Indians they might be — they might be friendly or hostile ; if the latter, not only would all his plans be frustrated, but the lives of him-self and party would be in danger. Guapo could not assure him on this head; he had been so long absent from the Great Montaña that he was ignorant of the places where the tribes of these parts might now be located. These tribes often change their homes. He knew that the Chunchos sometimes roamed so far up, and they were the most dangerous of all the Indians of the Montaña — haters of the whites, fierce and revengeful. It was they who sev-eral times destroyed the settlements and mission sta-tions. If Chunchos were in the woods they might look out for trouble. Guapo did not think there were any Indians near. He would have seen some traces of them before now; and he had observed none since their arrival. This assurance of the knowing Indian quite restored Don Pablo's confidence, and they talked no longer on the subject. After a while their atten-tion was again called to the vultures. These filthy creatures had returned to the deer, and were busily gorging themselves, when all at once they were seen to rise up as if affrighted. They did not fly far, — only a few feet, — and stood with outstretched necks looking towards the carrion, as if whatever had frightened them was there.

The bark hunters could perceive nothing. It was the body of a small deer, already half eaten, and no object bigger than a man's hand could have been concealed behind it. The zamuros, however, *had* seen something strange, else they would hardly have acted as they did; and, with this conviction, the bark hunters stopped their work to observe them.

After a while the birds seemed to take fresh courage, hopped back to the carrion, and recommenced
tearing at it. In another moment they again started
and flew back, but this time not so far as before ; and
then they all returned again, and, after feeding another short while, started back a third time.

This was all very mysterious ; but Guapo, guessing
what was the matter, solved the mystery by crying
out, —

" *Tatou-poyou !* "

" Where ? " inquired Don Pablo.

" Yonder, master — yonder, in the body of the
beast."

Don Pablo looked ; and, sure enough, he could see
something moving ; it was the head and shoulders of
an armadillo. It had burrowed and come up through
the body of the deer, thus meeting the vultures half
way. No doubt it was the mysterious mode by which
it had entered on the stage that had frightened them.

They soon, however, got over their affright, and
returned to their repast.

The armadillo — a very large one — had, by this
time, crept out into the open air, and went on eating.

For a while the zamuros took no heed of him,
deeming, perhaps, that, although he had come in by
the back door, he might have as good a right upon
the premises as themselves. Their pacific attitude,
however, was but of short duration ; something occurred to ruffle their temper — some silent affront
no doubt ; for the bark hunters heard nothing.
Perhaps the *tatou* had run against the legs of one
and scraped it with the sharp edge of his corselet.

Whether this was the cause or no, a scuffle commenced, and the beast in armor was attacked by all
the vultures at once.

Of course he did not attack in turn; he had no
means; he acted altogether on the defensive; and
this he was enabled to do by simply drawing in his
legs and flattening himself upon the ground. He
was then proof, not only against the beaks and weak
talons of a vulture, but he might have defied the
royal eagle himself.

After flapping him with their wings, and pecking
him with their filthy beaks, and clawing him with
their talons, the zamuros saw it was all to no purpose,
and desisted. If they could not damage him, however, they could prevent him from eating any more
of the deer; for the moment he stretched out his
neck several vultures sprang at him afresh, and
would have wounded him in the tender parts of his
throat had he not quickly drawn in his head again.
Seeing that his feast was at an end, — at least above
ground, — he suddenly raised his hind quarters, and
in a brace of seconds buried himself in the earth.
The vultures pecked him behind as he disappeared;
but the odd manner of his exit, like that of his *entrée*,
seemed to mystify them, and several of them stood
for some moments in neck-stretched wonder.

This scene had scarcely ended when a pair of
fresh armadillos were espied coming from the farther
edge of the opening, and, in fact, from the edge of a
precipice; for the river flowed close by, and its channel was at that point shut in by cliffs. These two
were large fellows, and were making speedily towards

the carrion, in order to get up before it was all gone. Guapo could stand it no longer. Guapo had tasted roast armadillo, and longed for more. In an instant, therefore, axe in hand, he was off to intercept the new comers. Don Pablo and Leon followed to see the sport and assist in the capture.

The armadillos, although not afraid of the vultures, seeing the hunters approach, turned tail and made for the precipice. Guapo took after one, while Don Pao.o and Leon pursued the other. Guapo soon over-hauled his one; but, before he could lay his hands upon it, it had already half buried itself in the dry ground. Guapo, however, seized the tail and held on; and, although not able to drag it out, he was resolved it should get no deeper.

The one pursued by Don Pablo had got close to the edge of the precipice before either he or Leon could come up with it. There it stood for a moment, as if in doubt what plan to pursue. Don Pablo and Leon were congratulating themselves that they had fairly " cornered " it; for the cliff was a clear fall of fifty feet, and, of course, it could get no farther in that direction, while they approached it from two sides so as to cut off its retreat. They approached it with caution, as they were now near the edge, and it would not do to move too rashly. Both were bent forward with their arms outstretched to clutch their prey ; they felt confident it was already in their grasp. Judge their astonishment, then, at seeing the creature suddenly clew itself into a round ball and ro.l over the cliff!

They looked below ; they saw it upon the ground

14

they saw it open out again, apparently unharmed ; for the next moment it scuttled off and hid itself among the rocks by the edge of the water.

They turned towards Guapo, who was still holding his one by the tail and calling for help. Although it was but half buried, all three of them could not have dragged it forth by the tail. That member would have pulled out before the animal could have been dislodged ; and such is not an unfrequent occurrence to the hunters of the armadillo. Don Pablo, however, took hold of the tail and held fast until Guapo loosened the earth with his axe, and then the creature was more easily " extracted." A blow on its head from Guapo made all right, and it was afterwards carried safely to the house and " roasted in the shell."

That was a great day among the " armadillos."

CHAPTER XXX.

THE OCELOT.

During the whole summer, Don Pablo, Guapo, and Leon continued bark gathering. Every day they went out into the woods, excepting Sunday, of course. That was kept as a day of rest; for, although far from civilized society, there was not the less necessity for their being Christians. God dwells in the wilderness as well as in the walled city; and worship to him is as pleasing under the shadow of the forest leaves as with sounding organ beneath the vaulted dome of the grand cathedral.

During week days, while the others were abroad, Doña Isidora and the little Leona were not idle at home; yet their whole time was not taken up by the mere concerns of the *cuisine*. They had an industry of their own, and, in fact, one that promised to be almost as profitable in its results as the bark gathering. This was neither more nor less than preparing *vanilla*.

Some days after arriving in the valley, while exploring a wood that lay at the back of the cultivated ground, Don Pablo discovered that every tree carried a creeper or parasite of a peculiar kind. It was a small creeper not unlike ivy, and was covered with flowers of a greenish-yellow color, mixed with white

Don Pablo at once recognized in this parasitical plant one of the many species of llianas that produce the delicious and perfumed vanilla. It was, in fact, the finest of the kind — that which, among the French, is called *leq* vanilla; and, from the fact that every tree had a number of these parasites, and no other climbing vines, Don Pablo came to the conclusion that they had been planted by the missionaries. It is thus that vanilla is usually cultivated, by being set in slips at the root of some tree which may afterwards sustain it.

In the course of the summer, these vanilla vines exhibited a different appearance. Instead of flowers, long, beanlike capsules made their appearance. These capsules, or pods, were nearly a foot in length, though not much thicker than a swan's quill. They were a little flattish, wrinkled, and of a yellow color, and contained inside, instead of beans, a pulpy substance, surrounding a vast quantity of small seeds, like grains of sand. These seeds are the perfumed vanilla so much prized, and which often yield the enormous price of fifty dollars a pound. To preserve these, therefore, was the work of Doña Isidora and Leona; and they understood perfectly how to do it.

First, they gathered the pods before they were quite ripe. These they strung upon a thread, taking care to pass the thread through that end nearest the foot stalk. The whole were next plunged for an instant into boiling water, which gave them a blanched appearance. The thread was then stretched from tree to tree; and the pods, hanging like a string of candles, were then exposed to the sun for several hours. Next day they were lightly smeared with an oiled feather, and then wrapped in oiled cotton of the *Bombax ceiba* to prevent the valves from opening. When they had remained in this state for a few days the string was taken out and passed through the other ends, so that they should hang in an inverted position. This was to permit the discharge of a viscid liquid from the foot stalk end ; and, in order to assist this discharge, the pods were several times lightly pressed between the fingers. They now became dry and wrinkled. They had also shrunk to less than half their original size, and changed their color to a reddish brown. Another delicate touch of the oil feather and the vanilla was ready for the market. Nothing remained but to pack them in small cases, which had already been prepared from the leaf of a species of palm tree.

In such a way did the lady Isidora and her daughter pass their time ; and before the summer was out they had added largely to the stock of wealth of our exiles.

Although these two always remained by the house, they were not without *their* adventures as well, one of which I shall describe. It occurred while they were getting in their crop of vanilla. Leona was in the porch in front, busy among the vanilla beans. She had a large needle and a thread of palm-leaf fibre, with which she was stringing the long pods, while her mother was inside the house packing some that had been already dried.

Leona rested for a moment, and was looking over the water, when all at once she exclaimed, —

" Maman — Maman ! come out and see ! O, what a beautiful cat ! "

The exclamation caused Doña Isidora to start, and with a feeling of uneasiness. The cause of her uneasiness was the word " cat." She feared that what the innocent child had taken for a " beautiful cat " might prove to be the dreaded jaguar. She ran at once out of the door, and looked in the direction pointed out by Leona. There, sure enough, on the other side of the water, was a spotted creature, looking in the distance very much like a cat ; but Doña Isidora saw at a glance that it was a far larger animal. Was it the jaguar ? It was like one in its color and markings. It was of a yellowish color, and covered all over with black spots, which gave it the semblance of the jaguar. Still Doña Isidora thought that it was not so large as these animals usually are ; and this, to some extent, restored her confidence. When first seen, it was close down to the water's edge, as if it had come there to drink ; and Doña Isidora was in hopes that, after satisfying its thirst, it would go away again. What was her consternation to see it make a forward spring, and, plunging into the water, swim directly for the house !

Terrified, she seized Leona by the hand and retreated inside. She shut the door and bolted it. If it were a jaguar, what protection would that be ? Such a creature could dash itself through the frail bamboo wall, or tear the door to pieces with his great claws in a moment. "If it be a jaguar," thought she, "we are lost!"

Doña Isidora was a woman of courage. She was determined to defend the lives of herself and daughter to the last. She looked around the house for a weapon. The pistols of Don Pablo were hanging against the wall. She knew they were loaded. She took them down and looked at the flints and priming, and then stationed herself at a place where she could see out through the interstices of the bamboos. The little Leona kept by her side, though she knew that in a struggle with a ferocious jaguar she could give no help.

By this time the animal had crossed the river, and she could see it spring out on the bank and come on towards the house. In a few seconds it was close to the porch, where it halted to reconnoitre. Doña Isidora saw it very plainly, and would now have had a very good chance to fire at it; but she did not wish to begin the combat. Perhaps it might go away again, without attempting to enter the house. In order not to draw its attention, she stood perfectly quiet, having cautioned Leona to do the same.

It was not a large animal, though its aspect was fierce enough to terrify any one. Its tiger-like eyes and white teeth, which it showed at intervals, were any thing but pleasant to look upon. Its size, however, was not so formidable; and Doña Isidora had understood the jaguar to be a large animal; but there is also a smaller species of jaguar. This might be the one.

After halting a moment, the creature turned to one

side, and then proceeded at a skulking trot around
the house. Now and then it stopped and looked
towards the building, as if searching for some aper-
ture by which it might get in. Doña Isidora followed
it round on the inside. The walls were so open that
she could mark all its movements ; and, with a pistol
in each hand, she was ready for the attack, determined to fire the moment it might threaten to spring
against the bamboos.

On one side of the house, at a few paces distant,
stood the mule. The horse had been taken to the
woods, and the mule was left alone. This animal
was tied to a tree, which shaded her from the sun.
As soon as the fierce creature got well round the
house it came in full view of the mule, which now
claimed its attention. The latter, on seeing it, had
started, and sprung round upon her halter, as if badly
terrified by the apparition.

Whether the beast of prey had ever before seen a
mule was a question. Most likely it had not ; for,
half innocently and half as if with the intention of
making an attack, it went skulking up until it was
close to the heels of the latter. It could not have
placed itself in a better position to be well kicked ,
and well kicked it was ; for just at that moment the
mule let fling with both her heels, and struck it upon
the ribs. A loud " thump " was heard by those
within the house ; and Doña Isidora, still watching
through the canes, had the satisfaction to see the
spotted creature take to its heels and gallop off as if
a kettle had been tied to its tail. It made no stop,
not even to look back ; but, having reached the edge

of the water, plunged in and swam over to the opposite shore. They could see it climb out on the other side ; and then, with a cowed and conquered look, it trotted off and disappeared among the palm trees.

Doña Isidora knew that it was gone for good, and, having now no further fear, went on with her work as before. She first, however, carried out a large measure of the *murumuru* nuts and gave them to the mule, patting the creature upon the nose and thanking her for the important service she had rendered.

When Don Pablo and the rest returned, the adventure was, of course, related ; but, from the description given of the animal, neither Don Pablo nor Guapo believed it could have been the jaguar. It was too small for that. Besides, a jaguar would not have been cowed and driven off by a mule. He would more likely have killed the mule and dragged its body off with him across the river, or perhaps have broken into the house and done worse.

The animal was, no doubt, the " ocelot," which is also spotted, or rather marked, with the eyelike rosettes which distinguish the skin of the jaguar. Indeed there are quite a number of animals of the cat genus in the forests of the Montaña ; some spotted like the leopard, others striped as the tiger, and still others of uniform color all over the body. They are, of course, all preying animals ; but none of them will attack man except the jaguar and the puma. Some of the others, when brought to bay, will fight desperately, as would the common wildcat under like circumstances ; but the largest of them will leave man alone if unmolested themselves. Not so with the jaguar, who will attack either man or beast, and put them to death, unless he be himself overpowered.

The jaguar, or, as he is sometimes called, " ounce," (*Felis onça,*) and by most Spanish Americans " tiger," is the largest and most ferocious of all the American *Felidæ.* He stands third in rank as to these qualities — the lion and tiger of the eastern continent taking precedence of him. Specimens of the jaguar have been seen equal in size to the Asiatic tiger; but the average size of the American animal is much less. He is strong enough, however, to drag a dead horse or ox to his den — often to a distance of a quarter of a mile ; and this feat has been repeatedly observed.

The jaguar is found throughout all the tropical countries of Spanish America, and is oftener called tiger (*tigre*) than jaguar. This is a misapplied name ; for although he bears a considerable likeness to the tiger, both in shape and habits, yet the markings of his skin are quite different. The tiger is striated, or striped, while the black on the jaguar is in beautiful eyelike rosettes. The leopard is more like the jaguar than any other creature ; and the panther and chee-tah of the eastern continent also resemble him. The markings of the jaguar, when closely examined, dif-fer from all of these. The spots on the animals of the old world are simple spots, or black rings ; while those of the American species are rings with a single spot in the middle, forming *ocellæ,* or eyes. Each, in fact, resembles a rosette.

Jaguars are not always of the same color. Some have skins of an orange yellow, and these are the most beautiful. Others are lighter colored ; and individuals have been killed that were nearly white. But there is a " black jaguar," which is thought to be of a different species. It is larger and fiercer than the other, and is found in the very hottest parts of the Great Montaña. Its skin is not quite jet black, but of a deep maroon brown ; and, upon close inspection, the spots upon it can be seen of a pure black. This species is more dreaded by the inhabitants of those countries than the other; and it is said always to attack man wherever it may encounter him.

In the forests of South America the jaguar reigns with undisputed sway. All the other beasts fear and fly from him. His roar produces terror and confusion among the animated creation, and causes them to fly in every direction. It is never heard by the Indian without some feeling of fear; and no wonder; for a year does not pass without a number of these people falling victims to the savage ferocity of this animal.

There are those, however, among them who can deal single handed with the jaguar, — regular " jaguar hunters " by profession, — who do not fear to attack the fierce brute in his own haunts. They do not trust to firearms, but to a sharp spear. Upon this they receive his attack, transfixing the animal with unerring aim as he advances. Should they fail in their first thrust, their situation is one of peril; yet all hope is not lost. On their left arm they carry a sort of sheepskin shield. This is held forward, and usually seized by the jaguar; and while he is busy with it the hunter gains time for a second effort, which rarely fails to accomplish his purpose.

The jaguars are killed for many reasons. Their beautiful skins sell for several dollars; besides, in many places a price is set upon their heads, on account of their destructive habits. Thousands are destroyed every year. For all this, they do not seem to diminish in numbers. The introduction of the large mammalia into America has provided them with increased resources; and in many places, where there are herds of half-wild cattle, the number of the jaguars is said to be greater than formerly. It is difficult for one living in a country where such fierce animals are unknown to believe that they may have an influence over man to such an extent as to prevent his settling in a particular place; yet such is the fact. In many parts of South America, not only planta-tions, but whole villages, have been abandoned solely from fear of the jaguars.

CHAPTER XXXI.

A FAMILY OF JAGUARS.

As yet none of the exiles had seen any tracks or indications of the terrible jaguar, and Don Pablo began to believe that there were none in that district of country. He was not allowed to remain much longer in this belief, for an incident occurred shortly after proving that at least one pair of these fierce animals was not far off.

It was near the end of the summer, and the cinchona trees on the side of the river on which stood the house had been all cut down and " barked." It became necessary, therefore, to cross the stream in search of others. Indeed, numerous " manchas " had been seen on the other side, and to these the " cascarilleros " now turned their attention. They, of course, reached them by crossing the tree bridge, and then keeping up the stream on the farther side.

For several days they had been at work in this new direction, and were getting bark in by the hundred weight.

One day Guapo and Leon had gone by themselves — Guapo to fell the trees as usual, and Leon, who was now an expert bark peeler, to use the scalping knife. Don Pablo had remained at home, busy with

work in the great magazine, for there was much to
do there in the packing and storing.

An hour or two after Guapo was seen to return
alone. He had broken the handle of his axe, and,
having several spare ones at the house, he had returned to get one. Leon had remained in the woods.

Now, Leon had finished his operations on such
trees as Guapo had already cut down, and, not finding a good seat near, had walked towards the precipice which was farther up the hill, and sat down upon
one of the loose rocks at its base. Here he amused
himself by watching the parrots and toucans that
were fluttering through the trees over his head.

He noticed that just by his side there was a large
hole or cave in the cliff. He could see to the farther
end of it from where he sat; but curiosity prompted
him to step up to its mouth, and give it a closer examination. On doing so, he heard a noise not unlike
the mew of a cat. It evidently came from the cave,
and only increased his curiosity to look inside. He
put his head to the entrance, and there, in a sort of
nest upon the bottom of the cave, he perceived two
creatures, exactly like two spotted kittens, only larger.
They were about half as big as fullgrown cats.

" Two beauties," said Leon to himself ; " they are
the kittens of some wild cat — that's plain. Now, we
want a cat very much at home. If these were brought
up in the house, why shouldn't they do ? I'll warrant
they'd be tame enough. I know mamma wants a cat.
I've heard her say so. I'll give her an agreeable
surprise by taking this pair home. The beauties ! "

Without another word Leon climbed up, and, taking hold of the two spotted animals, returned with them out of the cave. They were evidently very young creatures, yet for all that they growled, and spat, and attempted to scratch his hands. But Leon was not a boy to be frightened at trifles ; and, after getting one under each arm, he set off in triumph, intending to carry them direct to the house.

Guapo was in front of the house, busy in new hafting his axe. Don Pablo was at work in the store room. Doña Isidora and the little Leona were occupied with some affair in the porch. All were engaged one way or other. Just then a voice sounded upon their ears, causing them all to stop their work and look abroad. It even brought Don Pablo out of the storehouse. It was the voice of Leon, who shouted from the other side of the lake, where they all saw him standing, with a strange object under each arm.

" Hola ! " cried he. " Look, mamma ! See what I've got ! I've brought you a couple of cats — beauties, ain't they ? " And as he said this, he held the two yellow bodies out before him.

Don Pablo turned pale, and even the coppery cheek of Guapo blanched at the sight. Though at some distance, both knew at a glance what they were. Cats, indeed ! *They were the cubs of the jaguar !*

" My God ! " cried Don Pablo, hoarse with affright. " My God ! the boy will be lost ! " and as he spoke he swept the upper edge of the lake with an anxious glance.

" Run, little master ! " shouted Guapo. " Run for your life ; make for the bridge — for the bridge ! "

Leon seemed astonished. He knew by the words of Guapo, and the earnest gestures of the rest, that there was some danger — but of what? Why was he to run? He could not comprehend it. He hesitated, and might have staid longer on the spot, had not his father, seeing his indecision, shouted out to him in a loud voice, —

" Run, boy, run! The jaguars are after you! "

This speech enabled Leon to comprehend his situation for the first time; and he immediately started off towards the bridge, running as fast as he was able.

Don Pablo had not seen the jaguars when he spoke; but his words were prophetic, and that prophecy was speedily verified. They had hardly been uttered when two yellow bodies, dashing out of the brushwood, appeared near the upper end of the lake. There was no mistaking what they were. Their orange flanks and ocellated sides were sufficiently characteristic. *They were jaguars!*

A few springs brought them to the edge of the water, and they were seen to take the track over which Leon had just passed. They were following by the scent, — sometimes pausing, sometimes one passing the other, — and their waving tails and quick energetic movements showed that they were furious and excited to the highest degree. Now they disappeared behind the palm trunks, and the next moment their shining bodies shot out again like flashes of light.

Doña Isidora and the little Leona screamed with affright. Don Pablo shouted words of encouragement in a hoarse voice. Guapo seized his axe—

which fortunately he had finished hafting — and ran towards the bridge, along the water's edge. Don Pablo followed with his pistols, which he had hastily got his hands upon.

For a short moment there was silence on both sides of the river. Guapo was opposite Leon, both run- ning. The stream narrowed as it approached the ravine, and Leon and Guapo could see each other, and hear every word distinctly. Guapo now cried out, —

" Drop one ! young master — *only one !* "

Leon heard, and, being a sharp boy, understood what was meant. Up to this moment he had not thought of parting with his " cats " — in fact, it was because he had *not* thought of it. Now, however, at the voice of Guapo, he flung one of them to the ground, without stopping to see where it fell. He ran on, and in a few seconds again heard Guapo cry out, —

" *Now the other !* "

Leon let the second slip from his grasp, and kept on for the bridge.

It was well he had dropped the cubs, else he would never have reached that bridge. When the first one fell the jaguars were not twenty paces behind him. They were almost in sight, but by good fortune the weeds and underwood hid the pursued from the pur- suers.

On reaching their young, the first that had been dropped, both stopped, and appeared to lick and caress it. They remained by it but a moment. One parted sooner than the other — the female it was, no

15

doubt, in search of her second offspring. Shortly after the other started also, and both were again seen springing along the trail in pursuit. A few stretches brought them to where the second cub lay; and here they again halted, caressing this one as they had done the other.

Don Pablo and Doña Isidora, who saw all this from the other side, were in hopes that, having recovered their young, the jaguars might give over the chase, and carry them off. But they were mistaken in this. The American tiger is of a very different nature. Once enraged, he will seek revenge with relentless pertinacity. It so proved. After delaying a moment with the second cub, both left it, and sprang forward upon the trail, which they knew had been taken by whoever had robbed them.

By this time Leon had gained the bridge — had crossed it — and was lifted from its nearer end by Guapo. The latter scarce spoke a word — only telling Leon to hurry towards the house. For himself he had other work to do than run. The bridge he knew would be no protection. The jaguars would cross over it like squirrels, and then ——

Guapo reflected no further, but, bending over the thick branch, attacked it with his axe. His design was apparent at once. He was going to cut it from the cliff.

He plied the axe with all his might. Every muscle in his body was at play. Blow succeeded blow. The branch was already creaking, when, to his horror, the foremost of the jaguars appeared in sight on the opposite side. He was not discouraged. Again

fell the axe — again and again ; the jaguar is upon
the bank ; it has sprung upon the root of the tree !
It pauses a moment — another blow of the axe —
the jaguar bounds upon the trunk — its claws rattle
along the bark — it is midway over the chasm !
Another blow — the branch crackles — there is a
crash — it parts from the cliff — it is gone ! Both
tree and jaguar gone — down — down to the sharp
rocks of the foaming torrent !

A loud yell from the Indian announced his triumph.
But it was not yet complete. It was the female jaguar
— the smaller one — that had fallen. The male still
remained — where was he ? Already upon the opposite brink of the chasm !

He had dashed forward just in time to see his mate
disappearing into the gulf below. He saw and seemed
to comprehend all that had passed. His eyes glared
with redoubled fury. There was vengeance in his
look, and determination in his attitude.

For a moment he surveyed the wide gulf that separated him from his enemies. He seemed to measure
the distance at a glance. His heart was bold with
rage and despair. He had lost his companion — his
faithful partner — his wife. Life was nothing now
— he resolved upon revenge or death !

He was seen to run a few paces back from the
edge of the chasm, and then, turning suddenly, set
his body for the spring.

It would have been beautiful to have beheld the
play of his glistening flanks at that moment, had one
been out of danger ; but Guapo was not, and he had

no pleasure in the sight. Guapo stood upon the op-posite brink, axe in hand, ready to receive him.

The Indian had not long to wait. With one des-perate bound the jaguar launched his body into the air, and, like lightning, passed to the opposite bank. His fore feet only reached it, and his claws firmly grasped the rock. The rest of his body hung over, clutching the cliff.

In a moment he would have sprung up, and then woe to his antagonist! But he was not allowed that moment, for he had scarcely touched the rock when the Indian leaped forward and struck at his head with the axe. The blow was not well aimed, and although it stunned the jaguar, he still clung to the cliff. In setting himself for a second blow, Guapo came too near, and the next moment the great claws of the tiger were buried in his foot.

It is difficult to tell what might have been the result. It would, no doubt, have been different. Guapo would have been dragged over, and that was certain death; but at this moment a hand was protruded between Guapo's legs — the muzzle of a pistol was seen close to the head of the jaguar — a loud crack ran through the ravine, and when the smoke cleared away the jaguar was seen no more !

Guapo, with his foot badly lacerated, was **drawn back** from the cliff into the arms of Don Pablo.

CHAPTER XXXII.

THE RAFT.

THIS was the most exciting day that had been passed since their arrival in the Montaña ; and, considering the result, it was well that the occurrence had taken place. It had rid them of a pair of bad neighbors — there would soon have been four — that some time or other would have endangered the lives of some of the party. It was the opinion of Guapo that they need not, at least for a while, have any fear of jaguars. It was not likely there was another pair in that district ; although, from the roaming disposition of this animal, fresh ones might soon make their appearance ; and it was deemed best always to act as though some were already in the neighborhood.

The cubs were disposed of. It was not deemed advisable to bring them up as " cats." After what had occurred, that was voted, even by Leon, a dangerous experiment — too dangerous to be attempted. They were still on the other side of the river, and the bridge was now gone. If left to themselves, no doubt they would have perished, as they were very young things. Perhaps some carnivorous creature — wolf, coati, eagle, or vulture — would have devoured them, or they might have been eaten up by

the ants.   But this was not to be their fate.   Guapu
swam across and strangled them ; then, tying them
together, he suspended the pair over his shoulders,
and brought them with him to be exhibited as a curiosity.   Moreover, Guapo had a design upon their
skins.

It was not long after that a pleasanter pet than
either of them was found; and this was a beautiful
little saïmiri monkey, about the size of a squirrel,
which Guapo and Leon captured one day in the
woods.   They heard a noise as they were passing
along, and, going up to the spot, saw on the branch of
a low tree nearly a dozen little monkeys all rolled up
together in a heap, with their tails warped round
each other as if to keep themselves warm.   Nearly
another dozen were running about, whining and apparently trying to get in among the rest.   Guapo
and Leon made a sudden rush upon them, and were
able to capture three or four before the creatures
could free themselves ; but only one lived, and that
became a great pet and favorite.   It was a beautiful
little creature — a true saïmiri, or squirrel monkey,
called the " titi."   Its silky fur was of a rich olive-
green color; and its fine large eyes expressed fear
or joy — now filling with tears, and now brightening
again — just like those of a child.

During the summer our bark gatherers continued
their labor without interruption ; and on account of
the great plenty of the cinchona trees, and their
proximity to the house, they were enabled to accu-
mulate a very large store.   They worked like bees.

Although this forest life was not without its pleas-

ures and excitements, yet it began to grow very irk-
some both to Don Pablo and Doña Isidora. Life in
the wilderness, with its rude cares and rude enjoy-
ments, may be very pleasant for a while to those who
seek it as amateurs, or to that class who, as colonists,
intend to make it a permanent thing. But neither
Don Pablo nor his wife had ever thought of coloniza-
tion. With them their present industry was the result of accident and necessity. Their tastes and
longings were very different. They longed to return
to civilized life ; and, though the very misfortune
which had driven them forth into the wilderness had
also guided them to an opportunity of making a fortune, it is probable they would have passed it by had
they not known that, penniless as they were, they
would have fared still worse in any city to which
they might have gone. But before the first year was
out they yearned very much to return to civilization;
and this desire was very natural. But there were
other reasons that influenced them besides the mere
ennui of the wilderness. The lives of themselves
and their children were constantly in danger from
jaguars, pumas, and poisonous reptiles. Even man
himself might at any moment appear as their destroyer. As yet no Indian — not even a trace of one
— had been seen. But this was not strange. In the
tangled and impenetrable forests of the great Montaña
two tribes of Indians may reside for years within
less than a league's distance of each other without
either being aware of the other's existence. Scarcely any intercourse is carried on, or excursions made,
except by the rivers, for they are the only roads ; and

where two of these run parallel, although they may be only at a short distance from each other, people residing on one may never think of crossing to the other.

Notwithstanding that no Indians had yet appeared to disturb them, there was no certainty that these might not arrive any day and treat them as enemies. On this account Don Pablo and Doña Isidora were never without a feeling of uneasiness.

After mutual deliberation, therefore, they resolved not to prolong their stay beyond the early part of spring, when they would carry out their original de-sign of building a *balza* raft and commit themselves to the great river, which, according to all appearance and to Guapo's confident belief, flowed directly to the Amazon. Guapo had never either descended or ascended it himself, and on their first arrival was not so sure about its course ; but, after having gone down to its banks and examined its waters, his recollections revived, and he remembered many accounts which he had heard of it from Indians of his own tribe. He had no doubt but it was the same which, under the name of the " Purus," falls into the Amazon be-tween the mouths of the Madeira and the Coary.

Upon this stream, therefore, in a few months they would embark. But these intervening months were not spent in idleness. Although the season for bark gathering was past, another source of industry pre-sented itself. The bottom lands of the great river were found to be covered with a network of under-wood ; and among this underwood the principal plant was a well-known brier, *Smilax officinalis.* This is

the creeping plant that yields the celebrated " sarsaparilla ; " and Don Pablo, having made an analysis
of some roots, discovered it to be the most valuable
species; for it is to be remembered that, like the
cinchona, a whole genus, or rather several genera,
furnish the article of commerce. The brier which
produces the sarsaparilla is a tall, creeping plant,
which throws out a. large number of long, wrinkled
roots of a uniform thickness and about the size of a
goose quill. Nothing is required further than dig-
ging and dragging these roots out of the ground,
drying them a while, and then binding them in bundles with a small " sipo," or tough forest creeper.
These bundles are made up so as to render the roots
convenient for packing and transport.

During several months this branch of industry occupied Don Pablo, Guapo, and Leon ; so that, when
the time drew nigh for their departure, what with
the cinchona bark, the sarsaparilla, and the vanilla
beans, there was not an empty inch in the large
storehouse.

Guapo had not been all the time with them. For
several days Guapo was not to be seen at the house,
nor any where around it. Where had Guapo been
all this time ? I will tell you. Guapo *had been to
the mountains.*

Yes ; Don Pablo had sent him on an important
mission, which he had performed with secrecy and
despatch. Don Pablo, before braving the dangers of
the vast journey he had projected, had still a linger-
ing hope that something might have happened —
some change in the government of Peru — perhaps a

new viceroy — that might enable him to return with safety to his native land. To ascertain if such had taken place, Guapo had made his journey to the mountains.

He went no farther than the Puna — no farther than the hut of his friend the vaquero, who, by a previous understanding with Guapo, had kept himself informed about political matters.

There was no hope ; the same council, the same viceroy, the same price upon the head of Don Pablo, who, however, was believed to have escaped in an American ship, and to have taken refuge in the great republic of the North.

With this news Guapo returned ; and now the preparations for the river voyage were set about in earnest. A balza raft was built out of large trunks of the *Bombax ceiba*, which, being light wood, was the best for the purpose. Of course these trunks had been cut long ago with a view to using them in this way. A commodious cabin, or " toldo," was constructed on the raft, built of palm and bamboos, and thatched with the broad leaves of the bussu. A light canoe was also hollowed out, as a sort of tender to the raft ; and a couple of very large canoes, for the purpose of giving buoyancy to it, were lashed one upon each side. The " merchandise " was care-fully " stowed " and covered with " tarpaulings " of palm leaves, and the stores laid in with every provi-dential care and calculation.

You will be wondering what was done with the horse and mule — those creatures that had served the exiles so faithfully and so well. Were they left behind to become a prey to the jaguars and the large blood-sucking bats that kill so many animals in these parts ? No ; they were not to be left to such a fate. One of them — the mule — had been already dis· posed of. It was a valuable beast; and partly on that account, and partly from gratitude felt towards it for the well-timed kick it had given the ocelot, it was to be spared. Guapo had taken both the mule and the horse on his mountain journey, and presented the former to his friend the vaquero.

But the horse was still on hand. What was to be done with him ? Leave him behind? That would be certain death ; for no horse that was not cared for could exist in the Montaña ten days without being eaten up by the fierce creatures that inhabit it. The bats would surely have destroyed him. Well, what was done ? He could not be carried on the raft ; but he was though — *in a way.* Guapo was resolved that the bats should not have him, nor the jaguars neither. He was in fine condition — fat as a pig. The fruit of the murumuru had agreed with him. He was just in the condition in which an Indian thinks a horse " good for killing ; " and *Guapo killed him ;* yes, Guapo killed him. It is true it was a sor* of a Virginius tragedy, and Guapo had great difficulty in nerving himself for the task. But the blow gun was at length levelled, and the *curare* did its work. Then Guapo skinned him, and cut him into strips, and dried him into " charqui," and carried him on board the raft. That was the closing scene.

All left the house together, carrying with them the remains of their hastily-created *penates.* On reaching the end of the valley they turned and threw back a last glance at a home that had to them been a happy one ; and then, continuing their journey, they were soon upon the balza. The only living creature that accompanied them from their valley home was the pretty saïmiri, carried on the shoulder of the little Leona.

The cable of piassaba palm was carefully taken in and coiled, the raft was pushed out, and the next moment floated lightly upon the broad bosom of the river.

CHAPTER XXXIII.

THE GUARDIAN BROTHER.

THE current of the river flowed at the rate of about four miles an hour, and at this speed they travelled. They had nothing to do but guide the raft in the middle part of the stream. This was effected by means of a large stern oar fixed upon a pivot, and which served the purpose of a rudder. One was required to look after this oar, and Don Pablo and Guapo took turns at it. It was not a very trouble-some task, except where some bend had to be got round, or some eddy was to be cleared, when both had to work at it together. At other times the balza floated straight on, without requiring the least effort on the part of the crew; and then they would all sit down and chat pleasantly, and view the changing scenery of the forest-covered shores. Sometimes tall palms lined the banks, and sometimes great forest trees netted together by thick parasites that crept from one to the other, and twined around the trunks like monster serpents. Sometimes the shores were one unbroken thicket of underwood, where it would have been almost impossible to make a landing, had they wished it. At other places there were sand bars, and even little islets, with scarce any vegetation upon them; and they also passed many other islets

and large islands thickly wooded. The country generally appeared to be flat; though at one or two
places they saw hills that ran in to the banks of the
river.

Of course the change of scenery and the many
fresh vistas continually opening before them rendered
their voyage both cheerful and interesting. The
many beautiful birds, too, and new kinds of trees
and animals, which they saw, were a constant source
of varied enjoyment, and furnished them with themes
of conversation.

During the first day they made a journey of full
forty miles. Having brought their balza close to the
shore and secured it to a tree, they encamped for the
night. There was no opening of any extent, but for
some distance the ground was clear of underwood,
and the trunks of great old trees rose like columns,
losing themselves amidst the thick foliage overhead.
A dark forest only could be seen; and, as night drew
on, the horrid cries of the alouattes, or howling
monkeys, mingling with the voices of other nocturnal
animals, filled the woods. They had no fear of
monkeys; but now and then they thought they could
distinguish the cry of the jaguar, and of him they
had fear enough. Indeed the jaguar possesses the
power of imitating the cry of the other animals of
the forest, and often uses it to draw them within reach
of him.

In addition to the fire upon which they had cooked
their supper, as soon as night had fairly set in they
kindled others, forming a sort of semicircle, the chord
of which was the bank of the river itself. Within

this semicircle the hammocks were stretched from tree to tree ; and, as all were fatigued with the day's exertions, they climbed into them at an early hour, and were soon asleep. One alone sat up to keep watch. As they thought they had heard the jaguar, this was deemed best; for they knew that fire will not always frighten off that fierce animal. As the neighborhood looked suspicious, and also as it was their first encampment, they, like all travellers at setting out, of course were more timid and cautious.

To Leon was assigned the first watch; for Leon was a courageous boy, and it was not the first time he had taken his turn in this way. He was to sit up for about two hours, and then wake Guapo, who would keep the midnight watch; after which Don Pablo's turn would come, and that would terminate in the morning at daybreak. Leon was instructed to rouse the others in case any danger might threaten the camp.

Leon from choice had seated himself by the head of the hammock in which slept the little Leona; in order, no doubt, to be nearer her, as she was the most helpless of the party, and therefore required more immediate protection. He had both the pistols by him, ready to his hand and loaded; and in case of danger, he knew very well how to use them.

He had been seated for about half an hour, now casting his eyes up to the red and wrinkled trunks of the trees, and then gazing into the dark vistas of the surrounding forest, or at other times looking out upon the glistening surface of the river. Many a strange sound fell upon his ear. Sometimes the whole forest appeared to be alive with voices — the voices of beasts and birds, reptiles and insects; for the tree frogs and ciendas were as noisy as the larger creatures. At other times a perfect stillness reigned, so that he could distinctly hear the tiny hum of the mosquito; and then, all at once, would fall upon his ear the melancholy wailing of the nighthawk — the "*alma perdida*," or "lost soul" — for such is the poetical and fanciful name given by the Spanish Americans to this nocturnal bird.

While thus engaged, Leon began to feel very drowsy. The heavy day's work, in which he had borne part, had fatigued him as well as the others; and, in spite of the odd voices that from time to time fell upon his ear, he could have lain down upon the bare ground and slept without a feeling of fear. Snakes or scorpions, or biting lizards or spiders, would not have kept him from going to sleep at that moment. It is astonishing how the desire of sleep makes one indifferent to all these things, which at other times we so much dread. Leon did not fear them a bit, but kept himself awake from a feeling of pride and honor. He reflected that it would never do to be unfaithful to the important trust confided to him. No, that would never do. He rubbed his eyes, and rose up, and approached the bank, and dipped his hands in the water, and came back to his former place, and sat down again. Spite of all his efforts, however, he felt very heavy. O, when would the two hours pass, that he might rouse Guapo?

"Car-r-ambo! I nev-er was so s-s-sleepy. *Vamos!* Leon! you mustn't give in!"

And, striking himself a lively slap on the chest, he straightened his back, and sat upright for a while.

He was just beginning to get bowed about the shoulders again, and to nod a little, when he was startled by a short, sharp exclamation uttered by the little Leona. He looked up to her hammock. He could perceive it had moved slightly; but it was at rest again, and its occupant was evidently asleep.

"Poor little sis! she is dreaming," he muttered half aloud. "Perhaps some horrid dream of jaguars or serpents. I have half a mind to wake her. But, no; she sleeps too soundly; I might disturb them all;" and, with these reflections, Leon remained upon his seat.

Once more his head was beginning to bob, when the voice of Leona again startled him, and he looked up as before. The hammock moved slightly, but there was no appearance of any thing wrong. From where he sat he could not see well into it; but the outlines of the child's body were easily discernible through the elastic netting; and at the farther end he could just perceive one of her little feet, where it had escaped from the covering, and rested partly over the edge.

As he continued to gaze upon the delicate member, thinking whether he had not better cover it against the mosquitoes, all at once his eye was attracted by something red — a crooked red line that traversed from the toe downward along the side of the foot. It was red and glittering — it was *a stream of blood!*

His first feeling was one of horror. His next was

16

a resolve to spring to his feet and rouse the camp; but this impulse was checked by one of greater prudence. Whatever enemy had done it, thought he, must still be about the hammock; to make a noise would, perhaps, only irritate it, and cause it to inflict some still more terrible wound. He would remain quiet until he had got his eyes upon the creature, when he could spring upon it, or fire his pistol, before it could do further harm.

With these ideas, quickly conceived, he rose silently to his feet, and standing, or rather crouching, forward bent his eyes over the hammock.

CHAPTER XXXIV.

THE VAMPIRE.

LEON's head was close to that of the sleeper, whose sweet breath he felt, and whose little bosom rose and fell in gentle undulation. He scanned the inside of the hammock from head to foot. He gazed anxiously into every fold of the cover. Not an object could he see that should not have been there — no terrible creature — no serpent — for it was this last that was in his mind. But something must have been there. What could have caused the stream of blood, that now, being closer, he could more plainly see trickling over the soft blue veins ? Some creature must have done it.

" O, if it be the small viper," thought he, " or the coral snake, or the deadly macaurel ! If these —— "

His thoughts at this moment were interrupted. A light flapping of wings sounded in his ear — so light, that it appeared to be made by the soft pinions of the owl, or some nocturnal bird. It was not by the wings of a bird that that sound was produced, but by the wings of a hideous creature. Leon was conscious, from the continued flapping, that something was playing through the air, and that it occasionally approached close to his head. He gazed upward and around him, and at length he could distinguish a dark form passing between him and the light ; but it glided into the darkness again, and he could see it no more. Was it a bird ? It looked like one — it might have been an owl — it was full as large as one ; but yet, from the glance he had had of it, it appeared to be black or very dark, and he had never heard of owls of that color. Moreover, it had not the look nor flight of an owl. Was it a bird at all ? Or whatever it was was it the cause of the blood ? This did not appear likely to Leon, who still had his thoughts bent upon the snakes.

While he was revolving these questions in his mind, he again turned and looked towards the foot of the hammock. The sight caused him a thrill of horror. There was the hideous creature, which he had just seen, right over the bleeding foot. It was not perched, but suspended in the air on its moving wings, with its long snout protruded forward and pressed against the toe of the sleeper! Its sharp, white teeth were visible in both jaws ; and its small vicious eyes glistened under the light of the fires. The red hair covering its body and large membranous wings added to the hideousness of its aspect · and a more hideous creature could not have been conceived. *It was the vampire* — the blood-sucking *phyllostoma !*

A short cry escaped from the lips of Leon. I was not a cry of pain, but the contrary. The sigh of the great bat, hideous as the creature was, relieves him. He had all along been under the painful impression that some venomous serpent had caused the blood to flow ; and now he had no further fear on that score. He knew that there was no poison in the wound inflicted by the phyllostoma — only the loss of a little blood ; and this quieted his anxieties at once. He resolved, however, to punish the intruder ; and not caring to rouse the camp by firing, he stole a little closer, and aimed a blow with the but of his pistol. The blow was well aimed, and brought the bat to the ground ; but its shrill screeching awoke every body, and in a few moments the camp was in complete confusion. The sight of the blood on the foot of the little Leona quite terrified Doña Isidora and the rest ; but when the cause was explained, all felt reassured and thankful that the thing was no worse. The little foot was bound up in a rag ; and although, for two or three days after, it was not without pain, yet no bad effects came of it.

The " blood-sucking " bats do not cause death, either to man or any other animal, by a single attack. All the blood they can draw out amounts to only a few ounces, although after their departure the blood continues to run from the open wound. It is by repeating their attacks night after night that the strength of an animal becomes exhausted, and it dies from sheer loss of blood and consequent faintness. With animals this is far from being a rare occurrence. Hundreds of horses and cattle are killed every year in the South American pastures. These creatures suffer, perhaps, without knowing from what cause ; for the phyllostoma performs its cupping operation without causing the least pain — at all events the sleeper is very rarely awakened by it. It is easy to understand how it sucks the blood of its victim ;

for its snout and the leafy appendage around its mouth — from which it derives the name " phyllos- toma " — are admirably adapted to that end. But how does it make the puncture to " let " the blood ? That is as yet a mystery among naturalists, as it also is among the people who are habitually its victims Even Guapo could not explain the process. The large teeth — of which it has got quite a mouthful — seem altogether unfitted to make a hole such as is found where the phyllostoma has been at work. Their bite, moreover, would awake the soundest sleeper. Besides these, it has neither fangs, nor sting, nor proboscis, that would serve the purpose. How, then, does it reach the blood ? Many theories have been offered. Some assert that it rubs the skin with its snout until it brings it to bleeding ; others say that it sets the sharp point of one of its large tusks against the part, and then, by plying its wings, wheels round and round, as upon a pivot, until the point has penetrated — that during this operation the motion of the wings fans and cools the sleeping victim, so that no pain is felt. It may be a long while before this curious question is solved, on account of the difficulty of observing a creature whose habits are nocturnal, and most of whose deeds are " done in the dark."

People have denied the existence of such a crea- ture as the blood-sucking bat ; even naturalists have gone so far. They can allege no better grounds for their incredulity than that the thing has an air of the fabulous and horrible about it. But this is not philos- ophy. Incredulity is the characteristic of the half educated. It may be carried too far, and the fables of the vulgar have often a stratum of truth at the bottom. There is one thing that is almost intolerable, and that is the conceit of the " closet naturalist," who sneers at every thing as untrue that seems to show the least *design* on the part of the brute creation — who denies every thing that appears at all singular or fanciful, and simply because it appears so. With the truthful observations that have been made upon the curious domestic economy of such little creatures as bees, and wasps, and ants, we ought to be cautious how we reject statements about the habits of other animals, however strange they may appear.

Who doubts that a mosquito will perch itself upon the skin of a human being, pierce it with his proboscis, and suck away until it is gorged with blood ? Why does it appear strange that a bat should do the same ?

Now, your closet naturalist will believe that the bat *does* suck the blood of cattle and horses, but denies that it will attack man. This is sheer nonsense. What difference to the vampire, whether its victim be a biped or quadruped ? Is it fear of the former that would prevent it from attacking him ? Perhaps it may never have seen a human being before : besides, it attacks its victim while asleep, and is rarely ever caught or punished in the act. Where these creatures are much hunted or persecuted by man, they may learn to fear him, and their original habits may become changed ; but that is quite another thing. As Nature has formed them, the blood-sucking bats will make their attack indifferently, either upon man or large quadrupeds. There are a thousand proofs to be had in all the tropical regions of America. Every year animals are killed by the *phyllostoma hastatum*, not in hundreds, but in thousands. It is recorded that on one extensive cattle farm several hundred head were killed in the short period of six months by the bats ; and the vaqueros, who received a bounty upon every bat they should capture, in one year succeeded in destroying the enormous number of *seven thousand*. Indeed, " bat hunting " is followed by some as a profession, so eager are the owners of the cattle farms to get rid of these pests.

Many tribes of Indians and travellers suffer great annoyance from the vampire bats. Some persons never go to sleep without covering themselves with blankets, although the heat be ever so oppressive. Any part left naked will be attacked by the phyllostoma ; but they seem to have a preference for the tip of the great toe — perhaps because they have found that part more habitually exposed. Sometimes one sleeper is " cupped " by them, while another will not be molested ; and this, I may observe, is true also of the mosquitoes. There may be some difference as to the state of the blood of two individuals that leads to this fastidious preference. Some are far more subject to their attack than others — so much so, that they require to adopt every precaution to save themselves from being bled to death. Cayenne pepper rubbed over the skin is used to keep them off, and also to cure the wound they have made ; but even this sometimes proves ineffective.

Of course, there are many species of bats in South America besides the vampire ; in fact, there is no class of mammalia more numerous in genera and species, and no part of the world where greater numbers are found, than in the tropical regions of America. Some are insect eaters, while others live entirely on vegetable substances; but all have the same unsightly and repulsive appearance. The odor of some kinds is extremely fetid and disagreeable. Notwithstanding this, they are eaten by many tribes of Indians; and even the French Creoles of Guiana have their "bat soup," which they relish highly. The proverb, "*De gustibus non disputandum est*," seems to be true for all time. The Spanish Americans have it in the phrase, "*Cada uno a su gusto;*" "*Chacun à son goût*," say the French; and on hearing these tales about "ant paste," and "roast monkey," and "armadillo done in the shell," and "bat soup," you, boy reader, will not fail to exclaim, "Every one to his liking."

The vampire appeared to be to Guapo's liking. It was now his turn to keep watch; and as the rest of them got into their hammocks and lay awake for a while, they saw him take up the bat, spit it upon a forked stick, and commence broiling it over the fire. Of course *he ate it!*

When morning came, and they had got up, what was their astonishment to see no less than fourteen bats lying side by side! They were dead, of course: Guapo had killed them all during his watch. They had appeared at one period of the night in alarming numbers, and Guapo had done battle manfully without awaking any body.

Another curious tableau came under their notice

shortly after. Just as they were about to embark, a singular-looking tree was observed growing near the bank of the river. At first they thought the tree was covered with birds' nests, or pieces of some kind of moss. Indeed, it looked more like a tree hung over with rags than any thing else. Curiosity led them to approach it. What was their astonishment to find that the nests, moss, or rags were neither more nor less than a vast assemblage of bats suspended, and asleep! They were hanging in all possible positions; some with their heads down, some by the claws upon either wing, and some by both, while a great many had merely hooked over the branch the little horny curvature of their tails. Some hung down along the trunk, suspended by a crack in the bark, while others were far out upon the branches.

It was certainly the oddest "roost" that any of the party (Guapo, perhaps, excepted) had ever witnessed ; and, after gazing at it for some time, they turned away without disturbing the sleepers, and, getting on board once more, floated adown the stream swiftly and silently.

CHAPTER XXXV.

THE MARIMONDAS.

THAT day they made good progress, having dropped down the river a distance of fifty miles at least. They might even have gone farther; but a good camping-place offered, and they did not like to pass it, as they might not find another so convenient. It was a muddy bank, or rather a promontory, that ran out into the river, and was entirely without trees, or any other vegetation, as it was annually overflowed, and formed, in fact, part of the bed of the river. At this time the mud was quite dry and smooth, and appeared as if it had been paddled and beaten down by the feet of animals and birds. This was, in fact, the case; for the point was a favorite resting-place for the " chiguires," or " capivaras," on their passage to and from the water. There were tracks of tapirs, too, and peccaries, and many sorts of wading birds, that had been there while the mud was still soft.

There were no trees to which to hang their hammocks; but the ground was smooth and dry, and they could sleep well enough upon it. They would not be troubled with the bats, as these creatures keep mostly in the dark, shadowy places of the forest; and snakes would not likely be found out on the bare ground. They thought they would there be safer from jaguars

too. In fact it was from these considerations that
they had chosen the place for their camp. They
could go to the woods for an armful or two of sticks
to cook supper with, and that would suffice.

The balza was brought close in on the upper side
of the promontory, so as to be out of the current;
and then all landed and made their preparations for
passing the night. Guapo marched off with his axe
to get some firewood, and Leon accompanied him, to
assist in carrying it. They had not far to go — only
a hundred yards or so; for up at the end of the
promontory the forest began, and there were both
large trees and underwood.

As they walked forward one species of trees caught
their attention. They were palm trees, but of a sort
they had not yet met with. They were very tall,
with a thick, globe-shaped head of pinnate, plume-
like leaves. But what rendered these trees peculiar
was the stem. It was slender in proportion to the
height of the tree, and was thickly covered with long
needle-shaped spines, not growing irregularly, but set
in bands, or rings, around the tree. This new palm
was the " pupunha," or " peach palm," as it is called,
from the resemblance which its fruits bear to peaches.
It is also named " pirijao " in other parts of South
America, and it belongs to the genus "*Gullielma*."

At the tops of these trees, under the great globe
of leaves, Guapo and Leon perceived the nuts. They
were hanging in clusters, as grapes grow; but the
fruits were as large as apricots, of an oval, triangular shape, and of a beautiful reddish-yellow color.
That they were delicious eating, either roasted or

boiled, Guapo well knew ; and he was determined
that some of them should be served at supper. But
how were they to be reached ? No man could climb
such a tree as they grew upon. The needles would
have torn the flesh from any one who should have
attempted it.

Guapo knew this. He knew, moreover, that the
Indians, who are very fond of the fruit of this tree,
— so much so that they plant large *palmares* of it
around their villages, — have a way of climbing it to
get at the ripe clusters. They tie cross pieces of
wood from one tree to the other, and thus make a sort
of step ladder, by which they ascend to the fruit. It
is true they might easily cut down the trees, as the
trunks are not very thick ; but that would be killing
the goose that gave the golden eggs. Guapo, however, had no further interest in this wild orchard than
to make it serve his turn for that one night ; so, lay-
ing his axe to one of the " pupunhas," he soon levelled its majestic stem to the ground. Nothing more
remained than to lop off the clusters, any one of
which was as much as Leon could lift from the ground.
Guapo found the wood hard enough even in its green
state ; but when old it becomes black, and is then so
hard that it will turn the edge of an axe. There is,
perhaps, no wood in all South America harder than
that of the pirijao palm.

It is with the needle-like spines of this species that
many tribes of Indians puncture their skins in tattoo-
ing themselves ; and other uses are made by them of
different parts of this noble tree. The macaws, parrots, and other fruit-eating birds are fonder of the

nuts of the pupunha than perhaps any other species ; and so, too, would be the fruit-eating quadrupeds if they could get at them. But the thorny trunk renders them quite inaccessible to all creatures without wings, excepting man himself. No ; there is one other exception, and that is a creature closely allied to man ; I mean the *monkey*. Notwithstanding the thorny stem, which even man cannot scale without a contrivance, — notwithstanding the apparently inac‑ cessible clusters, inaccessible from their great height, — there is a species of monkey that manages now and then to get a meal of them. How do these mon‑ keys manage it ? Not by climbing the stem, for the thorns are too sharp even for them. How then ? Do the nuts fall to the ground and allow the monkeys to gather them ? No ; this is not the case. How then ? We shall see.

Guapo and Leon had returned to the camp, taking with them the pupunha fruit and the firewood. A fire was kindled, the cooking pot hung over it on a tripod, and they all sat around to wait for its boiling.

While thus seated, an unusual noise reached their ears, coming from the woods. There were parrots and macaws among the palms, making noise enough and fluttering about ; but it was not these. The noise that had arrested the attention of our travellers was a mixture of screaming, and chattering, and howling, and barking, as if there were fifty sorts of creatures at the making of it. The bushes, too, were heard " switching about ; " and now and then a dead branch would crack, as if snapped suddenly. To a stranger in these woods, such a blending of sounds would have appeared very mysterious and inexplicable. Not so to our party. They knew it was only a troop of monkeys passing along upon one of their journeys. From their peculiar cries, Guapo knew what kind of monkeys they were.

" *Marimondas,*" he said.

The marimondas are not true " howlers," although they are of the same tribe as the " howling monkeys," (*Stentor.*) They belong to the genus *Ateles*, so called because they want the thumb, and are therefore *imperfect* or *unfinished* as regards the hands. But what the ateles want in hands is supplied by another member — the tail; and this they have to all perfection. It is to them a fifth hand, and apparently more useful than the other four. It assists them very materially in travelling through the tree tops. They use it to bring objects nearer them. They use it to suspend themselves in a state of repose, and thus suspended they sleep; nay, more; thus suspended they often die! Of all the monkey tribe, the ateles are those that have most prehensile power in their tails.

There are several species of them known; the coaita, the whitefaced, the black cayou, the beelzebub, the chamek, the blackhanded, and the marimonda. The habits of all are very similar, though the species differ in size and color.

The marimonda is one of the largest of South American monkeys, being about three feet standing upon its hind legs, with a tail of immense length, thick and strong near the root, and tapering to a point. On its under side, for the last foot or so from the end, there is no hair, but a callous skin; and this is the part used for holding on to the branches. The marimonda is far from being a handsome monkey. Its long, thin arms and thumbless hands give it an attenuated appearance, which is not relieved by the immense disproportioned tail. It is reddish, or of a parched coffee color, on the upper part of the body, which becomes blanched on the throat, belly, and insides of the thighs. Its color, in fact, is somewhat of the hue of the half blood Indian and negro; hence the marimonda is known in some parts of Spanish America by the name of "mono zambo," or "zambo" monkey; a "zambo" being the descendant of Indian and negro parents.

The noise made by the marimondas which had been heard by our party seemed to proceed from the bank of the river, some distance above the promontory; but it was evidently growing louder every minute, and they judged that the monkeys were approaching.

In a few minutes they appeared in sight, passing along the upper part of a grove of trees that stood close to the water. Our travellers had now an excellent view of them, and they sat watching them with interest. Their mode of progression was extremely curious. They never came to the ground, but where the branches interlocked they ran from one to the other with the lightning speed of squirrels, or, indeed, like birds upon the wing. Sometimes, however, the boughs stood far apart. Then the marimonda, running out as far as the branch would bear him, would warp a few inches of his tail around it, and spring off into the air. In the spring he would give himself such an impetus as would cause the branch to revolve; and his body following this circular motion, with the long, thin arms thrown out in front, he would grasp the first branch that he could reach. This, of course, would land him on a new tree, and over that he would soon spring to the next.

Among the troop several females were perceived with their young. The latter were carried on the backs of the mothers, where they held on by means of their own little tails, feeling perfectly secure. Sometimes the mothers would dismount them, and cause them to swing themselves from branch to branch, going before to show them the way. This was witnessed repeatedly. In other places, where the intervening space was too wide for the females with their young to pass over, the males could be seen bending down a branch of the opposite tree, so as to bring it nearer and assist them in crossing. All these movements were performed amidst a constant gabble of conversation, and shouting, and chattering, and the noise of branches springing back to their places.

The grove through which the troop was passing ended just by the edge of the promontory. The palm trees succeeded, with some trees of large size that grew over them.

The marimondas at length reached the margin of the grove, and then they were all seen to stop, most of them throwing themselves heads down, and hang-ing only by their tails. This is the position in which they find themselves best prepared for any immediate action; and it is into this attitude they throw them-

17

selves when suddenly alarmed. They remained so for some minutes; and, from the chattering carried on among them, it was evident that they were engaged in deliberation. A loud and general scream proclaimed the result; and all of them, at one and the same instant, dropped down to the ground, and were seen crossing over among the palm trees.

They had to pass over a piece of open ground with only some weeds upon it; but their helplessness on the ground was at once apparent. They could not place their palms on the surface, but doubled them up, and walked, as it were, on the backs of their hands, in the most awkward manner. Every now and again they flung out their great tails, in hopes of grasping something that would help them along; and even a large weed was a welcome support to them. On the ground they were evidently "out of their element." In fact the *ateles* rarely descend from the trees, which are their natural *habitat*.

At length they reached the palms, and, seated in various attitudes, looked up at the tempting fruit, all the while chattering away. How were they to reach it? Not a tree that was not covered with long needles; not a bunch of the luscious fruit that was not far above the height of the tallest marimonda. How were they to get at it? That was the question. It might have been a puzzling question to so many boys — to the monkeys it was not; for in less than a score of seconds they had settled it in their minds how the pupunhas were to be plucked.

Rising high over the palms grew a large tree, with

long, outreaching branches. It was the "zamang" tree — a species of *mimosa*, and one of the most beautiful trees of South America. Its trunk rose full seventy feet without a branch; and then it spread out in every direction, in numerous horizontal limbs, that forked and forked again until they became slender boughs. These branches were clad with the delicate pinnate leaves that characterize the family of the mimosas.

Many of the pupunha palms grew under the shadow of this zamang, but not the tallest ones. These were farther out. There were some, however, whose tufted crowns reached within a few yards of the lower limbs of the mimosa.

The monkeys, after a short consultation, were seen scampering up the zamang. Only some of the old and strong ones went; the rest remained watching below.

From the earnestness of their looks it was evident they felt a lively interest in the result. So, too, did the party of travellers; for these watched so closely that the pot was in danger of boiling over.

The marimondas, having climbed the trunk, ran out upon the lowermost limbs until they were directly above the palms. Then one or two were seen to drop off and hang down by their tails. But although, with their fore arms at full stretch, they hung nearly five feet from the branch, they could not even touch the highest fronds of the palms, much less the fruit clusters that were ten or twelve feet farther down. They made repeated attempts, suspending themselves over the very tallest palms; but all to no purpose.

One would have supposed they would have given
it up as a bad job. So thought Doña Isidora, Leon,
and the little Leona. Don Pablo knew better by his
reading, and Guapo by his experience. When they
saw that no one of them could reach the nuts, several
were seen to get together on one of the branches.
After a moment one dropped down head foremost, as
before, and hung at his full length. Another ran
down the body of this one, and, taking a turn of his
tail round his neck and fore arm, skipped off and
also hung head downwards. A third joined himself
on to the second in a similar manner, and then a
fourth. The fore arms of the fourth rested upon the
fruit cluster of the pupunha.

The chain was now long enough for the purpose.
In a few minutes the last monkey on the chain, with
his teeth and hands, had separated the footstalk of
the spathes, and the great clusters — two of them
there were — fell heavily to the bottom of the tree.
The marimondas on the ground ran forward, and, in
the midst of loud rejoicings, began to pull off the
" peaches " and devour them.

But the monkeys above did not cease their labors.
There were many mouths to feed, and they wanted
more nuts. Without changing their position, they,
by means of their arms and legs, threw themselves
into a vibrating motion, and by this means the last on
the string soon seized upon another pupunha, and also
detacned its fruit. In this way they continued until
they nad stripped every tree within their reach ; when,
judging they had got enough, the lowermost monkey
climbed back upon himself, then up his companions

to the branch, and in the same style was followed by the other three in succession. As soon as they were clear of one another, the whole party came down by the trunk to the ground, and joined their comrades below in the luxurious repast

CHAPTER XXXVI.

THE MONKEY MOTHER.

Now, you will perhaps imagine that Guapo, having sat so quiet during all this scene, had no desire for a bit of roast monkey to supper. In that fancy, then, you would be quite astray from the truth. Guapo had a *strong* desire to eat roast marimonda that very night; and, had he not been held back by Don Pablo, he would never have allowed the monkeys to get quietly out of the zamang ; for, it being an iso-lated tree, it would have afforded him a capital op-portunity of " treeing " them. His blow gun had been causing his fingers to itch all the time ; and, as soon as Don Pablo and the rest were satisfied with observing the monkeys, Guapo set out, blow gun in hand, followed by Leon.

There was no cover by which he might approach the group ; and therefore no course was left for him but to run up as quickly forward as possible and take his chance of getting a shot as they made off.

This course he pursued ; but, before he was within any thing like fair range, the monkeys, uttering their shrill screams, scampered over the open ground much faster than before, and took to the grove from which they had approached the spot.

Guapo followed at a slashing pace, and was soon

under the trees, Leon at his heels. Here they were met by a shower of sticks, pieces of bark, half-eaten "peaches," and something that was far less pleasant to their olfactory nerves. All these came from the tops of the trees, — the very tallest ones, — to which the monkeys had retreated, and where they were now hidden among the llianas and leaves.

You may fancy that it is easy to pursue a troop of monkeys in a forest. But it is not easy — in most cases it is not *possible.* The tangled underwood below puts a stop to the chase at once, as the monkeys can make their way through the branches above much quicker than the hunter can through the creeping plants below.

The pursuit would have been all up with Guapo, for the marimondas had soon got some way beyond the edge of the grove ; but, just as he was turning to sulk back, his keen Indian eye caught sight of one that was far behind the rest — so far, indeed, that it seemed determined to seek its safety rather by hiding than by flight. It had got under cover of a bunch of leaves ; and there it lay quiet, uttering neither sound nor syllable. Guapo could just see a little bit of its side, and at this in an instant the gravatána was pointed. Guapo's chest and cheeks were seen to swell out to their fullest extent, and off went the arrow. A shriek followed ; the monkey was hit, beyond a doubt. Guapo coolly waited the result.

A movement was visible among the leaves ; the marimonda was seen to turn and double about, and pluck something from its side ; and then the broken arrow came glancing among the twigs and fell to the ground. The monkey was now perceived to be twisting and writhing upon the branches ; and its wild death scream was answered by the voices of the others farther of.

At length its body was seen more distinctly ; it no longer thought of concealment, but lay out along the limb; and the next moment it dropped off. It did not fall to the ground though ; it had no design of gratifying its cruel destroyer to that extent. No; it merely dropped to the end of its tail, which, lapped over the branch, held it suspended. A few convulsive vibrations followed, and it hung down dead.

Guapo was thinking in what way he might get it down ; for he knew that, unless he could reach it by some means, it would hang there until the weather rotted it off, or until some preying bird or the tree ants had eaten it. He thought of his axe. The tree was not a very thick one, and it was a softwood tree. It would be worth the labor of cutting it down.

He was about turning away to get the axe, when his eye was attracted by the motion of some object near the monkey.

" Another ! " he muttered ; and, sure enough, another — a little tiny creature — ran out from among the leaves, and, climbing down the tail and body of the one already shot, threw its arms around her neck and whined piteously. It was the young one. Guapo had shot the mother.

The sight filled Leon with pity and grief ; but Guapo knew nothing of these sentiments. He had already inserted another arrow into his gravatána, and was raising the tube to bend it, when all at once there was a loud rustling among the leaves above. A large marimonda, that had returned from the band, was seen springing out upon the branch. He was the husband and father.

He did not pause a moment. Instinct or quick perception taught him that the female was dead. His object was to save the young one.

He threw his long tail down, and, grasping the little creature in its firm hold, jerked it upward, and then, mounting it on his back, bore it off among the branches.

All this passed so quickly that Guapo had not time to deliver his second arrow. Guapo saw them no more.

The Indian, however, was not to be cheated out of his supper of roast monkey. He walked quietly back for his axe, and, bringing it up, soon felled the tree, and took the marimonda mother with him to the camp.

His next affair was to skin it, which he did by stripping the pelt from the head, arms, legs, and all ; so that, after being skinned, the creature bore a most hideous resemblance to a child.

The process of cooking came next ; and this Guapo made more tedious than it might have been, as he was resolved to dress the marimonda after the manner practised by the Indians, and which by them is esteemed the best. He first built a little stage out of split laths of the pupunha palm. For this a hard wood that will resist fire a long time is necessary ; and the pupunha was just the thing. Under this stage Guapo kindled a fire of dry wood and upon

the laths he placed his monkey in a sitting posture
with its arms crossed in front and its head resting
upon them. The fire was then blown upon until it
became a bright blaze, which completely enveloped
the half-upright form of the monkey. There was
plenty of smoke ; but this is nothing in the eyes of a
South American Indian, many of whom prefer the
" smoky flavor " in a roast monkey.

Guapo had now no more to do but wait patiently
until the body should be reduced to a black and
charred mass ; for this is the condition in which it is
eaten by these strange people. When thus cooked,
the flesh becomes so dry that it will keep for months
without spoiling.

The white people who live in the *monkey countries*
eat roast monkey as well as the Indians. Many of
them, in fact, grow very fond of it. They usually
dress it, however, in a different manner. They take
off the head and hands before bringing it to the table ;
so that the " childlike " appearance is less perceptible.

Some species of monkeys are more delicate food
than others ; and there are some kinds that *white*
monkey eaters will not touch.

As for the Indians, it seems with them to be " all
fish," &c. ; and they devour all kinds indifferently,
whether they be " howlers," or " ateles," or " capuchins," or " ouistitis," or " sajous," or " sakis," or
whatever sort. In fact, among many Indian tribes
monkey stands in the same place that mutton does in
England, and they consider it their staple article of
flesh meat. Indeed, in these parts no other animal
is so common as the monkey ; and, with the excep-

tion of birds and fish, they have little chance of getting any other species of animal food. The best
" Southdown " would perhaps be as distasteful to
them as monkey meat would be to you ; so here
again we are met by that same eternal proverb —
" *Chacun à son goût.*"

CHAPTER XXXVII.

AN UNEXPECTED GUEST.

GUAPO sat by the fire patiently awaiting the " doing " of the marimonda. The rest had eaten their
supper, and were seated some distance apart. They
were looking out upon the broad river, and watching
the movements of the various birds. They could see
tall scarlet flamingoes on the farther shore, and
smaller birds of the ibis kind. They could see the
" tiger crane," so called from its color and spots resembling the markings of the jaguar. Among some
tall canes on the banks the " ciganos," or gypsy birds,
fluttered about with their great crest, looking like so
many pheasants, but far inferior to these creatures in
their flesh. In fact, the flesh of the " cigano " is so
bitter and disagreeable that even *Indians will not
eat it.*

Sitting upon a naked branch that projected over the
water, they noticed the solitary sky-blue kingfisher,
(*Alcedon.*) Over the water swept the great harpy
eagle — also a fisher like his whiteheaded cousin of
the north ; and now and then flocks of muscovy
ducks made the air resound with their strong, broad
wings.

They saw also the " boatbill," or " crabeater,"
(*Cancroma,*) a curious wading bird of the heron

kind, with a large bill shaped like two boats laid with
their concave sides against each other. This, like the
kingfisher, sat solitarily upon a projecting stump, now
and then dashing into the shallow water, and scoop-
ing up the small fishes, frogs, and crustacea with its
huge mandibles.

Another curious bird was observed, which had
something of the appearance of the water hen — to
which kind it is also assimilated in its habits. It was
the " faithful jacana," or " chuza," as it is called in
some places. There are several species of " jacana "
in South America, and also some species in the tropical countries of the East. That known as the
" faithful jacana " has a body about the size of a
common fowl ; but its legs and neck are longer, so
that, when standing, it is a foot and a half in height.
The body is of a brownish color ; and there is a crest
of twelve black feathers on the nape of the neck,
three inches in length. ˙At the bend of the wings
there are horny spurs, half an inch long, with which
the bird can defend itself when attacked. It is, however, a pacific bird, and only uses them in defence.
The most singular character of the jacana is its long
toes and claws. There are four upon each foot —
three in front, and one directed backwards ; and, when
standing, these cover a base nearly as large as the
body of the bird ; and, indeed, upon ordinary ground
they interfere with the freedom of its walking. But
these spreading feet were not designed for ordinary
ground. They were given it to enable it to pass
lightly over the leaves of waterlilies, and other yield-
ing surfaces, through which a narrow-footed bird

would at once sink. Of course, as Nature designed them for this purpose, they answer admirably, and the jacana skims along the surface of lily-covered ponds or streams without sinking. From the leaves it picks up such insects and larvæ as lodge there, and which form its principal food.

The jacana utters a singular cry when alarmed. It remains silent during the whole day, and also at night, unless disturbed by the approach of some danger, when it utters its "alarm cry." So quick is its ear that it can detect the least noise or rustling caused by any one approaching. For this reason some tribes of Indians have tamed the jacana, and use it as a sentinel or "watchdog," to apprise them of the approach of their enemies during the darkness of the night. Another use is also made of it by the Spanish Americans. It is tamed and allowed to go about along with the domestic poultry. When these are attacked by hawks or other birds of prey, the jacana defends them with its sharp wing spurs, and generally succeeds in beating off the enemy. It never deserts the flock, but accompanies it in all its movements and will defend its charge with great fury and courage.

Besides the water birds which were noticed by our travellers, many kinds were seen by them upon the shore and fluttering among the trees. There were parrots in flocks, and macaws in pairs — for these birds usually go in twos; there were trogons, and great-billed toucans, and their kindred the aracaris; and there, too, were "umbrella chatterers," of which there is a species quite white; and upon a fruit-

covered tree, not far off, they saw a flock of the
snow-white " bell birds," (*Casmarhynchos.*) These
are about as large as blackbirds, with broad bills,
from the base of which grows a fleshy tubercle that
hangs down to the length of nearly three inches, like
that of the turkey cock. The name of " bell birds "
is given to them on account of the clear, bell-like
ring of their note, which they utter about the middle
of the day, when most other creatures of the tropical
world are in silence or asleep.

Of course Don Pablo as a naturalist was interested
in all those birds, and observed their habits and movements with attention. There was none of them about
which he had not some strange story to tell ; and in
this way he was beguiling the after-supper hour. It
was too early for them to go to rest ; indeed, it was
not quite sunset ; and Guapo for one had not yet had
his supper, although that meal was now very near at
hand. The marimonda was becoming charred and
black, and would soon be ready for mastication.

Guapo sat by the fire, now and again raking up
the cinders with a long pole which he held in his
hand, while his eyes from time to time rested on the
marimonda that was directly in front of him, *vis-à-vis*.

At length the monkey appeared to him to be
" done to a turn ; ' and, with his *macheté* in one hand
and a forked stick in the other, he was just bending
forward to lift it off the fire, when to his horror the
ground was felt to move beneath him, causing him to
stagger, and almost throwing him from his feet !
Before he could recover himself, the surface again
heaved up, and a loud report was heard like the

explosion of some terrible engine ; then another up-
heaval — another report ; the ground opened into a
long fissure ; the staging of palms, and the half-burned
cinders, and the charred monkey were flung in all
directions, and Guapo himself went sprawling upon
his back.

Was it an earthquake ? So thought the others, who
were now on their feet running about in great consternation, the females screaming loudly. So, too,
thought Guapo for the moment.

Their belief in its being an earthquake, however,
was of short duration. The shocks continued, the
dried mud flew about in large pieces, and the burned
wood and splinters were showered in the air. The
smoke of these covered the spot and prevented a
clear view ; but through the smoke the terrified spec-
tators could perceive that some large body was in
motion, apparently struggling for life. In another
moment it broke through the bending stratum of mud,
causing a long rift ; and there was displayed before
their eyes the hideous form of a gigantic crocodile !

Though not quite so terrible as an earthquake, it
was a fearful monster to behold. It was one of the
largest, being nearly twenty feet in length, with a
body thicker than that of a man. Its immense jaws
were of themselves several feet long ; and its huge
tusks, plainly seen, gave it a most frightful appearance. Its mouth was thrown open, as though it
gasped for air ; and a loud bellowing proceeded from
its throat, that sounded like a cross between the
grunting of a hog and the lowing of a bull. The air
was filled with a strong musky odor, which ema-

nated from the body of the animal; and, what with
the noise made by the crocodile itself, the screams
and shouts of the party, the yelling of the various
birds, — for they, too, had taken up the cue, — there
was for some moments an utter impossibility of any
voice being heard above the rest. It was indeed a
scene of confusion. Don Pablo and his companions
were running to and fro, Guapo was tumbling about
where he had fallen, and the great lizard was writhing and flapping his tail; so that pots, pans, half-
burned fagots, and even Guapo's monkey, were being
knocked about in every direction.

Of course such a violent scene could not be of
long duration. It must end one way or the other.
Guapo, who soon came to himself, now that he saw
what it was that had pitched him over, had already
conceived a plan for terminating it. He ran for his
axe, which fortunately lay out of the range of the
crocodile's tail; and, having laid his hands upon it, he
approached in a stealthy manner, with the intention
of striking a blow. He directed himself towards the
root of the reptile's tail, for he knew that that was
the only place where a blow of the axe would cripple
it; but, just as he was getting within reach, the crocodile suddenly shifted himself round, making his tail
fly like a piece of sprung whalebone. Guapo leaped
hastily back — as hastily, I will make bold to say, as
any Indian of his years could have done, but not
quick enough to clear himself quite. He wanted
about eight inches; but in this case inches were as
good as miles for the crocodile's purpose; for about
eight inches of the tip of his tail came " smack '

18

across Guapo's naked shins, and sent the old Indian head over heels.

It was just an accident that Guapo's shanks were not broken like sticks of sealing wax; and, had the blow been directed with the crocodile's full force, such would have been the unhappy result. As it was, they were only " scratched ; " and Guapo, leaping to his feet, ran to recover his axe ; for that weapon had flown several yards out of his hands at the blow.

By the time he laid hold of it, however, the *saurian* was no longer on dry ground. His newly-opened eyes — opened perhaps for the first time for months — caught sight of the water close by ; and, crawling forward a step or two, he launched his ugly, mud-bedaubed carcass into the welcome element. The next moment he had dived and was out of sight.

CHAPTER XXXVIII.

THE CROCODILE AND CAPIVARAS.

GUAPO was in no humor for enjoying the conversation of that evening. The crocodile had "choused" him out of his favorite supper. The monkey was literally knocked to "smithereens;" and the pieces that still adhered together were daubed all over with mud. It wasn't fit meat even for an Indian; and Guapo had to content himself with a dried plantain and a stew of jerked horse flesh.

Of course Don Pablo and the rest examined with curiosity the great hole in the mud that had contained the crocodile. There it had lain during months of the dry season in a state of torpidity, and would, no doubt, have remained still longer, but that it was aroused by the big fire that Guapo had built over it. The irritation produced by this had been the cause of its sudden resurrection; for the crocodiles that thus bury themselves usually come out after the beginning of the heavy rains.

It was a true long-snouted crocodile, as Don Pablo had observed in the short opportunity he had had, and not an alligator; for it must be here remarked that the true crocodile is found in many parts of Spanish America, and also in many of the West India islands. For a long time it was believed that only alligators

existed in America, and that the crocodiles were confined to the Eastern continent. It is now known that
at least one species of crocodile is an American animal; and several distinct species of alligators are
inhabitants of the new world. There is the alligator of the Mississippi, which is the "caïman," or
"cayman," of the Spanish Americans; there is the
spectacled alligator, (*A. sclerops*,) a southern species,
so called from a pair of rings around its eyes, having
a resemblance to spectacles; and there is a still
smaller species called the "bava," which is found in
Lake Valencia and in many South American rivers.
The last kind is much hunted by the Indians, who,
although they eat parts of all these creatures, are
fonder of the flesh of the bava than of any of the
others.

They had not intended to keep watch this night, as
the naked promontory seemed to be a safe place to
sleep upon; but now, after their adventure with the
crocodile, they changed their minds, and they resolved
to mount guard as before. The monster might easily
crawl out of the water again; and, judging from the
size of his mouth, it is not improbable to suppose
that he might have swallowed one of the smaller individuals of the party at a single effort. Lest he might
return to use either his teeth or his tail, the watch was
set as on other nights — Leon taking the first turn,
Guapo the second, and Don Pablo sitting it out till
daybreak. The night passed through, however, without any unusual disturbance; and, although an occasional plunge was heard in the water close by, no
more was seen of the crocodile until morning.

I have said *until* morning — for he was seen then. Yes, indeed! That beauty was not going to let them off without giving them another peep at him—not he! They were awake and up before day; and as the fire had been kept burning all night, they had now nothing more to do than rake up the embers and hang on the coffee kettle. It was not yet bright day when breakfast was already cooked, and they sat down to eat it.

While engaged in this operation they noticed a string of flamingoes on the muddy promontory, at the end where it joined the land. They were ranged in line, like soldiers, some of them balanced on one long, thin leg, as these birds do. They appeared in the gray light to be unusually tall; but when it became a little clearer our travellers could perceive that they were not upon the ground, but standing upon an old log. This, of course, made them look taller. They were just in the very track by which Guapo and Leon had passed to get the wood the evening before. Now, neither Guapo nor Leon remembered any log. They were certain there was none there, else they would have cut it up for firewood; that was a sure thing; and it was very mysterious who could have rolled a log there during the night.

While discussing this point it became clearer; and, to the astonishment of all, what they had taken to be an old log turned out to be nothing else than their old friend the crocodile! I have said to the astonish-ment of all; that is not strictly correct. Guapo saw nothing to astonish him in that sight. He had wit nessed a similar one many a time ; and so does every one who travels either on the Amazon or the Orinoco.

These flamingoes were perfectly safe, so far as the crocodile was concerned, and they knew it. As long as they kept out of the reach of his jaws and tail he could not hurt them. Although he could bend himself to either side, so as to " kiss " the tip of his own tail, he could not reach any part of his back, exert himself as he might. This the flamingoes and other birds well know ; and these creatures, being fond of a place to perch upon, often avail themselves of the long serrated back of the crocodile, or the caïman.

As the day became brighter the flamingoes sat still — not appearing to be alarmed by the movements at the camp, which was about a hundred yards distant from their perch. It was likely they had never been frightened by the hunter ; for these birds in districts where they are hunted are exceedingly shy. All at once, however, as if by a given signal, the whole flock rose together, and flew off with loud screams. The crocodile, too, was seen to move ; but it was not this which had scared them off. It was after they had gone that he had stirred himself; and, even had it not been so, they would not have regarded his movements, as these birds are often seen perched upon a *crawling* crocodile !

No. Something else had affrighted them, and that was a noise in the bushes beyond, which was now distinctly heard at the camp. There was a rustling of leaves and a crackling of branches, as if more than one creature made the noise. So it appeared; for the next moment nearly a score of animals dashed out of the bushes and ran on towards the water.

These creatures were odd enough to fix the atten‐ tion of the party at the camp. They were about the size of small hogs, very much of the same build, and covered with a thin, sandy, bristly hair, just like some hogs are. They were not " pigheaded," however. Their heads were exactly like those of the gray rab‐ bit; and instead of hoofs, they were toed and clawed. This gave them altogether a lighter appearance than hogs, and yet they did not run as fast, although when first noticed they appeared to be doing their best.

Our travellers knew them at once; for they were animals that are common upon the rivers in all the warm parts of South America. They were " *capi‐ varas*," or " chiguires," as they are also called. These creatures are peculiar to the American conti‐ nent. They are, in fact, " guinea pigs " on a large scale, and bear the greatest resemblance to those well‐ known animals, except in size and color; for the capivaras are of a uniform sandy brown. They are of the same genus as the guinea pigs, though the sys‐ tematizers have put them into a separate one, and have also made a third genus to suit another ani‐ mal of very similar shape and habits. This is the " moco," which is between the guinea pig and capi‐ vara in size, and of a grayish-olive color. All three are natives of South America, and in their wild state are found only there; though from the absurd name, " guinea pig," you may be led to think that this little creature came originally from Africa.

The three are all " rodent " animals, and the capivara is the largest " rodent " that is known. It, moreover, is amphibious, quite as much so as the tapir;
and it is found only near the banks of rivers. It is
more at home in the water than on dry land, or perhaps it has more numerous enemies on land; though
— poor, persecuted creature! — it is not without some
in either element, as will be seen by what follows.

The drove of capivaras counted nearly a score ;
and they were making for the water as fast as their
legs could carry them. The crocodile lay directly
across their path ; but their black eyes, large and
prominent, seemed to be occupied with something
behind ; and they had run up almost against the body
of the reptile before they saw it. Uttering a sort of
squeak, they made a half pause. Some sprang up
and leaped over ; others attempted to go round. All
succeeded except one ; but the crocodile, on seeing
their approach, — no doubt it was for this he had
been in wait all the morning, — had thrown himself
into the form of a half moon ; and as they passed he
let fly at them. His powerful tail came " flap "
against the nearest, and it was pitched several yards,
where, after a kick or two, it lay upon its side, as
dead as a herring, a door nail, or even Julius Cæsar ;
take your choice.

CHAPTER XXXIX.

FIGHT OF THE JAGUAR AND CROCODILE.

THE chiguires that escaped past the crocodile the next instant plunged into the river, and disappeared under the water. They would come to the surface for breath in ten or twelve minutes, but at such a distance off that they needed no longer fear pursuit from the same enemy.

Our travellers took no notice of them from the moment they were fairly out of the bushes. They saw that the crocodile had knocked one of them over; but the eyes of Guapo and Don Pablo were directed upon a different place — the point at which the chiguires had sallied out of the underwood. These knew that the animals had not issued forth in their natural way, as if they were going to the stream to drink, or in search of food. No — quite different. Their bristles were erect — they were excited — they were terrified — beyond a doubt they were pursued !

Who or what was their pursuer ? It might be an ocelot, or the yaguarundi, or some one of the smaller cats ; for many of these prey on the defenceless capivara. It *might* be one of these, thought Don Pablo and Guapo ; but what if it was not ? What else could it be ? What else ? *The jaguar !*

It *was* the jaguar ! As they stood gazing with looks

full of apprehension, the leaves of the underwood were seen to move, and then a beautiful but terrible object, the spotted head of a jaguar, was thrust forth. It remained a moment as if reconnoitring ; and then the whole body, bright and glistening, glided clear of the leaves, and stood boldly out in front of the underwood. Here it halted another moment — only a moment. The crocodile had turned itself, and was about closing its jaws upon the body of the chiguire, when the jaguar, seeing this, uttered a loud scream, and, making one bound forward, seized the dead animal almost at the same instant.

They were now face to face — the great lizard and the great cat ; and their common prey was between them. Each had a firm hold with his powerful jaws, and each appeared determined to keep what he had got. The yellow eyes of the jaguar seemed to flash fire, and the black, sunken orbs of the saurian glared with a lurid and deadly light. It was a terrible picture to look upon.

For some seconds both remained apparently gazing into each other's eyes, and firmly holding the prey between them. The tail of the jaguar vibrated in sudden angry jerks, while that of the crocodile lay bent into a semicircle, as if ready to be sprung at a moment's notice.

This inaction did not last long. The fury of the jaguar was evidently on the increase. He was indignant that he, the king of the American forest, should thus meet with opposition to his will ; and, indeed, the crocodile was about the only creature in all the wide Montaña that dare oppose him in open fight

But he was determined to conquer even this enemy, and for that purpose he prepared himself.

Still holding on to the capivara, and watching his opportunity, he sprang suddenly forward, throwing one of his great paws far in advance. His object was to *claw the eye* of his adversary ; for 'he well knew that the latter was vulnerable neither upon its long snout, nor its gaunt jaws, nor even upon the tough scaly skin of its throat. Its eyes alone could be injured, and these were the objects of the jaguar's attack.

The thrust was a failure. The crocodile had anticipated such a manœuvre, and, suddenly raising himself on his fore legs, threw up one of his great scaly hands and warded off the blow. The jaguar, fearing to be clutched between the strong fore arms of the saurian, drew back to his former position.

This manœuvre and its counter manœuvre were repeated several times ; and although each time the struggle lasted a little longer than before, and there was a good deal of lashing of tails, and tearing of teeth, and scratching of claws, still neither of the combatants seemed to gain any great advantage., Both were now at the height of their fury, and a third enemy approaching the spot would not have been heeded by either.

From the first the head of the crocodile had been turned to the water, from which he was not distant over ten feet. He had, in fact, been carrying his prey towards it when he was interrupted by the attack of the jaguar ; and now at every fresh opportunity he was pushing on, bit by bit, in that direction. He knew that in his own proper element he would be more than a match for his spotted assailant, and no doubt he might have escaped from the contest by surrendering his prey. Had he been a smaller crocodile he would have been only too glad to have done so; but 'trusting to his size and strength, and perhaps not a little to the justice of his cause, he was determined not to go without taking the capivara along with him.

The jaguar, on the other hand, was just as determined he should not. He, too, had some rights. The capivara would not have been killed so easily had he not frightened it from behind; besides, the crocodile was out of his element. He was poaching on the domain of the forest monarch.

Bit by bit the crocodile was gaining ground — at each fresh pause in the struggle he was forging forward, pushing the chiguire before him, and of course causing his antagonist to make ground backwards.

The jaguar at length felt his hind feet in the water; and this seemed to act upon him like a shock of electricity. All at once he let go his hold of the capivara, ran a few feet forward, and then, flattening his body along the ground, prepared himself for a mighty spring. Before a second had passed, he launched his body high into the air, and descended upon the back of the crocodile just over his fore shoulders. He did not settle there, but ran nimbly down the back of the saurian towards its hinder part, and his claws could be heard rattling against its scaly skin. In a moment more he was seen close squatted along the crocodile's body, and with his teeth tearing fiercely at the root of its tail. He knew that, after the eyes, this was the most vulnerable part of his antagonist, and if he had been allowed but a few minutes' time he would soon have disabled the crocodile ; for to have seriously wounded the root of his tail, would have been to have destroyed his essential weapon of offence.

The jaguar would have succeeded had the encounter occurred only a dozen yards farther from the water. But the crocodile was close to the river's edge, and perceiving the advantage against him, and that there was no hope of dismounting his adversary, he dropped the capivara, and, crawling forward, plunged into the water. When fairly launched, he shot out from the shore like an arrow, carrying the jaguar along, and the next moment he had dived to the depth of the stream. The water was lashed into foam by the blows of his feet and tail ; but in the midst of the froth the yellow body of the jaguar was seen rising to the surface, and after turning once or twice, as if searching for his hated enemy, the creature headed for the bank and climbed out. He stood for a moment looking back into the stream. He appeared less cowed than angry and disappointed. He seemed to vow a future revenge ; and then seizing the half-torn carcass of the capivara, he threw it lightly over his shoulder and trotted off into the thicket.

Our travellers had not watched this scene either closely or continuously. They had been too busy all the time. From its commencement they had been doing all in their power to get away from the spot ;

for they dreaded lest the jaguar might either first overpower the crocodile and then attack them, or, being beaten off by the latter, might take it into his head to revenge himself by killing whatever he could. With these apprehensions, therefore, they had hastily carried every thing aboard, and, drawing in their cable, pushed the balza from the shore. When the fight came to an end, they had got fairly into the current, and, just as the jaguar disappeared, the raft was gliding swiftly down the broad and rippling stream.

CHAPTER XL.

ADVENTURE WITH AN ANACONDA.

For several days they voyaged down stream, with-out any occurrence of particular interest. Once or twice they saw Indians upon the shore ; but these, in-stead of putting off in their canoes, seemed fright-ened·at so large a craft, and remained by their " ma-loccas," or great village houses, in each of which sev-eral families live together. Not caring to have any dealings with them, our travellers were only too glad to get past without molestation ; and, therefore, when they ·passed any place where they thought they ob-served the signs of Indians on the bank, they kept on for hours after without stopping.

A curious incident occurred one evening as they were bringing the balza to her moorings, which com-pelled them to drop a little farther down stream, and, in fact, almost obliged them to float all night, which would have been a dangerous matter, as the current at the place happened to be sharp and rapid.

They had been on the lookout for some time for a good camping-place, as it was their usual hour to stop.

No opening, however, appeared for several miles. The banks on both sides were thickly wooded to the river's edge, and the branches of the trees even drooped into the water. At length they came in sight of a natural raft that had been formed by driftwood in a bend of the stream; and as the logs lay thickly together, and even piled upon each other, it appeared an excellent place to encamp on. It was, at all events, better than to attempt to penetrate the thick iungles which met them every where else · and so the balza was directed towards the raft, and soon floated alongside it.

They had already got ashore on the raft, which was dry and firm, and would have served their purpose well enough; when, all at once, Guapo was heard uttering one of those exclamations which showed that all was not right. The rest looked towards him for an explanation. He was standing by the edge of the floating timber, just where the balza touched it, with his arms stretched out in an attitude that betokened trouble. They all ran up. They saw what was the matter at a glance. Thousands of red ants were climbing from the raft to the balza! Thousands — nay, it would be nearer the truth to say millions!

At one glance Don Pablo saw that it would be a terrible calamity should these creatures gain a lodgment on the balza. Not only were they the dreaded stinging ants, but in a short time nothing on board would be left. In a few hours they would have eaten all his stores — his bark, his vanilla, and his roots. Already quite a number had got upon the canoe, and were crossing it towards the body of the balza.

Without saying another word, he ordered all to get on board as quickly as possible, each taking some utensil that had already been carried on shore. He and Guapo flew to the poles; and, having hastily unfastened and drawn in the cable, they pushed the balza out into the stream; then, while Guapo managed the great oar, Don Pablo, assisted by Leon and by Doña Isidora, went to work with scoops and pails, dashing water upon the ants, until every one of them had disappeared, drowned in the canoe or washed off into the river. Fortunate for them, they had observed this strange enemy in time. Had they not done so, — in other words, had they gone to sleep, leaving the balza where it was during the night, — they would have awakened in the morning to find their stores completely destroyed — their labor of a year brought to nothing in the space of a single night. This is no uncommon occurrence to the merchant or the colonist of tropical America.

They had made a narrow escape, but a fortunate one. They were not without their troubles, however. No open ground could be found for miles below; and, as it was growing dark, they approached the thickly-wooded bank, and, after a good deal of scratching among the branches, at length succeeded in making the cable fast to a tree. The balza then swung round and floated at the end of the cable, half of it being buried under the long, hanging branches.

They spent their night on board ; for it was no use attempting to get on shore through the underwood ; and even if they had, they could not have encamped very comfortably in a thicket. On the other hand, the balza did not afford the best accommodation for sleeping. The little " toldo," or cabin, was not large enough to swing a hammock in. It would only

19

contain a few persons seated close together; and it had been built more for the purpose of keeping the sun off during the hot hours of the day than for sleeping in. The rest of the balza was occupied with the freight; and this was so arranged, with sloping sides, thatched with the bussu leaves, that there was no level place where one could repose upon it. The night, therefore, was passed without very much sleep having been obtained by any one of the party. Of course, the moment the first streaks of day began to appear along the eastern sky, they were all awake and ready to leave their disagreeable anchorage.

As they were making preparations to untie the cable, they noticed that just below where the balza lay a horizontal limb stretched far out over the river. It was the lowermost limb of a large zamang tree that stood on the bank close to the edge of the water. It was not near the surface, but a good many feet above. Still it was not certain that it was high enough for the roof of the toldo to clear it. That was an important question; for, although the current was not very rapid just there, it was sufficiently so to carry the balza under this branch before they could push it out into the stream. Once the cable was let go, they must inevitably pass under the limb of the zamang; and, if that caught the toldo, it would sweep off the frail roof like so much spider's web This would be a serious damage, and one to be avoided if possible.

Don Pablo and Guapo went to the end of the balza nearest the branch, and stood for some time surveying it. It was about eight or ten yards distant ; but in the gray dawn they could not judge correctly of its height, and they waited till it grew a little clearer. At length they came to the conclusion that the branch was high enough. The long pendulous leaves — characteristic of this great *mimosa* — and the droop-ing branchlets hung down much below the main shaft ; but these, even if they touched the roof, would do no injury. It was therefore determined to let go the cable.

It was now clear day, for they had been delayed a good while ; but at length all was ready, and Guapo untied the cable and drew the end on board. The balza began to move, slowly at first, for the current under the bushes was very slight.

All at once the attention of the voyagers was called to the strange conduct of the pet monkey. That little creature was running to and fro, first upon the roof of the toldo, then down again, all the while uttering the most piercing shrieks, as if something was biting off its tail. It was observed to look for-ward and upward towards the branch of the zamang, as if the object it dreaded was in that quarter. The eyes of all were suddenly bent in the same direction. What was their horror on beholding, stretched along the branch, the hideous body of an enormous ser-pent ! Only part of it could be seen ; the hinder half and the tail were bidden among the bromelias and vines that in huge masses clustered around the trunk of the zamang, and the head was among the leaflets of the mimosa ; but what they saw was enough to convince them that it was·a snake of the

largest size — the great *"water boa"* — the anaconda !

That part of the body in sight was full as thick as
a man's thigh, and covered with black spots, or
blotches, upon a ground of dingy yellow. It was seen
to glisten as the animal moved ; for the latter was in
motion, crawling along the branch *outward !* The
next moment its head appeared under the pendulous
leaves ; and its long, forking tongue, protruding several inches from its mouth, seemed to feel the air in
front of it. This tongue kept playing backwards and
forwards, and its viscid covering glittered under the
sunbeam, adding to the hideous appearance of the
monster.

To escape from passing within its reach would be
impossible. The balza was gliding directly under it.
It could launch itself aboard at will ; it could seize
upon any one of the party without coming from the
branch ; it could coil its body around them and crush
them with the constricting power of its muscles. It
could do all this ; for it had crushed before now the
tapir, the roebuck, perhaps even the jaguar himself.

All on board the boat knew its dangerous power
too well ; and of course terror was visible in every
countenance.

Don Pablo seized the axe, and Guapo laid hold of
his *macheté.* Doña Isidora, Leon, and the little
Leona were standing — fortunately they were — by
the door of the toldo ; and, in obedience to the cries
and hurried gestures of Don Pablo and the Indian,
they rushed in and flung themselves down. They
had scarcely disappeared inside when the forward

part of the balza, upon which stood Don Pablo and Guapo, came close to the branch, and the head of the serpent was on a level with their own. Both aimed their blows almost at the same instant; but their footing was unsteady; the boa drew back at the moment, and both missed their aim. The next moment the current had carried them out of reach, and they had no opportunity of striking a second blow.

The moment they had passed the hideous head again dropped down, and hung directly over, as if waiting. It was a moment of intense anxiety to Don Pablo. His wife and children! Would it select one as its victim and leave the others, or ——

He had but little time for reflection. Already the head of the snake was within three feet of the toldo door. Its eyes were glaring; it was about to dart down.

"O God, have mercy!" exclaimed Don Pablo, falling upon his knees. "O God!"

At that moment a loud scream was heard. It came from the toldo; and at the same instant the saïmiri was seen leaping out from the door. Along with the rest, it had taken shelter within; but, just as the head of the snake came in sight, a fresh panic seemed to seize upon it, and, as if under the influence of fascination, it leaped screaming in the direction of the terrible object. It was met half way. The wide jaws closed upon it, its shrieks were stifled, and the next moment its silken body, along with the head of the anaconda, disappeared among the leaves of the mimosa. Another moment passed, and the balza swept clear of the branch and floated triumphantly into the open water.

Don Pablo sprang to his feet, ran into the toldo, and, after embracing his wife and children, knelt down and offered thanks to God for their almost miraculous deliverance.

CHAPTER XLI.

A BATCH OF CURIOUS TREES.

OF course the escape from danger so imminent, after the first moments were over, produced a sort of reaction in the feelings of all, and they were now rather joyous than otherwise. But with all there was a mixture of regret when they thought of the fate of little " titi." It had been their only pet, and had grown to be such a favorite that its loss was now mourned by every one ; and its absence caused them to feel as though one of the company had been left behind. Several times during that day poor " titi " was the subject of conversation ; indeed, they could hardly talk about any thing else. Little Leona was quite inconsolable ; for the pretty creature had loved Leona, and used to perch on her shoulder by the hour, and draw her silken ringlets through its tiny hand, and place its dainty little nose against the rich velvet of her cheek, and play off all sorts of antics with her ears. Many an hour did " titi " and Leona spend together. No wonder that the creature was missed.

During the whole of that day they travelled through a country covered with dense forest. The river was a full half mile wide ; but sometimes there were islands, and then the current became narrowed on each side, so that, in passing, the balza almost touched the trees on one side or the other. They saw many kinds of trees growing together, and rarely a large tract covered with any one species of timber; for this, as already remarked, is a peculiarity of the Amazon forests. Many new and curious trees were noticed, of which Don Pablo gave short botanical descriptions to the others, partly to instruct them and partly to while away the hours. Guapo, at the rudder, listened to these learned lectures, and sometimes added some information of his own about the properties of the trees, and the uses to which they were put by the Indians. This is what is termed the popular part of the science of botany; and perhaps it is more important than the mere classification of genera and species, which is usually all the information that you get from the learned and systematic botanists.

Among the trees passed to-day was one called the "volador," (*gyrocarpus.*) This is a large forest tree, with lobed leaves, of a heart shape. But it is the seeds which are curious, and which give to the tree the odd name of "volador," or "flier." These seeds have each a pair of membranaceous and striated wings, which, when the seeds fall, are turned to meet the air at an angle of forty-five degrees; and thus a rotatory motion is produced, and the falling seeds turn round and round like little fly wheels. It is altogether a curious sight, when a large volador is shaken in calm weather, to see the hundreds of seeds whirling and wheeling towards the ground, which they take a considerable time in reaching. The volador is not confined to South America; I have seen it in Mexico and other parts of North America.

Another singular tree noticed was a tree of the barberry family, (*berberis*,) known among the Spanish Americans as *barba de tigre*, or "tiger's beard." This name it derives from the fact of its trunk — which is very large and high — being thickly set all over with sharp branching thorns, that are fancied to resemble the whiskers of the jaguar, or South American "tiger."

A third remarkable tree (or bush) observed was the *Bixa orellana*, which yields the well-known *arnatto* dye. This bush is ten or twelve feet in height, and its seeds grow in a burlike pericarp. These seeds are covered with a reddish pulp, which produces the dye. The mode of making it is simple. The Indian women throw the seeds into a vessel of hot water, and stir them violently for about an hour, until they have taken off the pulp. The water is then poured off, and the deposit, separated from the seeds, is mixed with oil of turtle eggs, or crocodile fat, and kneaded into cakes of three or four ounces' weight. It is then "anoto," sometimes written "arnatto," sometimes "arnotto," sometimes "onoto," and sometimes "anato." The first is the proper spelling. In Brazil it is called "urucu," whence the French name "rocou;" and the Peruvians have still another designation for it—"achoté." Of course each tribe of Indians calls it by a separate name. The botanic name, *Bixa*, is the ancient name by which it

was known to the Indians of Hayti; for it is found in
most parts of tropical America growing wild, although
it is also cultivated.   It is an article in great demand
among all the Indians of South America, who use it
for painting their bodies and dyeing the cotton cloth
of which they make their garments.

But these people are very skilful in drawing pig-
ments from plants and trees of many kinds; in fact,
their practical chemistry, so far as it relates to dyes
and poisons, is quite surprising; and from time to
time Guapo pointed out trees that were used by them
for such purposes.

One was a climbing plant, whose tendrils reached
to the tops of the highest trees.   It had beautiful violet-colored flowers, an inch long; and Don Pablo saw
that it was a species of *bignonia.*   Guapo called it
" chica."   When in fruit, it carries a pod two feet in
length, full of winged seeds.   But Guapo said it was
not from the seeds that the dye was obtained, but
from the leaves, which turn red when macerated in
water.   The coloring matter comes out of the leaves
in the form of a light powder, and is then shaped
into cakes, which sell among the Indians for the value
of a dollar each.   This color has a tinge of lake in
it, and is prized even more highly than the anoto.
Indeed red dyes among all savage nations seem to
hold a higher value than those of any other color.

Another dye tree was the " huitoc."   This one is
a slender tree, about twenty feet high, with broad
leaves shooting out from the stem, and nuts growing
at their bases, after the manner of the bread fruit.

These nuts resemble black walnuts, and are of a russet color outside; but the pulp inside, which produces the huitoc, is of a dark-blue, or purple tint.

The " wild indigo tree " was also seen growing in the woods, with a leaf narrow at the base and broad at the extremity. With these and many other dyes the Indians of the Montaña paint their bodies in fan tastic modes. So much are they addicted to these customs, that, among the Indians who labor at the missions, some have been known to work nearly a month to procure paint enough to give their body a single coat, and the missionaries have made a merchandise of this gigantic folly. But the paint is not always to be looked upon in the light of a mere folly or vanity. Sometimes it is used to keep off the " zancudos," or mosquitoes, so numerous and annoying in these regions.

Another singular tree was observed, which Guapo called the " marima," or "shirt tree." The use of this he explained. The tree stands fifty or sixty feet high, with a diameter of from two to three. When they find them of this size the Indians cut them down, and then separate the trunk into pieces of about three feet long. From these pieces they strip the bark, but without making any longitudinal incision, so that the piece of bark when taken off is a hollow cylinder. It is thin and fibrous, of a red color, and looks like a piece of coarsely-woven sackcloth. With this the shirt is made, simply by cutting two holes in the sides to admit the arms; and the body being passed into it, it is worn in time of rain. Hence the saying of the old missionaries, that in the

" forests of America garments were found ready made on the trees."

Many other trees were noticed, valuable for their fruits, or leaves, or bark, or roots, or their wood. There was the well-known " seringa," or India rubber tree ; the great courbaril, the " dragon's blood " tree, not that celebrated tree of the East, (*Dracæna*,) but one of a different genus, (*Croton*,) from whose white bark flows a red, bloodlike juice.

They saw, also, a species of cinnamon tree, (*Laurus cinnamonoides*,) though not the cinnamon of commerce ; the large tree that bears the Brazilian nutmeg, (the Puxiri ;) and that one, also, — a large forest tree, — that bears the nuts known as " Tonka beans," and which are used in the flavoring of snuff.

But of all the trees which our travellers saw on that day, none made such an impression upon them as the " juvia," or Brazil nut tree, (*Bertholletia excelsa*.) This tree is not one with a thick trunk ; in fact, the largest ones are not three feet in diameter ; but it rises to a height of one hundred and twenty feet. Its trunk is branchless for more than half that height, and the branches then spread out and droop, like the fronds of the palm. They are naked near their bases, but loaded towards the top with tufts of silvery-green leaves, each two feet in length. The tree does not blossom until its fifteenth year, and then it bears violet-colored flowers ; although there is another species, the . " sapucaya," which has yellow ones. But it is neither the trunk, nor the branches, nor the leaves, nor yet the flowers of this tree that render it such an object of curiosity. It is the great woody and spherical pericarps that contain the nuts or fruits that are wonderful. These are often as large as the head of a child, and as hard as the shell of the cocoa nut! Inside is found a large number — twenty or more — of those triangular-shaped nuts which you may buy at any Italian warehouse under the name of " Brazil nuts."

CHAPTER XLII.

THE FOREST FESTIVAL.

IN consequence of their having rested but poorly on the preceding night, it was determined that they should land at an early hour; and this they did, choosing an open place on the shore. It was a very pretty spot, and they could see that the woods in the background were comparatively open, as though there were some meadows or prairies between. These openings, however, had been caused by fire. There had been a growth of cane. It had been burned off, and as yet was not grown up again, though the young reeds were making their appearance like a field of green wheat. In some places, and especially near the river, the ground was still bare. This change in the landscape was quite agreeable to our travellers, so much so that they resolved to exercise their limbs by taking a short stroll; and, having finished their late dinner, they set out. They all went together, leaving the balza and camp to take care of themselves.

After walking a few hundred yards their ears were assailed by a confused noise, as if all the animals in the forest had met and were holding a *conversazione.* Some low bushes prevented them from seeing what it meant; but, on pushing their way through, they saw whence and from what sort of creatures the noise proceeded.

Standing out in the open ground was a large and tall juvia tree. Its spreading branches were loaded with great globes as big as human heads — each one, of course, full of delicious nuts. These were now ripe, and some of them had already fallen to the ground.

Upon the ground an odd scene presented itself to the eyes of our travellers. Between birds and animals assembled there, there were not less than a dozen kinds, all as busy as they could be.

First, then, there were animals of the rodent kind. These were pacas, (*Cælogenus paca,*) agoutis, (*Chloromys*,) and capivaras. The pacas were creatures a little larger than hares, and not unlike them, except that their ears were shorter. They were whitish on the under parts, but above were of a dark-brown color, with rows of white spots along each side. They had whiskers like the cat, consisting of long white bristles; and their tails, like those of hares, were scarcely visible. The agoutis bore a considerable resemblance to the pacas. Like these, they are also rodent animals, but less in size; and, instead of being spotted, they are of a nearly uniform dark color, mixed with reddish brown. Both pacas and agoutis are found in most parts of tropical America. There are several species of each, and with the chinchillas and viscachas, already described, they occupy the place in those regions that the hares and rabbits do in northern climates. Indeed, European settlers usually know them by the names of hare, or rabbit, and hunt them in the same way. The flesh of most species is very good eating, and they are, there-

fore, much sought after both by the natives and colonists.

Along with these, near the juvia tree, were several
capivaras, already noticed. But still more singular
creatures on the ground were the monkeys. Of these
there were different kinds ; but that which first drew
the attention of our party was the great Capuchin
monkey, (*Brachyurus chiropotes.*) This creature is
not less than three feet in height, and of a reddish-
maroon color. Its body is entirely different from the
" ateles " monkeys, being stouter and covered with a
fuller coat of hair ; and its tail is large and bushy,
without any prehensile power. It is, in fact, less of
a tree monkey than the *ateles*, although it also lives
among the branches. The most striking peculiarities
of the Capuchin are its head and face. In these it
bears a stronger resemblance to the human being than
any other monkey in America. The top of its head
is covered with a crop of coarse hair, that lies somewhat after the fashion of human hair ; but, what most
contributes to the human expression is a large full
beard and whiskers reaching down to the breast, and
arranged exactly after the fashion of the huge beards
worn by Orientals and some Frenchmen. There were
only two of these Capuchins on the ground — a male
and female — for this species does not associate in
bands. The female one was easily distinguished by
her smaller size, and her beard was considerably less
than that of the male. The beards seemed to be
objects of special attention with both — especially the
male ; as every now and then he was observed to
stroke it down with his hand, just as a dandy may be

seen doing with his mustache or his well-brushed
whiskers.

Another peculiar habit of the Capuchins was noticed. There was a little pool of water close by.
Every now and then they ran to this pool and took a
drink from it. But in drinking they did not apply
their lips to the pool, or lap like a dog. No; they
lifted the water in the hollow of their hands — hence
their specific name of *chiropotes*, or " hand-drinking
monkeys." They raised the water to their lips with
great care, taking pains not to let a drop of it fall
on their precious beards. From this habit of going
so often to quench their thirst, the Capuchin monkeys
have in some parts got the name of " hard-drinking
monkeys."

Apart from these was a troop of monkeys of a
very different species. They were nearly of the
same size, but more of the shape of the " ateles ; "
and their long tails, naked underneath and curling
downward near the points, showed that, like them,
too, they possessed prehensile power in that member.
Such was the fact, for they were " howling monkeys ; " and some species of these can use the tail
almost as adroitly as the " ateles " themselves. Those
that our travellers saw were the " guaribas," nearly
black in color, but with their hands covered with yellow hair — whence their name among the naturalists
of " yellow-handed howler," (*Stentor flavimanus.*)
They were seated in a ring when first observed, and
one — apparently the chief of the band — was ha-
ranguing the rest ; but so rapid were his articulations,
and so changeable the tones of his voice, that any

20

one would have thought the whole party were chattering together. This, in effect, did occur at intervals, and then you might have heard them to the
distance of more than a mile. These creatures are
enabled to produce this vast volume of voice in consequence of a hollow, bony structure at the root of
the tongue, which acts as a drum, and which gives
them the appearance of a swelling, or goître, in the
throat. This is common to all the howling monkeys,
as well as the guaribas.

Besides the howlers there were other species —
there were tamarins, and ouistitis, and the black
coaitas of the genus " ateles," all assembled around
the juvia tree. There were parrots, and macaws,
and other nut-eating birds. High above in the air
soared the great eagle, watching his opportunity to
swoop down on the pacas or agoutis, his natural
prey. It was altogether a singular assemblage of
wild animals — a zoölogical garden of the wilderness.

Our party, concealed by bushes, looked on for
some time. They noticed that not one of all the
living things was *under* the tree. On the contrary,
they formed — monkeys, cavies, parrots, and all — a
sort of ring around it, but at such distance that none
of the branches were above them. Why was this?
Guapo knew the reason well, and before leaving their
place of observation the others had an explanation
of it.

While they stood gazing, one of the great globes
was seen to fall from the tree above. The loud report as it struck the earth could have been heard a

iong way off. It caused the whole assemblage of living creatures to start. The macaws flapped their wings, the monkeys ran outward and then stopped, and a simultaneous cry from the voices of both birds and beasts echoed on all sides; and then there was a general chattering and screaming, as though the fall of the great pericarp had given pleasure to all parties.

It was very evident from this circumstance why both beasts and birds kept so far out from the tree. One of these fruits coming down like a nine-pound shot would have crushed any of them to atoms. Indeed, so heavy are they, that one of them falling from a height of fifty or sixty feet will dash out the brains of a man; and the Indians who gather them go under the trees with great wooden helmets that cover both the head and shoulders. It would be no boy's play to " go a nutting " in a wood of juvia trees.

But how did the monkeys and birds get at the nuts? Neither of these could break open the outer shell. This is full half an inch thick, and so hard that it can scarcely be cut with a saw. How could either monkeys or birds open it? That was the question put to Guapo.

" Watch them," said Guapo.

All kept their eyes bent attentively on what was going on; and, to their astonishment, they observed that neither the monkeys nor the birds had any thing to do with the opening of the shells. That was entirely the work of the rodent animals — the pacas, cavies, and agoutis. These with their fine cutting teeth laid open the thick pericarps; and whenever one was seen to have succeeded, and the triangular nuts were scattered upon the ground, then there was a general rush, and macaws, parrots, and monkeys scrambled for a share. The monkeys, however, did their part of the work. Whenever a fruit fell from the tree, one or two of them, deputed by the others, were seen to run in and roll it out, all the while exhibiting symptoms of great terror. They would then lift it in their hands, several of them together, and dash it repeatedly upon a stone. Sometimes, when the shell was not a strong one, they succeeded in breaking it in this way; but oftener they were not able, and then it was left to the rodent animals, who were watched at their operations, and usually robbed of the fruits of their labor. Such were the singular incidents witnessed at this festival of juvia nuts.

But the scene was brought to a sudden termination. A cry was heard that rose far above all the other noises — a cry more terrible than the screams of the parrots, or the shrieks of the howling monkeys — it was the cry of the jaguar. It came from a piece of woods close to the juvia tree, and the branches were heard to crackle as the dreaded utterer advanced.

In a moment the ground was cleared of every creature. Even the winged birds had flown up from the spot and perched upon the branches; the cavies took to the water; the pacas and agoutis to their burrows; and the monkeys to the tops of the adjacent trees; and nothing remained on the ground but the empty shells of the juvias.

Our party did not stay to notice the change. They, too, had been warned by the roar of the tiger, and, hastily leaving the spot, returned to their place of encampment. On reaching it, they kindled a large circle of fire to keep them in safety during the night. They saw no more of the jaguar, although at intervals through the midnight hours they were awakened by his loud and savage cry resounding through the openings of the forest.

CHAPTER XLIII.

.

ACRES OF EGGS.

The next evening our travellers encamped on a
sandbar, or rather a great bank of sand, that ran for
miles along one side of the river. Of course they
had nothing to hang their hammocks to ; but that was
a matter of no importance ; for the sand was dry and
soft, and of itself would make a comfortable bed, as
pleasant to sleep on as a hair mattress. They only
wanted wood enough to cook with and to keep up
their fire during the night, so as to frighten off the
wild beasts.

This night they kept watch as usual, Leon taking
the first turn. In fact, they found that they must do
so every night — as in each of the camps where they
had slept some danger had threatened ; and they
thought it would be imprudent for all to go to sleep
at the same time. The heaviest part of the sentinel's
duty fell to Guapo's share ; but Guapo had long accustomed himself to go without sleep, and did not
mind it ; moreover Don Pablo took longer spells at
the stern oar during the day, and allowed Guapo
many a " cat nap."

Leon seated himself upon a pile of sand that he
had gathered up, and did his best to keep awake ;
but in about an hour after the rest were asleep he

felt very drowsy — in fact, quite as much so as on the night of the adventure with the vampire. He used pretty much the same means to keep himself awake, but not with so good success ; for on this occasion he fell into a nap that lasted nearly half an hour, and might have continued still longer had he not slid down the sand hill and tumbled over on his side. This awoke him ; and feeling vexed with himself, he rubbed his eyes as if he was going to push them deeper into their sockets.

When this operation was finished, he looked about to see if any creature had ventured near. He first looked towards the woods — for of course that was the direction from which the tigers would come, and these were the only creatures he feared ; but he had scarcely turned himself when he perceived a pair of eyes glancing at him from the other side of the fire. Close to them another pair, then another and another ; until, having looked on every side, he saw himself surrounded by a complete circle of glancing eyes ! It is true they were small ones, and some of the heads which he could see by the blaze were small. They were not jaguars, but they had an ugly look — they looked like the heads of serpents. Was it possible that a hundred serpents could have surrounded the camp ?

Brought suddenly to his feet, Leon stood for some moments uncertain how to act. He fully believed they were snakes — anacondas or water snakes, no doubt — that had just crept out of the river ; and he felt that a movement on his part would bring on their united and simultaneous attack upon the sleeping

party. Partly influenced by this fear, and again exhibiting that coolness and prudence which we have
already noticed as a trait of his character, he remained for some moments silent and motionless.
Having already risen to his feet, his eyes were now
above the level of the blaze; and, as they got the
sleep well scared out of them, he could see things
more distinctly. He now saw that the snakelike
heads were attached to large oval-shaped bodies,
and that, besides the half hundred or so that had
gathered around the fires, there were whole droves of
the same upon the sandy beach beyond. The white
surface was literally covered as far as he could see
on all sides of him with black moving masses; and
where the rays of the moon fell upon the beach there
was a broad belt, that glistened and sparkled as though
she shone upon pieces of glass kept constantly in
motion!

A singular sight it was, and to Leon, who had
never heard of such before, a most fearful one. For
the life of him he could not make out what it all
meant, or by what sort of odd creatures they were
surrounded. He had but an indistinct view of them,
but he could see that their bodies were not larger
than those of a small sheep; and from the way in
which they glistened under the moon, he was sure
they were water animals and had come out of the
river.

He did not stay to speculate any longer upon them.
He resolved to wake Guapo; but in doing so the
whole party were aroused, and started to their feet in
some alarm and confusion. The noise and movement

had its effect on the nocturnal visitors; for, before Leon could explain himself, those immediately around the fires, and for some distance beyond, rushed to the edge, and were heard plunging by hundreds into the water.

Guapo's ear caught the sounds, and his eye, now ranging along the sandy shore, took in at a glance the whole thing.

" Carapas," he said, laconically.

" Carapas ? " inquired Leon.

" O ! " said Don Pablo, who understood him. " Turtles, is it ? "

" Yes, master," replied Guapo. " This is, I sup-pose, one of their great hatching-places. They are going to lay their eggs somewhere in the sand above. They do so every year."

There was no danger from the turtles, as Guapo assured every body ; but the fright had chased away sleep, and they all lay awake for some time, listening to Guapo's account of these singular creatures, which we shall translate into our own phraseology.

These large turtles, which in other parts of South America are called " arraus," or simply " tortugas," assemble every year in large armies from all parts of the river. Each one of these armies chooses for itself a place to breed — some sandy island or great sand bank. This they approach very cautiously, ly-ing near it for some days, and reconnoitring it with only their heads above the water. They then crawl ashore at night in vast multitudes, just as the party saw them, and each turtle, with the strong, crooked claws of her hind feet, digs a hole for herself in the

sand. These holes are three feet in diameter and
two deep. In this she deposits her eggs, — from
seventy to one hundred and twenty of them, — each
egg being white, hard shelled, and between the size
of a pigeon's and pullet's. She then covers the whole
with sand, levelling it over the top so that it may
look like the rest of the surface, and so that the
precious treasure may not be found by vultures,
jaguars, and other predatory creatures. When this
is done the labor of the turtle is at an end. The
great army again betakes itself to the water, and
scatters in every direction. The sun, acting upon
the hot sand, does the rest ; and in less than six
weeks the young turtles, about an inch in diameter,
crawl out of the sand and at once make for the
water. They are afterwards seen in pools and lakes,
where the water is shallow, far from the place where
they have been hatched ; and it is well known that
the first years of their life are not spent in the bed
of the great river. How they find these pools, or
whether the mothers distinguish their own young and
conduct them thither, as the crocodiles and alligators
do, is a mystery. With these last the thing is more
easy, as the crocodile mothers deposit their eggs in
separate places, and each returns for her young when
they are hatched, calls them by her voice, and guides
them to the pool where they are to remain until partly grown. But among the thousands of little turtles
hatched at one place and time, and that seek the
water all together, how would it be possible for the
turtle mother to distinguish her own young ? Yet an
old female turtle is frequently seen swimming about

with as many as a hundred little ones after her.
Now, are these her own? or are they a collection
picked up out of the general progeny? That is an
undetermined question. It would seem impossible
that each turtle mother should know her own young;
yet amidst this apparent confusion there may be
some maternal instinct that guides her to distinguish her own offspring from all the rest. Who
can say?

It is not often, however, that the turtle is permitted
to have offspring at all. These creatures are annually robbed of their eggs in millions. They have
many enemies, but man is the chief. When a turtle
hatching-place is discovered, the Indians assemble,
and, as soon as all the eggs have been deposited,
they uncover and collect them. They eat them; but
that is not the principal use to which they are put.
It is for the making of oil, or "tortoise butter," they
are collected. The eggs are thrown into a large
trough, or canoe, where they are broken up with a
wooden spade and stirred about for a while. They
then remain exposed to the sun until the oily part
collects on the surface, which is then skimmed off
and well boiled. The "tortoise butter" is now made,
and, after being poured into earthen jars, or bottles,
(*botijas*,) it is ready for market. The oil is clear,
of a pale-yellow color, and some regard it as equal
to the best olive oil, both for lamps and for cooking.
Sometimes, however, it has a putrid smell, because
many of the eggs are already half hatched before
the gathering takes place.

What would be the result were these eggs not

gathered by the Indians ? Perhaps in the different rivers of South America more than a hundred millions of them are deposited every year. In the Orinoco alone, in three principal hatching-places, it has been calculated that at least thirty-three millions are annually destroyed for the making of tortoise butter. Fancy, then, one hundred millions of animals, each of which grows to the weight of fifty or sixty pounds, being produced every year, and then the increase in production which these would make if left to themselves ! Why, the rivers would be crowded ; and it would be true what old Father Gumilla once asserted, that " it would be as difficult to count the grains of sand on the shores of the Orinoco as to count the immense number of tortoises that inhabit its margins and waters. Were it not for the vast consumption of tortoises and their eggs, the river, despite its great magnitude, would be unnavigable ; for vessels would be impeded by the enormous multitude of the tortoises."

But Nature has provided against this " over-population " of the turtles by giving them a great many enemies. The jaguars, the ocelots, the crocodiles, the cranes, and the vultures all prey upon them ; and perhaps if man were to leave them alone the result would be, not such a great increase in the number of the turtles, but that the creatures who prey upon them would come in for a larger share.

The " carapa," or arrau turtle, is, when fullgrown, forty or fifty pounds in weight. It is of a dark-green color above, and orange beneath, with yellow feet. There are many other species of fresh-water turtles

in the rivers of South America ; but these breed sep•
arately, each female choosing her own place, and
making her deposit alone. Indeed, some of the
smaller species, as the " terekay," are more esteemed both for their flesh and eggs ; but, as a large
quantity of these eggs is never found together, they
are not collected as an article of trade, but only to
be roasted and eaten. The white does not coagulate
in roasting or boiling, and only the yolk is eaten ; but
that is esteemed quite as palatable as the eggs of the
common fowl. The flesh of all kinds is eaten by
the Indians, who fry it in pots, and then pour it, with
its own oil, into other vessels, and permit it to cool.
When thus prepared, it will keep for a long time,
and can be taken out when required for use.

Most of the above particulars were communicated
by Guapo ; and when he had finished talking all the
others went to sleep, leaving Guapo to his midnight
vigil.

CHAPTER XLIV.

A FIGHT BETWEEN TWO VERY SCALY CREATURES.

WHEN they awoke in the morning they found Guapo busy over the fire. He had already been at the turtles' nests, and had collected a'large basketful of the eggs, some of which he was cooking for break fast. In addition to the eggs, moreover, half a dozen large turtles lay upon their backs close by. The flesh of these Guapo intended to scoop out and fry down, so as to be carried away as a sort of stock of preserved meat; and a very excellent idea it was. He had caught them during his watch as they came out of the water.

All the turtles had gone off, although this is not always the case; for frequently numbers that have not finished covering their eggs during the night may be seen hard at work in the morning, and so intent on it that they do not heed the presence of their worst enemies. These the Indians denominate "mad tortoises."

This morning, however, no "mad tortoises" were to be seen; but when our travellers cast their eyes along the beach they saw quite a number that ap-peared to be turned upon their backs just like those that Guapo had capsized. They were at some distance from the camp; but curiosity prompted our travellers to walk along the beach and examine them. Sure enough there were nearly a dozen large tortoises regularly laid on their backs and unable to stir; but, besides these, there were several tortoise shells out of which the flesh had been freshly scooped; and these were as neatly cleaned out as if the work had been done by an anatomist. All this would have been a mystery but for the experience of Guapo; but Guapo knew it was the jaguar that had turned the tortoises on their backs, and that had cleaned out and eaten the flesh from the empty shells.

Now, it is no easy thing for a man, provided with the necessary implements, to separate the flesh of a tortoise from its shell; and yet the jaguar, with his paw, can in a few minutes perform this operation most adroitly, as our travellers had full proof. All that they saw had been done that same night; and it gave them no very pleasant feeling to know that the jaguar had been at work so near them. This animal, as Guapo said, in attacking the turtles, first turns them over, so as to prevent their escape; for the "carapas" are of those tortoises that, once upon their backs on level ground, cannot right themselves again. He then proceeds to tear out the flesh, and eats it at his leisure. Oftentimes he capsizes a far greater number than he can eat, and even returns to the spot to have a second meal of them; but frequently the Indians wandering along the river find the tortoises he has turned over, and of course make an easy capture of them.

Guapo, upon this occasion, took advantage of the

jaguar's skill, and carried to the camp all that the latter had left. It was Guapo's design to make a large quantity of "turtle sausage meat," so that they might have a supply for many days, as by this time even Guapo himself was getting tired of the horse-flesh "charqui."

They were about returning to camp when their attention was drawn to two dark objects upon the sand beach, a little farther on. These objects were in motion, and at first they believed they were a pair of "mad tortoises" that had not yet returned to the water, although they were close to its edge.

Led on by curiosity, our party approached them, and saw that one only was a tortoise, and one of the largest kind, being nearly three feet in diameter. The other animal was a small caïman, or alligator.

As our travellers drew near they saw that these two creatures were engaged in a fierce and deadly combat. Now, it is a curious fact that the larger alligators and crocodiles are among the most destructive enemies which the turtles have, eating thousands of the latter while they are still tiny little creatures and unable to defend themselves; and, on the other hand, that the turtles prey extensively on the young of both alligators and crocodiles, eating them whenever they can catch them! I say this is a curious fact in natural history, and it seems a sort of retaliatory principle established between these two kinds of reptiles, as if they ate one another's offspring *en revanche.* There is no feeling of revenge, however, in the matter. It is merely an instinct of appetite by which both kinds will eat almost any small fry they come across. In fact the alligators and crocodiles not only eat the young of the turtles, but their own young as well — that is, the *old males* do ; and it has been stated that the males of some species of tortoises have a similar unnatural appetite.

The turtle of which we are speaking is one of the most carnivorous of the whole race, and one of the fiercest in its nature too ; so much so that it has earned the name of the " fierce tortoise," (*Testudo ferox.*) It will eat fish and small crustacea, and almost any living thing it finds in the water which is not too large for it. It is extremely expert in catching its prey. It lies concealed at the bottom among the roots of flags and nymphæ, and, when any small fish chances to pass it, by means of its long neck darts out its head and seizes upon its unsuspecting victim. Once the bill of the " fierce turtle " has closed upon any object, its hold is secure. You may cut its head off, but otherwise it cannot be forced to let go until it has either captured its prey or taken the piece with it. It will " nip " a stout walking cane between its mandibles as if it was no more than a rush.

A very good story is told of a thief and a tortoise. The thief was prowling about the larder of a hotel, in search of plunder, when he came upon a large market basket filled with provisions. He immediately inserted his hand to secure the contents, when he felt himself suddenly seized by the fingers and bit.en sc severely that he was fain to draw back his hand in the most hasty manner possible. But along with the hand he drew out a " snapping " turtle. To

21

get rid of the " ugly customer " was his next care but, in spite of all his efforts, the turtle held on, determined to have the finger. The scuffle, and the shouts which pain compelled the thief to give utterance to, awoke the landlord and the rest of the household; and before the thief could disengage himself and escape, he was secured and given into custody.

Well, it was just a tortoise of this species, a " snapping turtle," and one of the largest size, that our travellers now saw doing battle with the caïman. The caïman was not one of large size, else the turtle would have fled from it; not that even the largest caïmans are feared by the fullgrown *carapas*. Nc the strong plate armor of the latter protects them both from the teeth and tail of this antagonist. The jaguar, with his pliable paws, and sharp, subtle claws, is to them a more dreaded assailant than the crocodile or caïman.

The one in question was some six or seven feet long, and altogether not much heavier than the turtle itself. It was not for the purpose of eating each other they fought. No; their strife was evidently on other grounds. No doubt the caïman had been attempting to plunder the new-laid eggs of the tortoise, and the latter had detected him in the act. At all events, the struggle must have been going on for some time, for the sand was torn up and scored in many places by the sharp claws of both.

The battle appeared to be still at its height when our party arrived on the spot. Neither tortoise nor caïman paid any attention to their presence, but fought on pertinaciously. The aim of the caïman appeared to be to get the head of the tortoise in his mouth; but whenever he attempted this the latter suddenly drew his head within the shell, and repeatedly disappointed him. The tortoise, on its part, rose at intervals upon its hind feet, and, making a dash forward, would dart forth its long neck and clutch at the softer parts of its antagonist's body, just under the throat. Several times it had succeeded in this manœuvre, and each time it had brought the piece with it, so that the caïman was already somewhat mangled. Another manœuvre of the tortoise was to seize the tail of its antagonist. Instinct seemed to teach it that this was a vulnerable part; and for the purpose of reaching the tail, it constantly kept crawling and edging round towards it. Now, there is no movement so difficult for a reptile of the crocodile kind as to turn its body on dry land. The peculiar formation of the vertebræ both of its neck and spine renders this movement difficult; and in "changing front," the reptile is forced to describe a full circle with its unwieldy body — in fact to turn "all of a piece." The tortoise, therefore, had the advantage; and, after several efforts, he at length succeeded in outflanking his antagonist and getting right round to his rear. He lost no time, but, raising himself to his full height, and making a dart forward, seized the tail and held on. He had caught by the very tip; and it was seen that his horny mandibles had taken a proper hold.

Now commenced a somewhat ludicrous scene. The caïman, though but a small one, with the immense muscular power which he possessed in his tail, if not able to detach his antagonist, was able to give him a sound shaking; and the turtle was seen vibrating from side to side, dragged along the sand. He held his broad yellow feet spread out on all sides, so as to preserve his equilibrium; for he well knew that to lose that would be to lose his life. Should he get turned on his back it would be all over with him; but he carefully guarded against such a fatal catastrophe. Of course there were intervals when the caïman became tired and remained still for a moment; and at each of these intervals the tortoise renewed his hold, and, in fact, as our party now perceived, was slowly, though surely, *eating the tail !* ·

When this had continued a short while, the great saurian seemed to despair. The pain, no doubt, caused him to weep "crocodile's tears," though none were seen; but his eyes glared with a lurid light, and he began to look around for some means of escape from his painful position. His eyes fell upon the water. That promised something, although he knew full well the turtle was as much at home there as he. At all events, his situation could not be a worse one, and, with this or some such reflection, he made a "dash" for the water. He was but a few feet from it; but it cost him a good deal of pulling, and dragging, and clawing the sand before he could get into it. In fact the tortoise knew that its position could not be benefited by the change, and would have pre ferred fighting it out on dry land; and to do this he set *his* claws as firmly as possible, and pulled the tail in the opposite direction.

The strength of the caïman at length prevailed. He got his body into the water, and, with a few strokes of his webbed feet, jerked the turtle after, and both were now fairly launched. Once in the river, the caïman seemed to gain fresh vigor. His tail vibrated violently and rapidly, throwing the tortoise from side to side until the foam floated around them, and then both suddenly sank to the bottom.

Whether they continued " attached," or became " separated " there, or whether the turtle killed the lizard, or the lizard the turtle, or " each did kill the other," no one ever knew, as it is highly probable that no human eye ever saw either of them again.

At all events, no one of *our* party saw any more of them ; and, having watched the surface for some time, they turned in their steps and walked back to the camp.

CHAPTER XLV.

A PAIR OF VALIANT VULTURES.

THEY had got into a part of the river that seemed
to be a favorite resort with turtles and crocodiles, and
creatures of that description. At different times they
saw turtles of different kinds; among others, the
' painted turtle," a beautiful species that derives its
name from the fine coloring of its shell, which appears as if it had been painted in enamel. Of crocodiles, too, they saw three or four distinct species,
and not unfrequently the largest of all, the great
black crocodile, (*Jacare nigra.*) This was sometimes seen of the enormous length of over twenty
feet. Terrible looking as these crocodiles are, they
are not masters of every creature upon the river.
There are even birds that can sorely vex them, and
compel them to take to the water to save themselves
from a fearful calamity — blindness.

One day, while descending the river, our travellers
were witness to an illustration of this.

They were passing a wide sand bank that shelved
back from the river, with a scarcely perceptible slope,
when they saw, at a distance of about two hundred
yards from the water's edge, a crocodile making for
the river. He looked as though he had just awaked
from his torpid sleep; for his body was caked all

over with dry mud, and he seemed both hungry and thirsty. It was like enough he was coming from some inland pond, where the water had dried up, and he was now on his way to the river.

All at once two dark shadows were seen passing over the white surface of the sand bank. In the heaven two large birds were wheeling about, crossing each other in their courses, and holding their long necks downwards, as if the crocodile was the object of their regard.

The latter, on seeing them, paused, and lowered his body into a squatted or crouching attitude, as if in the birds he recognized an enemy. And yet what could such a large creature fear from a pair of " king vultures " ? for king vultures they were, as was easily seen by their red-orange heads and cream-colored plumage. What could a crocodile, full ten feet long, fear from these, even had they been eagles, or the great condor himself? No matter; he was evidently frightened at them; and each time that they drew near in their flight, he stopped and flattened his body against the sand, as if that might conceal him. As soon as they flew off again to a more distant point of their aerial circle, he would once more elevate himself on his arms, and make all haste towards the water.

He had got within about a hundred yards of the river, when the birds made a sudden turn in the sky, and, swooping down, alighted upon the sand, directly before the snout of the crocodile. The latter stopped again, and kept his eyes fixed upon them. They did not leave him long to rest; for one of them, making

a few hops towards him, came so close that it might
have been supposed the crocodile could have seized
it in his jaws. This, in fact, he attempted to do ; but
the wary bird threw up its broad wings, and flapped
to one side out of his reach. Meanwhile, the other
had hopped close up to his opposite shoulder ; and
while the crocodile was engaged with the first one,
this made a dash forward, aiming its great open beak
at the eye of the reptile. The crocodile parried the
thrust by a sudden turn of his head ; but he had
scarcely got round, when the second vulture, watching its opportunity, rushed forward at the other eye.
It must have succeeded in pecking it, for the great
lizard roared out with the pain, and, rushing forward
a bit, writhed and lashed the sand with his tail.

The vultures paid no attention to these demonstra-
tions, but only kept out of the way of the teeth and
claws of their antagonist ; and then, when he became
still again, both returned to the attack as before. One
after the other was seen dashing repeatedly forward
— using both legs and wings to effect their object,
and each time darting out their great beaks towards
the eyes of the reptile. The head of the latter kept
continuously moving from side to side ; but move
where it would, the beaks of the vultures were ready
to meet it, and to pierce into the sockets of those deep
lurid eyes.

This terrible contest lasted all the time the balza
was floating by. It was a slow current at this place,
and our travellers were a long time in passing, so
that they had a good opportunity of witnessing the
strange spectacle. Long after they had glided past,

they saw that the conflict continued. They could still perceive the black body of the reptile upon the white sand bank, writhing and struggling, while the flapping wings of the vultures showed that they still kept up their terrible attack. But the head of the crocodile was no longer directed towards the water. At the first onset the reptile had used every effort to retreat in that direction. He knew that his only safety lay in getting into the river and sinking beyond the reach of his adversaries. At every interval between their assaults he had been seen to crawl forward, stopping only when compelled to defend himself. Now, however, his head was seen turned from the water ; sometimes he lay parallel with the stream, and sometimes he appeared to be heading back for the woods, while his struggles and contortions betrayed the agony he was undergoing. But his turning in this way was easily accounted for. He knew not in what direction lay the river. He could no longer see. His eyes were mutilated by the beaks of the birds. *He was blind !*

Guapo said the vultures would not leave him until they had made a meal of his eyes ; and that was all they wanted. He would then remain on shore, perhaps without finding his way back to the water, and most likely be attacked by jaguars, or other preying creatures, who could conquer him the easier now that he was deprived of his sight.

As the balza glided on, Guapo told our travellers many strange stories of crocodiles. He stated, what is well known to be true, that, in the rivers of South America, many people are every year killed by these

ravenous creatures; in fact, far more than have ever
fallen victims to the salt-sea sharks.   In some places
they are much fiercer than in others; but this may
arise from different species being the inhabitants of
these different places. There is the true crocodile, with
long sharp snout and large external tusks; and the
caïman, with a snout broader and more pike shaped;
and the former is a much more courageous and man-
eating creature. Both are often found in the same
river; but they do not associate together, but keep in
distinct bands, or societies; and they are often mistaken for each other. This may account for the difference of opinion that exists in regard to the fierce
ness of these reptiles — many asserting that they are
utterly harmless, and will not attack man under any
circumstances; while others, who have witnessed
their attacks, of course bearing testimony to the contrary. There are many places in South America
where the natives will fearlessly enter a lake or river
known to be full of crocodiles, and drive these crea
tures aside with a piece of a stick; but there are
other districts where nothing will tempt an Indian to
swim across a river infested with these reptiles. In
the Amazon districts, in every Indian village, several
people may be seen who have been maimed by crocodiles. No wonder that among author travellers
there should be such a difference of opinion.

Guapo stated that, when an Indian has been seized
by a crocodile in its great jaws, he has only one
chance of escape, and that is by thrusting his fingers
into the eyes of the reptile. This will invariably
cause it to let go its hold, and generally frighten it, so

as to enable the person to escape. It of course requires great presence of mind to effect this, as the
person who has been seized will himself be in great
pain from the tearing teeth of the monster, and, perhaps, will have been drawn under the water before he
can gather his senses.   But it has often occurred that
Indians, and even women, have escaped in this way.

The eyes of the crocodile are its most tender parts ;
in fact, the only parts that cån be made to feel pain.
A crocodile may be disabled by cutting at the root of
its tail, but it can only be frightened by an attack
upon the eyes ; and this appears to be a well-known
fact, not only to the Indians, but to all its other enemies among the birds and quadrupeds.

The young crocodiles are often attacked, and have
their eyes pecked out, by the small gallinazo, or
" zamuro " vultures, (*aura* and *cathartes*,) just in the
same way that we have seen one of a larger size
become the victim of the more powerful king vultures,
(*Sarcoramphus papa.*)

CHAPTER XLVI.

THE "GAPO."

AFTER many days of rafting our travellers arrived in a most singular country. They were now approaching the mighty Amazon ; and the river upon which they had hitherto been travelling appeared to divide into many branches, where it formed *deltas* with the Amazon. Every day, and sometimes two or three times in the day, they passed places where the river forked, as though each branch passed round an island ; but our travellers perceived that these branches did not meet again, and they conjectured that they all fell into the Amazon by separate embouchures. They were often puzzled to know which one to take, as the main river was not always broadest, and they might get into one that was not navigable below. A curious region it was through which they passed ; for, in fact, they were now travelling in the country of the " Gapo."

What is the " Gapo " ? you will ask. The " Gapo,' then, is the name given to vast tracts of country upon the Amazon and some of its tributary streams that are annually inundated and remain under water for several months in the year. It extends for hundreds of miles along the Amazon itself, and up many of the rivers, its tributaries also, for hundreds of miles.

But the whole country does not become one clear sheet of water, as is the case with floods in other parts of the world. On the contrary, high as is the flood, the tree tops and their branches rise still higher, and we have in the " Gapo " the extraordinary spectacle of a flooded forest, thousands of square miles in extent!

In this forest the trees do not perish, but retain life and verdure. In fact, the trees of this part are peculiar, most of them differing in kind from the trees of any other region. There are species of palms growing in the " Gapo " that are found nowhere else; and there are animals and birds, too, that remain in this region during the whole season of flood. It has been further asserted that there are tribes of " Gapo " Indians, who live in the middle of the inundation, making their dwellings upon the trees, and who can pass from branch to branch and tree to tree almost as nimbly as monkeys. This may or may not be true. It would not be a new thing, if true; for it is well known that the Guarano Indians, at the mouth of the Orinoco, dwell among the tops of the murichi palms (*Mauritia flexuosa*) during many months of the season of flood. These people build platforms on the palms, and upon these erect roofs and sling their hammocks, and, with little fireplaces of mud, are enabled to cook their provisions upon them. But they have canoes, in which they are able to go from place to place and capture fish, upon which they principally subsist. The murichi palm furnishes them with all the other necessaries of life.

This singular tree is one of the noblest of the palms. It rises to a height of more than one hundred feet, and grows in immense *palmares*, or palm woods, often covering the bank of the river for miles. It is one of those called " fan palms ; " that is, the leaves, instead of being pinnate, or feathery, have long naked stocks, at the end of which the leaflets spread out circularly, forming a shape like a fan. One of the murichi leaves is a grand sight. The leaf stalk, or petiole, is a foot thick where it sprouts from the trunk ; and before it reaches the leaflets it is a solid beam of ten or twelve feet long, while the circular fan or leaf itself is nine or ten in diameter! A single leaf of the murichi palm is a full load for a man.

With a score of such leaves, shining and ever verdant as they are, at the top of its column-like trunk, what a majestic tree is the murichi palm !

But it is not more beautiful than useful. Its leaves, fruit, and stem are all put to some use in the domestic economy of the Indians. The leaf stalk, when dried, is light and elastic, like the quill of a bird, owing to the thin, hard, outer covering, and soft, internal pith. Out of the outer rind, when split off, the Indian makes baskets and window blinds. The pithy part is separated into laths, about half an inch thick, with which window shutters, boxes, birdcages, partitions, and even entire walls are constructed. The epidermis of the leaves furnishes the strings for hammocks and all kinds of cordage. From the fruits a favorite beverage is produced ; and these fruits are also pleasant eating, somewhat resembling apples.

They are, in appearance, like pine cones, of a red
color outside, and yellow pulp. The trunk itself furnishes a pith, or marrow, that can be used as sago:
and out of the wood the Indian cuts his buoyant canoe.
In short, there are tribes of Indians that not only
live, in a literal sense, *on* the murichi palms, but that
almost subsist on them.

Although the flood had, to a considerable extent
subsided, the river, in most places, was still beyond
its banks ; and this made it difficult for our travellers
to find a place for their night camps. Several nights
they were obliged to sleep, as they best could, on the
balza, the latter being secured to a tree. Sometimes, by pushing some distance up the mouth of an
" igaripé," or creek, they were able to find dry
ground on which to encamp. During their passage
through this labyrinth of rivers they travelled but
very slowly, and their provisions were fast running
out. There was no chance for increasing their stock,
as they could not find either wild hogs (peccaries) or
capivaras. These creatures, although they can swim
well enough, would only be found upon the banks of
the river when it returned within its proper channel.

Now and then Guapo brought down a parrot, a macaw, or an aracari with his blow gun ; but these
were only temporary supplies. They had often
heard howling monkeys in the trees, but had not been
able to see them ; and none of the party would have
refused to eat roast monkey now, as they had all tried
it and found it quite palatable. Guapo, blow gun in
hand, was continually peering up among the tree

tops in search of monkeys or other game.   He was,
at length, rewarded for his vigilance.

One night they had pushed the balza up an " igar-
ıpé " for a hundred yards or so, where a dry bank
gave them an opportunity of landing.   The creek itself was not much wider than the balza, and tall trees
stood upon both banks.   In one or two places the
thorny " jacitara " palm — which is a sort of climbing
plant, often hanging over the branches of other trees
— nearly reached across the stream.   These curious
palms had even to be cautiously pushed to one side
as the balza passed ; for the arrowy claws upon them,
if once hooked into the clothes of the passengers.
would either have dragged the latter from off the raft
or have torn out the piece of cloth.

CHAPTER XLVII.

THE ARAGUATOES.

Our party had passed several of these jacitaras, made the balza fast, landed, and were just cooking their scanty supper, when they heard a band of howling monkeys afar off in the woods. There was nothing unusual in this ; for these creatures are heard at all times among the forests of the Amazon, especially at sunrise and before sunset, or whenever there is any appearance of the approach of a rain storm. Our travellers would not have noticed their voices on this occasion but that they seemed to be approaching in that direction ; and, as they were coming along the bank of the main river, Guapo concluded that, on arriving at the " igaripé," they would turn up it and pass near where the balza was, and thus he might have them within reach of his gravatána. It was certain they were coming down the river side, of course upon the tree tops, and would, no doubt, turn up as Guapo expected ; for the trees on the opposite side of the igaripé stood too far apart even for monkeys to spring across.

After waiting for half an hour or so, the hideous howling of the monkeys could be heard at no great distance, and they were taking the desired route. In fact, in a few minutes after, the troop appeared upon

22

some tall trees that stood on the edge of the creek, not fifty yards from where the balza was moored. They were large animals, of that lanky and slender shape that characterizes the prehensile-tailed monkeys; but these were different from the *ateles* already mentioned. They were true howlers, as they had already proved by the cries they had been uttering for the half hour past. There are several species of howling monkeys, as we have already stated. Those that had arrived on the igaripé Guapo pronounced to be *araguatoes*. Their bodies are of a reddish-brown color on the body and shoulders, lighter underneath, and their naked, wrinkled faces are of a bluish black, and with very much of the expression of an old man. Their hair is full and bushy, and gives them some resemblance to a bear; whence their occasional name of " bear ape," and also their zoölogical designation, *Simia ursina.* The araguato is full three feet without the tail, and that powerful member is much longer.

When the band made its appearance on the igaripé, they were seen to come to a halt, all of them gathering into a great tree that stood by the water's edge. This tree rose higher than the rest; and the most of the monkeys, having climbed among the top branches, were visible from the balza. There were about fifty in the troop, and one, that seemed larger than any of the others, appeared to act as leader. Many of them were females; and there were not a few that had young ones, which they carried upon their backs just as the Indian mothers and those of other savage nations carry their children. Most of the little monkeys lay along the backs of their mothers clasping them around the neck with their fore arms, while their hind ones girdled the middle of the body. But it was in their tails the little fellows seemed to place most reliance. The top parts of these were firmly lapped around the thick base of the tails of the old ones, and thus not only secured their seat, but made it quite impossible for them to drop off. No force could have shaken them from this hold without dragging out their tails or tearing their bodies to pieces. Indeed, it was necessary they should be thus firmly seated, as the exertions of the mothers — their quick motions, and long, springing leaps from tree to tree — would otherwise have been impossible.

On reaching the bank of the igaripé the aragua-toes were evidently at fault. Their intention had been to proceed down along the main river; and the creek now interfered. Its water lay directly across their course; and how were they to get over it? Swim it, you may say. Ha! little do you know the dread these creatures have of water. Yes; strange to say, although many species of them pass their lives upon trees that overhang water, or even grow out of it, they are as much afraid of the water beneath them as if it were fire. A cat is not half so dainty about wetting her feet as some monkeys are; and, besides, a cat can swim, which the monkeys cannot — at best so badly that in a few minutes they would drown. Strange, is it not, that among animals, those that approach nearest to man, like him are not gifted by nature with the power of swimming? It is evident, then, that that is an art left to be discovered by the intellect of man. To fall into the water would be a sad mishap for a monkey, not only on account of the ducking, but of the danger. There is not much likelihood of an araguato falling in. Even though one branch may have broken and failed it, in the great concave sphere which it can so quickly trace around it by means of its five long members it is sure of finding a second. No ; the araguatoes might spend a lifetime in the flooded forest without even wetting a hair further than what is wetted by the rain.

From their movements, it was evident the igaripé had puzzled them ; and a consultation was called among the branches of the tall tree already mentioned. Upon one of the very highest sat the large old fellow who was evidently leader of the band. His harangue was loud and long, accompanied by many gestures of his hands, head, and tail. It was no doubt exceedingly eloquent. Similar speeches, delivered by other old araguato chiefs, have been compared to the creaking of an ungreased bullock cart, mingled with the rumbling of the wheels.

Our party thought the comparison a just one. The old chief finished at length. Up to this point not one of the others had said a word. They all sat silent, observing perfect decorum — indeed, much greater than is observed in the great British Parliament or the Congress of America. Occasionally one of the children might utter a slight squeak or throw out its hand to catch a mosquito ; but in such cases a slap from the paw of the mother or a rough shaking soon reduced it to quiet. When the chief had ended speaking, however, no debate in either Congress or Parliament could have equalled the noise that then arose. Every araguato seemed to have something to say, and all spoke at the same time. If the speech of the old one was like the creaking of a bullock cart, the voices of all combined might appropriately be compared to a whole string of these vehicles, with half the quantity of grease and a double allowance of wheels.

Once more the chief, by a sign, commanded silence, and the rest became mute and motionless as before.

This time the speech of the leader appeared to refer to the business in hand — in short, to the crossing of the igaripé. He was seen repeatedly pointing in that direction as he spoke, and the rest followed his motions with their eyes.

CHAPTER XLVIII.

BRIDGING AN IGARIPÉ.

THE tree upon which the araguatoes were assem·
bled stood near the edge of the water, but there was
another still nearer.   This was also a tall tree, free
of branches for a great way up.   On the opposite
bank of the igaripé was a very similar tree, and the
long horizontal branches of the two were separated
from each other by a space of about twenty feet.   It
was with these two trees that the attention of the araguatoes appeared to be occupied ; and our travellers
could tell by their looks and gestures that they were
conversing about, and calculating the distance between, their upper branches.   For what purpose ?
Surely they do not expect to be able to make a crossing between them ?   No creature without wings
could pass from the one to the other !   Such were the
questions and doubts expressed by Leon, and, indeed,
by all except Guapo ; but Guapo had seen araguatoes before, and knew some of their tricks.   Guapo,
therefore, boldly pronounced that it was their intention to cross the igaripé by these two trees.   He was
about to explain the manner in which they would accomplish it, when the movement commenced, and
rendered his explanation quite unnecessary.

At a commanding cry from the chief, several of

the largest and strongest monkeys swung themselves into the tree that stood on the edge of the water. Here, after a moment's reconnoissance, they were seen to get upon a horizontal limb, one that projected diagonally over the igaripé. There were no limbs immediately underneath it on the same side of the tree; and for this very reason had they selected it. Having advanced until they were near its top, the foremost of the monkeys let himself down upon his tail, and hung head downward. Another slipped. down the body of the first, and clutched him around the neck and fore arms with his strong tail, with his head down also. A third succeeded the second, and a fourth the third, and so on until a string of monkeys dangled from the limb. A motion was now produced by the monkeys striking other branches with their feet, until the long string oscillated back and forwards like the pendulum of a clock. This oscillation was gradually increased, until the monkey at the lower end was swung up among the branches of the tree on the opposite side of the igaripé. After touching them once or twice, he discovered that he was within reach; and the next time when he had reached the highest point of the oscillating curve, he threw out his long thin fore arms, and, firmly clutching the branches, held fast.

The oscillation now ceased. The living chain stretched across the igaripé from tree to tree, and, curving slightly, hung like a suspension bridge. A loud screaming, and gabbling, and chattering, and howling proceeded from the band of araguatoes, who, up to this time, had watched the manœuvres of their comrades in silence — all except the old chief, who occasionally had given directions, both with voice and gestures. But the general gabble that succeeded was, no doubt, an expression of the satisfaction of all that the *bridge was built.*

The troop now proceeded to cross over, one or two old ones going first, perhaps to try the strength of the bridge. Then went the mothers, carrying their young on their backs, and after them the rest of the band.

It was quite an amusing scene to witness, and the behavior of the monkeys would have caused any one to laugh. Even Guapo could not restrain his mirth at seeing those who formed the bridge biting the others that passed over them, both on the legs and tails, until the latter screamed again.

The old chief stood at the near end and directed the crossing. Like a brave officer, he was the last to pass over. When all the others had preceded him he crossed after, carrying himself in a stately and dignified manner. None dared to bite at *his* legs They knew better than play off their tricks on *him* and he crossed quietly and without any molestation.

Now, the string still remained suspended between the trees. How were the monkeys that formed it to get themselves free again? Of course the one that had clutched the branch with his arms might easily let go; but that would bring them back to the same side from which they had started, and would separate them from the rest of the band. Those constituting the bridge would, therefore, be as far from crossing as ever.

There seemed to be a difficulty here ; that is, to some of our travellers. To the monkeys themselves there was none. They knew well enough what they were about, and they would have got over the appar. ent difficulty in the following manner : The one at the tail end of the bridge would simply have let go his hold, and the whole string would then have swung over and hung from the tree on the opposite bank, into which they could have climbed at their leisure. I say they *would* have done so had nothing interfered to prevent them from completing the manœuvre ; but an obstacle intervened which brought the affair to a very different termination.

Guapo had been seated along with the rest; grava-tána in hand. He showed great forbearance in not having used the gravatána long before, for he was all the while quite within reach of the araguatoes ; but this forbearance on his part was not of his own free will. Don Pablo had, in fact, hindered him, in order that he and the others should have an opportunity of witnessing the singular manœuvres of the monkeys.

Before the scene was quite over, however, the Indian begged Don Pablo to let him shoot, reminding him how much they stood in need of a little " monkey meat." This had the effect Guapo desired ; the consent was given, and the gravatána was pointed diagonally upwards. Once more Guapo's cheeks were distended ; once more came the strong, quick puff ; and away went the arrow. The next moment it was seen sticking in the neck of one of the monkeys.

Now, the one which Guapo had aimed at and hit was that which had grasped the tree on the opposite

side with its arms. Why did he choose this moro
than any other? Was it because it was nearer, or
more exposed to view? Neither of these was the
reason. It was, that had he shot any of the others in
the string — they being supported by their tails — it
would not have fallen ; the tail, as we have already
seen, still retaining its prehensile power even to death.

But that one which held on to the tree by its fore
arms would in a second or two be compelled,
from weakness, to let go, and the whole chain would
drop back on the near side of the igaripé. This was
just what Guapo desired, and he waited for the result.
It was necessary only to wait half a dozen seconds.
The monkey was evidently growing weak under the
influence of the *curare*, and was struggling to retain
its hold. In a moment it must let go.

The araguato at the " tail end " of the bridge, not
knowing what had happened, and thinking all was
right for swinging himself across, slipped his tail
from the branch just at the very same instant that the
wounded one let go, and the whole chain fell " souse "
into the water. Then the screaming and howling
from those on shore, the plunging and splashing of
the monkeys in the stream, mingled with the shouts of
Leon, Guapo, and the others, created a scene of noise
and confusion that lasted for several minutes. In the
midst of it, Guapo threw himself into the canoe, and,
with a single stroke of his paddle, shot right down
among the drowning monkeys. One or two escaped
to the bank and made off ; several went to the bottom ,
but three, including the wounded one, fell into the
clutches of the hunter.

Of course roast monkey was added to the supper,
but none of the travellers slept very well after it,
as the araguatoes, lamenting their lost companions,
kept up a most dismal wailing throughout the whole
of the night.

CHAPTER XLIX.

THE MANATI.

THE araguatoes, with dried plantains and cassava, were the food of our travellers for several days after. On the evening of the third day they had a change. Guapo succeeded in capturing a very large turtle, which served for relish at several meals. His mode of taking the turtle was somewhat curious, and de· serves to be described.

The balza had been brought to the bank, and they were just mooring it, when something out on the water attracted the attention of Leon and Leona. It was a small, darkish object, and would not have been observed but for the ripple that it made on the smooth surface of the river ; and by this they could tell that it was in motion.

" A water snake ! " said Leon.

" O ! " ejaculated the little Leona ; " I hope not, brother Leon."

" On second thoughts," replied Leon, " I don't think it is a snake."

Of course the object was a good distance off, else Leon and Leona would not have talked so coolly about it. But their words had reached the ear of Doña Isidora, and drawn her attention to what they were talking about.

" No ; it is not a snake," said she. " I fancy it is a turtle."

Guapo up to this had been busy with Don Pablo in getting the balza made fast. The word " turtle," however, caught his ear at once, and he looked up, and then out on the river in the direction where Leon and Leona were pointing. As soon as his eye rested upon the moving object he replied to the remark of Doña Isidora.

" Yes, my mistress," said he, " it is a turtle, and a big one too. Please all keep quiet; I think I can get him."

How Guapo was to get the turtle was a mystery to all. The latter was about thirty paces distant; but it would be difficult, if not impossible, to hit his small snout — the only part above water — with the arrow of the blow gun. Moreover, they thought that the arrow would not penetrate the hard, bony substance, so as to stick there and infuse its poison into the wound.

These conjectures were true enough; but his gravatána was not the weapon which Guapo was abou'. to use. He had other weapons as well ; a fish spear, or harpoon, and a regular bow and arrows, which he had made during his leisure hours in the valley.

The latter was the weapon with which the tortoise was to be killed.

Taking the bow, and adjusting an arrow to the string, Guapo stepped forward to the water's edge. All watched him, uttering their hopes of his success. It was still not clear with them how the turtle was to

be killed oy an arrow shot from a bow any more than
by one sent from a blow gun. Would it not glance
from the shell even should he succeed in hitting it
under water ?   Surely it would.

As they stood whispering their conjectures to one
another, they observed Guapo, to their great astonishment, *pointing his arrow upward*, and making as if
he was going to discharge it in the air ! This he, in
fact, *did* do a moment after ; and they would have
been puzzled by his apparently strange conduct had
they not observed, in the next instant, that the arrow,
after flying high up, came down again head foremost,
and stuck upright in the back of the turtle !

The turtle dived at once, and all of them expected
to see the upright arrow carried under water.   What
was their surprise as well as chagrin to see that it
had fallen out and was floating on the surface !   Of
course the wound had only been a slight one, and the
turtle would escape and be none the worse for it.

But Guapo shared neither their surprise nor chagrin.   Guapo felt sure that the turtle was his, and
said nothing, but, jumping into the canoe, began to
paddle himself out to where the creature had been
last seen.   What could he be after ? thought they.

As they watched him they saw that he made for
the floating arrow.   " O ! " said they, " he is gone to
recover it."

That seemed probable enough ; but, to their astonishment, as he approached the weapon it took a start
and ran away from him ! Something below dragged
it along the water.   That was clear ; and they began
to comprehend the mystery.   The *head* of the arrow

was still sticking in the shell of the turtle. It was only the shaft that floated, and that was attached to the head by a string. The latter had been but loosely put on, so that the pressure of the water, as the turtle dived, should separate it from the shaft, leaving the shaft with its cord to act as a buoy and discover the situation of the turtle.

Guapo, in his swift canoe, soon laid hold of the shaft, and, after a little careful manœuvring, succeeded in landing his turtle high and dry upon the bank. A splendid prize it proved. It was a "jurara" tortoise — the "tataruga," or great turtle of the Portuguese ; and its shell was full three feet in diameter.

Guapo's mode of capturing the "jurara" is the same as that generally practised by the Indians of the Amazon, although strong nets and the hook are also used. The arrow is always discharged upwards, and the range calculated with such skill that it falls vertically on the shell of the turtle, and penetrates deep enough to stick and detach itself from the shaft. This mode of shooting is necessary, else the jurara could not be killed by an arrow, because it never shows more than the tip of its snout above water, and any arrow hitting it in a direct course would glance harmlessly from its shell. A good bowman among the Indians will rarely miss shooting in this way — long practice and native skill enabling him to guess within an inch of where his weapon will fall

In the towns of the Lower Amazon, where turtles are brought to market, a small square hole may be observed in the shells of these creatures. That is the mark of the arrowhead.

Guapo lost no time in turning his turtle inside out, and converting part of it into a savory supper, while the remainder was fried into sausage meat, and put away for the following day.

But on that following day a much larger stock of sausage meat was procured from a very different animal, and that was a " cow."

' How ? " you exclaim; " a cow in the wild forests of the Amazon ! Why, you have said that no cattle — either cows or horses — can exist there without man to protect them, else they would be devoured by pumas, jaguars, and bats. Perhaps they had arrived at some settlement where cows were kept ? "

Not a bit of it; your conjecture, my young friend, is quite astray. There was not a civilized settlement for many hundreds of miles from where Guapo got his cow, nor a cow neither, of the sort you are think-ing of. But there are more kinds of cows than one; and perhaps you may have heard of a creature called the " fish cow." Well, that is the sort of cow I am speaking of. Some term it the " sea cow;" but this is an improper name for it, since it also inhabits fresh-water rivers throughout all tropical America. It is known as the *Manati;* and the Portuguese call it "*peixe boi*," which is only " fish cow?" done into Portuguese.

It is a curious creature, the fish cow, and I shall offer you a short description of it. It is usually about seven feet in length, and five round the thickest part of the body, which latter is quite smooth, and tapers off into a horizontal flat tail, semicircular in shape. There are no hind limbs upon the animal, but just behind the head are two powerful fins of an oval shape. There is no neck to be perceived; and the head, which is not very large, terminates in a large mouth and fleshy lips, which are not unlike those of a cow; hence its name of "cow fish." There are stiff bristles on the upper lip, and a few thinly-scattered hairs over the rest of the body. Behind the oval fins are two *mammæ*, or breasts, from which, when pressed, flows a stream of beautiful white milk. Both eyes and ears are very small in proportion to the size of the animal; but, nevertheless, it has full use of these organs, and is not easily approached by its enemy.

The color of the skin is a dusky lead, with some flesh-colored marks on the belly; and the skin itself is an inch thick at its thickest part, on the back. Beneath the skin is a layer of fat, of great thickness, which makes excellent oil when boiled. As we have said, the manati has no appearance of hind limbs. Its fore limbs, however, are highly developed for a water animal. The bones in them correspond to those in the human arm, having five fingers with the joints distinct, yet so enclosed in an inflexible sheath that not a joint can be moved.

The cow fish feeds on grass, coming in to the borders of the lakes and rivers to procure it. It can swim very rapidly by means of its flat tail and strong fins, and is not so easily captured as might be supposed. All the art of the hunter is required to effect

23

its destruction. The harpoon is the weapon usually employed; though sometimes they are caught in strong nets stretched across the mouths of rivers, or the narrow arms of lakes. The flesh of the manati is much esteemed, and tastes somewhat between beef and pork, altogether different from " fish." Fried in its own oil, and poured into pots or jars, it can be preserved for many months.

As already stated, on the day after Guapo shot the turtle, — in fact the next morning, — just as they were going to shove off, some of the party, in gazing from the edge of the balza, noticed a queer-looking animal in the clear water below. It was no other than a " fish cow;" and, as they continued to examine it more attentively, they were astonished to observe that, with its short, paddle-like limbs, it hugged two miniature models of itself close to its two breasts. These were the "calves," in the act of sucking; for such is the mode in which the manati nourishes her young.

All the others would have watched this spectacle for a while, interested in the maternal and filial traits thus exhibited by a subaqueous creature; but while they stood looking into the water, something glanced before their eyes and glided with a plunge to the bottom. It was the harpoon of Guapo.

Blood rose to the surface immediately, and there was a considerable plashing as the strong manati made its attempt to escape; but the head of the harpoon was deeply buried in its flesh, and, with the attached cord, Guapo soon hauled the animal ashore. It was as much as he and Don Pablo could do to drag it on dry land; but the knife soon took it to pieces; and then several hours were spent in making it fit for preservation. Its fat and flesh yielded enough to fill every spare vessel our travellers had got ; and, when all were filled, the balza was pushed off, and they continued their voyage, without any fear of short rations for many days to come.

CHAPTER L.

THE CLOSING CHAPTER.

AFTER many days of difficult navigation, the balza floated upon the broad and mighty Amazon, whose yellowish-olive flood flowed yet fifteen hundred miles farther to the Atlantic Ocean.

The current was in most places over four miles an hour, and the navigation smooth and easy, so that our travellers rarely made less than fifty miles a day. There was considerable monotony in the landscape, on account of the absence of mountains; as the Amazon, through most of its course, runs through a level plain. The numerous bends and sudden windings of the stream, however, continually opening out into new and charming vistas, and the ever-changing variety of vegetation, formed sources of delight to the travellers.

Almost every day they passed the mouth of some tributary river — many of these appearing as large as the Amazon itself. Our travellers were struck with a peculiarity in relation to these rivers — that is, their variety of color. Some were whitish, with a tinge of olive, like the Amazon itself; others were blue and transparent; while a third kind had waters as black as ink. Of the latter class is the great river of the Rio Negro, which, by means of a tributary, (the Cassiquiare,) joins the Amazon with the Orinoco.

Indeed, the rivers of the Amazon valley have been classed into *white*, *blue*, and *black*. *Red* rivers, such as are common in the northern division of the American continent, do not exist in the valley of the Amazon.

There appears to be no other explanation for this difference in the color of rivers, except by supposing that they take their hue from the nature of the soil through which these channels run.

But the *white* rivers, as the Amazon itself, do not appear to be of this hue merely because they are " muddy." On the contrary, they derive their color, or most of it, from some impalpable substance held in a state of irreducible solution. This is proved from the fact, that even when these waters enter a reservoir, and the earthy matter is allowed to settle, they still retain the same tinge of yellowish olive. There are some white rivers, as the Rio Branco, whose waters are almost as white as milk itself.

The *blue* rivers of the Amazon valley are those with clear transparent waters, and the courses of these lie through rocky countries, where there is little or no alluvium to render them turbid.

The *black* streams are the most remarkable of all. These, when deep, look like rivers of ink ; and when the bottom can be seen, which is usually a sandy one, the sand has the appearance of gold. Even when lifted in a vessel, the water retains its inky tinge, and resembles that which may be found in the pools of peat bogs. It is a general supposition in South America that the black-water rivers get their color from the extract of sarsaparilla roots growing on their banks. It is possible the sarsaparilla roots may have something to do with it, in common with both the roots and leaves of many other vegetables. No other explanation has yet been found to account for the dark color of these rivers, except the decay of vegetable substances carried in their current; and it is a fact, that all the black-water streams run through the most thickly-wooded regions.

A curious fact may be mentioned of the black rivers; that is, that mosquitoes — the plague of tropical America — are not found on their banks. This is not only a curious, but important fact, and might be sufficient to determine any one on the choice of a settlement. You may deem a mosquito a very small thing, and his presence a trifling annoyance. Let me tell you that settlements have been broken up and deserted on account of the persecution experienced from these little insects! They are the real " wild beasts " of South America, far more to be dreaded than pumas, or crocodiles, or snakes, or even the fierce jaguar himself.

Day after day our travellers kept on their course, meeting with many incidents and adventures — too many to be recorded in this little volume. After passing the mouth of the Rio Negro, they began to get a peep now and then of high land, and even mountains, in the distance; for the valley of the Amazon, on approaching its mouth, assumes a different character from what it has farther up stream. These mountains bend towards it both from the

Brazilian country on the south, and from Guia ia on the north, and these are often visible from the bosom of the stream itself.

It was about a month from their entering the main stream of the Amazon, and a little more than two from the first launching of their vessel, when the balza was brought alongside the wharf of Grand Para, and Don Pablo and his party stepped on shore at this Brazilian town. Here, of course, Don Pablo was a free man — free to go where he pleased — free to dispose of his cargo as he thought best. But he did *not* dispose of it at Grand Para. A better plan presented itself. He was enabled to freight part of a vessel starting for New York; and thither he went, taking his family and cargo along with him. In New York he obtained a large price for his bark, roots, and beans; in fact, when all were disposed of, he found himself nearly twenty thousand dollars to the good. With this to live upon, he determined to remain in the great republic of the north until such time as his own dear Peru might be freed from the Spanish oppressor.

Ten years was the period of his exile. At the end of that time the Spanish American provinces struck almost simultaneously for liberty; and in the ten years' struggle that followed, not only Don Pablo, but Leon, — now a young man, — bore a conspicuous part. Both fought by the side of Bolivar at the great battle of Junin, which crowned the patriot army with victory.

At the close of the war of independence, Don Pablo was a general of division, while Leon had reached the grade of a colonel. But as soon as the fighting was over, both resigned their military rank, as they were men who did not believe in soldiering as a *mere profession.* In fact, they regarded it as an unbecoming profession in time of peace ; and in this view *I* quite agree with them.

Don Pablo returned to his studies ; but Leon organ-ized an expedition of *cascarilleros,* and returned to the Montaña, where for many years he employed himself in " bark hunting." Through this he became one of the richest of Peruvian " ricos."

Guapo, who at this time did not look a year older than when first introduced, was as tough and sinewy as ever, and was at the head of the cascarilleros ; and many a *coceada* did Guapo afterwards enjoy with his mountain friend — the vaquero — while passing back-ward and forward between Cuzco and the Montaña.

Doña Isidora lived for a long period an ornament to her sex, and the little Leona had *her* day as the " belle of Cuzco."

But Leon and Leona both got married at length ; and were you to visit Cuzco at the present time, you might see several little Leons and Leonas, with round, black eyes, and dark waving hair — all of them de-scendants from our family of

" FOREST EXILES."

www.ingramcontent.com/pod-product-compliance
Lightning Source LLC
Chambersburg PA
CBHW021711110726